Frankenstein in London
(The Empire of the
Necromancers 3)

Frankenstein in London
(The Empire of the Necromancers 3)

by

Brian Stableford

A Black Coat Press Book

"Where Zombies Armies Clash By Night" previously appeared in *Tales of the Shadowmen* No. 6 and "The Necromancers of London" in *Tales of the Shadowmen* No. 7.

Visit our website at www.blackcoatpress.com

Introduction

In Paul Féval's *John Devil*,[1] that legendary pseu-
donym is adopted by Comte Henri de Belcamp in support of his mother's career as a notorious member of
London's underworld, where she is known by her mai-
den name, Helen Brown. After attempting to rescue her
from an Australian prison camp, Henri takes news of his
mother's death to his long-estranged father, the Marquis
de Belcamp, in the small town of Miremont, and is reconciled with him. Meanwhile, Henri is secretly engaged
in financing the construction of an unprecedentedly powerful steamship with which he intends to rescue Napoleon from St. Helena and conquer India; in pursuit of
this plan, he takes over a secret Bonapartist organization,
the Knights of the Deliverance. Henri is assisted in this
project by his long-term companion Sarah O'Brien, the
daughter of a murdered Irish general.

When a potential traitor to the Deliverance, the opera singer Constance Bartolozzi, is murdered in London,
the case is investigated by Gregory Temple, the senior
detective at Scotland Yard, assisted by his junior, James
Davy. John Devil is identified as the murderer. Temple
strongly suspects that the person behind that name is Helen Brown's son, known to him as Tom Brown, but the

---

[1] Black Coat Press, 2004. ISBN 978-1-932983-15-9.

evidence seems to point to Temple's former assistant, Richard Thompson (who is secretly married to Temple's daughter, Suzanne). Actually, James Davy—who is another of Henri de Belcamp's many aliases—has framed his predecessor, exploiting the account of his methods Temple has published in a book on the art of detection. Henri/Davy persuades Thompson to flee to France, where Suzanne is a guest at the Château Belcamp, but he is captured and convicted of the Bartolozzi murder.

When Henri is reconciled with his father, Sarah rents the so-called "new château" on the Belcamp estate under the name of Lady Frances Elphinstone. Henri commissions the murders of his dead mother's wealthy brothers, but there is one further obstacle to the fortune Henri intends to collect by this means, in the name of Tom Brown: Constance Bertolozzi's daughter, Jeanne Herbet, who also lives in Miremont. Jeanne is the designated heir of both brothers, neither of whom knows which of them is her father. Henri falls in love with Jeanne after impulsively saving her life, and decides to marry her fortune rather than murdering her.

Henri eventually marries Jeanne under the alias of an English entrepreneur, Percy Balcomb, in which guise he slips out of the jail where Henri is supposedly confined. Henri is in prison because the obsessive Temple, having failed to prove that he murdered General O'Brien or Constance Bartolozzi, found out where the bodies of his hired killers were buried. Temple has obtained this information from the drunken mistress of the vertically-challenged petty criminal Ned Knob, who was a witness to the murders and disposed of the bodies. Ned had also schooled the false witnesses at Richard Thompson's trial, using members of a troupe of vagabond actors.

On the eve of Thompson's execution, Henri inveigles his way into Newgate Prison, helping him to escape by taking his place. When Temple tries the same trick, Henri confronts his nemesis in the condemned cell, almost driving him insane by telling him that Tom Brown is not, after all, one of his pseudonyms but an actual half-brother, sired by Temple. After escaping in Temple's place, however, Henri finds that everything is going awry. The Deliverance is betrayed, his new steamship is destroyed, and his mother has returned from Australia, accusing him of having abandoned her. He finds it politic to commit suicide—or, at least, to appear to do so.

Part One of *The Empire of the Necromancers*, *The Shadow of Frakenstein*,[2] picks up the story four years later, in November 1821. Ned Knob, now directing the acting troupe, is unexpectedly confronted with his predecessor in that role, "Sawney" Ross, who has been hanged but now appears to be alive again, though somewhat slow-witted. When the reanimated Ross is collected by a diminutive French physician, Germain Patou,[3] Ned follows them to a boat where they are met by a man in a Quaker hat like the one Henri wore in his guise as John Devil.

After being knocked unconscious, Ned wakes up in Newgate and is interrogated by Gregory Temple, now working for the secret police. Temple is supposed to be investigating a series of body-snatching incidents, but his attention has been caught by a report of the Quaker hat. Following his release, Ned tracks Patou to a house

[2] Black Coat Press 2006. ISBN 978-1-934543-63-2.
[3] From Paul Féval's *The Vampire Countess*, Black Coat Press, 2003. ISBN 978-0-9740711-5-2.

in Purfleet. There, he renews his acquaintance with Henri and witnesses the resurrection of a man from the dead using an elaborate electrical technique recently discovered by a Swiss scientist.

The demonstration is interrupted when Henri's ship is attacked by a rival group under the command of the only one of the reanimated Grey Men to have recovered all his faculties: a person who styles himself General Mortdieu. Mortdieu's hirelings seize the electrical apparatus from the house, taking it to their own ship, the *Outremort*. Ned is arrested again, but makes a deal with Temple. As the *Outremort* is about to depart from her berth in Greenhithe, a three-cornered battle develops between Mortdieu's hirelings, Henri's followers and Temple's men. The fight eventually arrives at an impasse, but a hastily-contrived treaty permits Mortdieu to sail away, taking Patou with him.

Later, Gregory Temple is woken one night by Henri, who tells him that they must join forces, at least temporarily. Temple's grandson has been kidnapped from the Château Belcamp, where Thompson and Suzanne are now resident, along with two younger children of much richer parents; one is the son of Henri and Jeanne, the other the son of the former Sarah O'Brien, now the widow of a German Count.

Temple and Henri set out to make their separate ways to Miremont, where Temple has to break the news to Jeanne that she is not a widow. Henri is delayed and Temple has to respond to the first ransom note with no one to help him but Ned Knob. He is taken prisoner in his turn. Temple's captors are members of a long-dormant society of heretic monks known as *Civitas Solis*, who are even more interested in securing the secret of resurrection than in the ransom money that will help finance their exploitation of it.

Henri's delay has been caused by his traveling under the name George Palmer, in which guise he was involved with a *vehm* (a secret society of vigilantes) at the time of General O'Brien's murder, and in whose eyes he is still a wanted man. Having made his peace with the vehmgerichte, however, Henri is able to attack *Civitas Solis* and liberate Temple and the captive children before disappearing again, intent on joining forces with Civitas Solis in the expectation of using them as he had formerly used the Deliverance.

Part Two, *Frankenstein and the Vampre Countess*,[4] opens in the vicinity of Spezia in Northern Italy in the summer of 1822. Ned Knob has been commissioned by Gregory Temple to keep watch on a villa rented by Victor Frankenstein, the original inventor of the technology of resurrection carried forward by Germain Patou, and his friend Robert Walton. Frankenstein is about to resume his own experiments, aided by a group of Englishmen headed by Lord Byron and Percy Shelley. Ned is also reporting his findings to Henri de Belcamp.

Ned is not the only spy interested in Frankenstein's work. He is approached with an offer of cooperation by a man who calls himself Guido, who eventually turns out to be a Magyar working for a reputed vampire—one of "nature's Grey Men" rather than a legendary bloodsucker. He also meets a burly but uncommonly articulate Grey Man who is somewhat resentful of being portrayed as a murderous "daemon" in the sensationalized version of Frankenstein's story that Robert Walton issued by way of Mary Shelley; Frankenstein's first creation pre-

---

[4] Black Coat Press, 2009. ISBN 978-1-934543-89-4.

fers to think of himself as the Adam of a new race and is attempting to negotiate a reconciliation with his creator. Ned has a less amicable encounter with a fanatical warrior monk named Malo de Treguern,[5] who appears to be working for a more orthodox and more inquisitorially-inclined arm of the Roman Church than *Civitas Solis*.

Owing to the interaction of these various interested parties and Percy Shelley's collapse as a result of a wound inflicted by a member of the local militia, Frankenstein's villa is besieged and his attempts to renew his experiments are thwarted. Frankenstein and most of his associates escape, but will have to find a more hospitable spot to resume work. Ned hears of Shelley's death by drowning a few days later, but does not believe the rumor.

Later, Gregory Temple visits the aged Jean-Paul Sévérin,[6] who was once one of the best swordsmen in France, in quest of information regarding Germain Patou, offering to trade information regarding an alleged vampire that Sévérin, his son-in-law, René de Kervoz, and Patou once encountered—an encounter that was responsible for Patou's initial interest in the biology of resurrection.

The female vampire in question, known as Comtesse Marcian Gregoryi,[7] has returned to France, seemingly no older although two decades have passed; she has hired Robert Surrisy as her lawyer with a view to buying the new château at Miremont. Coco-Lacour of the Sûreté, Malo de Treguern and Lord Byron also take

---

[5] From Paul Féval's *Revenants*, Black Coat Press, 2005. ISBN 978-1-932983-70-8.

[6] From *The Vampire Countess*, q.v.

[7] From *The Vampire Countess*, q.v.

an interest in the matter. Temple and Séverin are attacked by hirelings of the Comtesse's associate, Guido, who is similarly intent on finding Patou and who attempts to kidnap Séverin's grand-daughter in order to force information out of the old man. The attempt is thwarted by Frankenstein's first creation, who is now going by the name of Lazarus.

With Lazarus' aid, Temple tracks the master vampire who employs the Comtesse as his cat's-paw to Miremont, but is outmaneuvered by him and tricked into introducing him into a party held in the new château; he and the other guests—who include Byron and the enigmatic Colonel Bozzo-Corona [8]—are saved in the nick of time by Séverin and Malo de Treguern, whose timely intervention puts the vampire to flight. Temple and Byron make a brief but friendly contact, and admit to one another that they both have agents on a ship named the *Belleville*, bound for the Caribbean...

Now read on...

Bran Stableford

---

[8] From Paul Féval's *The Black Coats* series (*'Salem Street, The Invisible Weapon, The Parisian Jungle, The Companions of the Treasure, Heart of Steel, The Cadet Gang*), all from Black Coat Press.

PART ONE:
WHERE ZOMBIES ARMIES CLASH BY NIGHT

Chapter One
Trial by Ordeal

Ned Knob had woken up on many an occasion with a thumping headache occasioned by being hit over the head with a blunt instrument, but he had never learned to like the experience. Indeed, it never seemed to become any more tolerable. He always took care to thank Providence for giving him such a hard head—which had so far proved resistant to everything cruel Fate could throw at him—but, like the good Radical he was, he thought of Providence in terms of heredity and education rather than whimsical deity, so he always tempered his gratitude with regret for the fact that such an evolution had been necessary.

Ned had never known his father, but he had always admired the fortitude and discipline of his mother, who had never allowed him to touch a drop of gin, lest it deplete her own ration, and had sent him to the best school she knew: the academy of thievery operated in Will Sharper's Spirit Shop by the legendary Thomas Paddock, alias John Devil—from which he had eventually passed on, not without difficulty, to the university run by Paddock's mercurial successor, Tom Brown, alias John Devil the Quaker, also known as Comte Henri de Belcamp, late of the Knights of Deliverance and currently active in *Civitas Solis*. That admiration had, however, been similarly tempered with regret for the fact that his dear mother had required such fortitude and discipline in order to maintain her composure.

Having made his list of all the things for which he was required by his continued consciousness to be thankful, and added in the required leavening of regret, Ned tried to remember who had hit him, and under what circumstances. Unfortunately, his memory was reluctant to provide him with that information, at least for the moment.

He knew that he had been traveling on the French merchant ship *Belleville*, bound for Port-au-Prince in the Republic of Haiti, and that he had been so sick for the first week of the journey—his first ever crossing of any stretch of water broader than the English Channel—that he had been unable to keep his food down until the ship's supplies had deteriorated to standard naval fare. He also knew that he had contrived to forge a temporary alliance of sorts with Edward Trelawny, Lord Byron's emissary to the Republic, even though that worthy gentleman liked and trusted him far less than the not-so-late Percy Shelley, whom he had met in Spezia not so long ago. Alas, the trauma of being hit had robbed him of access to any shorter-term memories. He had one other avenue of information open to him, though, and he tried to engage it by opening his eyes.

The sky was a remarkably bright shade of blue and the tropical Sun must have been blazing with its most fervent ardor, but the direct light of the fiery orb could not reach him, by virtue of an expansive green parasol held by the exceedingly pretty young woman at whose feet he lay. She appeared to be in her mid-20s, and her skin was very dark, although the cast of her features was not entirely Negroid. He assumed that she was a mongrel of some kind—although she was evidently no mere cur, as he had been before transforming himself into "Gentleman Ned." She was, in every possible respect, a lady.

Ned remembered having seen the young woman once or twice on the deck of the *Belleville*, but she too had spent by far the greater part of her time in one of the glorified coffins that the *Belleville*'s captain—a Corsican who had once served Napoleon as a privateer, by the name of Argile—called "first class cabins." Ned had never been introduced to her, and had not dared to approach her without an introduction, partly because she had been accompanied on the occasions when he had seen her by an enormous bodyguard. He did not know the woman's name, but he had observed, with some interest, that at least some of Captain Argile's multicolored crew had treated her with an exaggerated respect mingled with fear, and that the few God-fearing individuals among them had crossed themselves defensively on catching sight of her.

The young woman was looking at him now, studying him carefully, but not contemptuously. Ned realized that he had not been laid at her feet in order to signify his relatively lowly status, but in order that his battered head might share the protection of the parasol. It was not until he sat up that he realized that the two of them were adrift in a small dinghy, which had a short mast but no sail, and rowlocks but no oars. The sea surrounding them was calm, and its deep blue would have seemed infinitely peaceful had it not been for the fins of two large sharks, which occasionally broke through the quiet waves as the predators circled the boat. Sharks had often followed the *Belleville*, from whose high deck they had seemed quite ineffectual, but at closer range their presence was considerably more disturbing.

Ned scanned the interior of the dinghy for a second time, making perfectly certain that it had nothing at all by the way of equipment or supplies, save for a small leather bottle that the unknown woman was cradling in her bosom, as if it were extremely precious. Ned deduced that the bottle contained water. He understood that, given the circumstances, his companion would be every bit as reluctant to share its contents with him as his mother would once have been to offer him a sip of gin—but when he raised his hand, tentatively, she handed it over without hesitation. She was obviously a very exceptional person. He responded to her generosity by sipping very carefully, taking the minimum that he needed.

He knew, as he did thus, that he was literally prolonging the torture to which they had been condemned. To be set adrift in a small boat in the Atlantic Ocean—for the Caribbean Sea, properly speaking, lay to the south of the line of islands that stretched from the Leewards through Puerto Rico and Hispaniola to Cuba—was, in essence, a form of execution, favored by mutineers, pirates and other agents of injustice who liked to pretend that they were better than mere murderers, or had some other reason for adopting a policy of cruel diplomacy. Notionally, castaways were delivered into the custody of God, who had the prerogative of treating them mercifully, should they be deemed deserving—except that God obviously had a blind spot when it came to victims of that sort, even when they were afforded the mocking grace of a bottle of water and a parasol. Despite the lesson preached by the heroic tale of Robinson Crusoe, Ned knew, even castaways fortunate enough to reach "desert islands" almost always perished, slain by thirst, heat and disease.

On the other hand, Ned reminded himself, determinedly, the real man on whose adventure Defoe had based his legend, Alexander Selkirk, really had survived for years on such an island, sustained by a population of goats and the company of his cats. "Pirates," he contrived to say, hoarsely, as memory began to filter back. "The *Belleville* was attacked by night—by pirates."

"It was," the mysterious woman confirmed.

"But the English and French navies suppressed piracy in these seas 100 years ago, and put an end to it forever," Ned remarked, nursing a sense of grievance that even the little history he knew should have misled him so treacherously.

"The English and French navies have been busy fighting one another for the greater part of the last thirty years," she told him. "When cats are away, it's not merely mice that come out to play—and piracy will endure forever, no matter what navies might claim." Her English seemed very fluent, although she spoke with a marked French accent. After a pause, she added: "These were privateers, though, rather than mere sea-wolves, for all that they're based in La Tortue. They were sent after the *Belleville* as mercenaries."

"By whom?" Ned asked, in bewilderment.

"Don't you know?" she countered. "You are, after all, a secret agent of His Britannic Majesty, King George."

Ned's hand moved reflexively toward the breast of his jacket. His second set of identification papers had not, of course, been carried in the inner pocket of the garment, but sewn into the lining, so subtly as to be hardly tangible—but someone had obviously found them. He only had to twitch the jacket to know that the lining had been slit and the papers removed. He looked into the woman's lovely dark eyes, suspiciously.

"It wasn't me," she said. "The pirates took care to search you. You were probably fortunate—had you not had the secret papers, they'd probably have cut your throat, and saved me from my obligation."

"What obligation?" he asked, still utterly bewildered.

She did not answer directly, but she did ask: "Why did you defend me, Monsieur Knob? Why did you prevent the *mestizo* assassins from carrying out their mission? Does the English King have some reason for wanting me alive?"

Fortunately, these questions acted as a trigger, releasing a trickle of memory.

Ned had been in his so-called cabin, asleep, when someone on deck had raised a belated alarm, informing him that the ship was under attack. He had slipped on his jacket and picked up the swordstick that he had bought from a shop in Jermyn Street before embarkation, in anticipation of the fact that he might need a disguised weapon in Port-au-Prince. He had gone out into the narrow corridor that connected the cabins, treading softly but ready for action.

There had been a lantern in the corridor—a further testimony to the cabins' supposed "first class" status—but its candle had burned low. Even so, he had been able to see two shadowy figures descending the staircase that led up to the deck, moving as stealthily as he was, clutching cutlasses. By the time he had drawn his blade from its wooden sheath, they had already passed the door of Trelawny's cabin, which was situated between his own and the stairway, and had seemed to be headed straight for him with murderous intent. He had, inevitably, backed away along the corridor while striking a defensive stance, glad that the corridor was so narrow that the attackers could only come at him one at a time.

Ned was no polished fencer, but Thomas Paddock's school had offered courses in dirty fighting that were the equal of any in the world. He remembered seeing the first of the cut-throats smile as the lantern-light had revealed his exceedingly small stature. He had been mistaken for a child or a dwarf before, but even when he really had been a child the appearance had been deceptive. The cutlass-bearer had moved forward recklessly, expecting an easy kill, and Ned had planted his own blade in the imbecile's heart with a riposte of which Henri de Belcamp himself would have been proud.

The second man, alas, had thus been forewarned of what he was facing, and had skipped over his fallen colleague's body with ominous agility. The corridor along which he was backing had a right-angled bend in it, and Ned had been driven into the corner, backed up against the door of one of the other cabins. There he had made his stand, against a slender, long-armed fellow who had a cudgel as well as a cutlass, and knew how to use both weapons. In defending himself against the blade, Ned had been forced to expose himself to the cudgel.

He could not remember exactly how the flurry of blows had come out, but he did remember the door of the cabin opening, allowing him a useful backward step at a critical moment. He *thought* that he might have contrived a lethal thrust of his own, at the very moment when the cudgel had come down on his well-seasoned head. What seemed more important for the moment, however, was what the pretty woman might have thought.

Apparently, finding him with his back to her door, fending off two assassins whom she believed—rightly or wrongly—to have been commissioned to murder her, she had seen him as her defender, risking his own life for hers, rather than merely as a ruffian raised in Sharper's with no other thought in his head but to defend himself. More than that—for some unfathomable reason, she thought that he might actually have been commissioned by the English crown to protect her.

Ned prided himself on his adaptability to any and all circumstances, so what he actually replied was: "It was not for the King of England's sake that I defended you, Mademoiselle, but out of loyalty to a higher duty. I'm not a gentleman by birth, but I am one by vocation, and I could never allow a lady to be attacked without doing everything in my power to protect her."

The woman studied him even more intently for some ten or 12 seconds, with dark eyes that seemed suddenly to become supernaturally intense. Eventually, she said: "Do you really expect me to believe that a white man would feel any ready-made desire or compulsion to defend the honor or life of a *zambo* woman from other half-breeds?"

Ned had not even bothered to take note of whether or not the two men he had fought had been white, black or anything in between, and he had not the slightest idea what a "*zambo*" was. "I've lived most of my life within spitting distance of the London docks," he told her, accurately enough, in a metaphorical sense. "I've long grown used to the company of men and women of every color and creed—there's no color bar, and precious little discrimination, in Sharper's. I might have been temporarily reduced to taking the King's shilling in order to support myself, but in my heart I'm a Radical, a diehard follower of Tom Paine. So yes, Mademoiselle, I would feel exactly such a desire and exactly such a compulsion—but if it relieves your conscience, you need feel no obligation. As a matter of fact, I thought the blackguards were trying to murder me, and was defending myself. If I rendered you some service in the process, then I'm sincerely glad of it—but I'll admit that it was accidental, and that what I said just now was mere bravado."

The pretty woman nodded, as if satisfied that he was now being honest—as, indeed, he was. "Is that why Monsieur Trelawny told the mercenary captain that you were not to be trusted, and were probably a traitor to your own ostensible cause?" she asked.

"Did he?" Ned queried, genuinely astonished and offended. "I would not have thought him capable of that degree of treachery."

"He had his own life to save, and his intervention might well have done as much to save you from immediate execution as your apparent status as an agent of the crown. It was Trelawny who persuaded Amédée Desart that you and I ought to be set adrift, subjected to trial by ordeal, rather than summarily killed. I have a similarly ambiguous status myself—and a reputation that complicated my situation further."

It was Ned's turn to study her. "If you were captured by the pirates after I was knocked out," he said, "why did they not simply complete the mission in which the first two assassins had failed?"

"Wheels within wheels," she said. "There are mercenaries and mercenaries. The two men who came to kill me did not have the same paymasters as the master of the pirate vessel. Desart was after the precious fraction of the *Belleville*'s cargo; he probably didn't know that I was aboard. He probably has a dozen *mestizos* in his crew, but knows nothing about their feuds and cared even less—until their subsidiary enterprise posed a tacit challenge to his despotic authority."

"I didn't know that *Belleville* had a precious cargo," Ned observed, thoughtfully. "I thought the bulk of what she was carrying comprised agricultural machinery."

"That is the precious fraction to which I referred," the woman told him. "There are Frenchmen willing to supply Boyer with economic necessities, and there are Frenchmen who are desperate to bring his infant republic to its knees by any means humanly possible. Wheels within wheels, as I say."

Jean-Pierre Boyer, Ned knew, was the President of the recently reborn Republic of Haiti, first proclaimed by Toussaint L'Ouverture, then smashed—albeit briefly—by Charles Leclerc, on the orders of Napoleon Bonaparte. It had been reasserted in the wake of the Emperor's defeat at the hands of the English, much to the chagrin of the restored Bourbon monarchy. It was not difficult to understand, in those tangled circumstances, how the presence on the *Belleville* of an English secret agent bound for Port-au-Prince might have seemed significant in all sort of strange ways.

"Might I ask what your own ambiguous status is, Mademoiselle?" Ned asked, politely.

"Do you really not know my name?" she countered. "You're a poor spy, if so—and you must really have been seasick when you hid away in your cabin for the first week of the voyage."

"I'm not so poor a spy as all that," he told her, "but your presence on the ship was of no relevance to my mission, and I really was horribly seasick. My being raised so close to the docks was no guarantee of immunity to the typical agues of seamen, unfortunately. Might you not trust me a little, given that we're in the same tumbrel, headed for the same cruel guillotine? Is there really any point in your keeping secrets, even if I am an agent of the English secret police?"

"We're not going to die, Monsieur Knob," she said—although he could not for the life of him see any such hope as he scanned the circular horizon, where the lighter blue of the sky met the darker blue of the sea with an ominous uniformity. "And you're right—even if I did not owe you an obligation for saving my life, there would be no point is concealing my identity at the stage in the game. My status is ambiguous because I'm an American citizen, born in New Orleans, although my loyalty is to my parents' people. I'm a *zambo*—a *maroon*, if you prefer, although that's a far more general term. The men who came to kill me were *mestizos*—sworn enemies of the *zambos* on hereditary and historical grounds—who would have considered my murder a triumph for their cause. I have no papers linking me to the American government, alas, but I do have a reputation as a practitioner of *vaudou*. My name is Marie Laveau."

Ned's first thought, absurdly, was that the surname should surely have been Leveau, as *veau* was a masculine noun—but this was the Caribbean, where grammatical niceties probably did not apply. He did, however, know what a *maroon* was: the result of interbreeding between runaway slaves and the native islanders whom Europeans persisted in calling "Indians." He had also heard the term *vaudou* before, in sinister and superstitious contexts.

"Are you saying that you're some kind of witch?" he asked. "Is that why we aren't going to die."

"Put crudely," she said, "yes. Whites and mulattos consider *vaudou* to be a kind of witchcraft, or black magic, while blacks consider it a kind of hybrid religion. There are many varieties of it, even in Haiti, and in New Orleans the situation is even more confused, because of its confusion with Cuban Santeria. As to what it really is...well, some of its hybrid forms incorporate the traditions of the Tairo, reputedly handed down from Queen Anacaona herself, of whom I'm said to be a descendant, and a reincarnation. There's no proof of that, by European or American standards—the Tairo's genealogical records were purely oral, and now that the tribe is extinct, save for its *zambo* and *mestizo* relics...well, a great deal has to be taken on trust, even if one holds the secrets."

"I'm sorry," Ned said, "but I don't understand many of the terms you're citing. Who are—or were—the Tairo?"

"The original inhabitants of the island that Columbus called Hispaniola—the island he mistook for the Garden of Eden, although that didn't stop him making war on the island's Queen, Anacaona. Her forces initially defeated his, despite Spanish steel and firepower, but he had secret weapons of whose power even he was ignorant: measles and smallpox. What military power failed to do, disease achieved. Anacaona's depleted forces were eventually defeated, and she was executed. The Spaniards were obsessed with gold, stealing all they could find and opening mines of their own; they had no interest in the Tairo's knowledge and arts apart from that. What they did discover of the Tairo's beliefs and practices, their priests condemned as devilry, which they considered it their holy duty to obliterate.

"When the Tairo retreated to the hills and forests, the Spaniards followed their usual policy of importing African slaves to labor in their mines and their plantations. As usual, many ran away and found refuge with the Tairo, with whom they interbred to produce the *zambo*—the *maroons* of Hispaniola. In the meantime, the Spaniards interbred too, with both the Tairo, producing *mestizos*, and the blacks, producing mulattos. Although they were second-class citizens, despised by the whites, the *mestizos* and the mulattos remained agents of the colonial force, electing in their turn to despise the *zambo*, and developing a fierce hatred for them, and for the remnants of Tairo wisdom that the *zambo* preserved within their own version of *vaudou*.

"*Vaudou* was, of course, primarily a black institution, but it mutated in various ways among such marginal populations as the *zambo* and the mulattos, accommodating itself to circumstance. My *vaudou* is not the same as black or mulatto *vaudou*, and is opposed by them as fiercely as heresies invisible to external eyes have been opposed within Christendom. As Spanish authority was succeeded by French authority in the western half of the island, which became Saint-Domingue, the situation was complicated further, but the underlying factors remained the same. The American Revolution and the French Revolution were followed by a Haitian Revolution—but neither the American nor the French revolutionaries were sympathetic to the Haitian one...and you must surely know the rest, Monsieur Knob, if you are any sort of agent at all."

"I'm a spy, not a diplomat," Ned reminded her, wryly. "But yes, I'm vaguely familiar with recent political developments, and the re-establishment of Boyer's republic. I know that Saint-Domingue was the richest of all France's colonies, supplying enormous quantities of sugar, tobacco and other produce, and that the restored monarchy would be very glad indeed to re-establish control of it, formally or informally. England and America, for their own reasons, would prefer that no such control was re-exerted, although neither nation would go so far as to attempt an actual conquest of all or part of the island. All in all, it's what we in England call a *can of worms*."

"It's more like a bucketful of snakes," she told him. "Mercifully, you killed the *mestizos'* agents, and Desart was more inclined to put my powers to a trial by ordeal than simply slit my throat. He threw you in, I suppose, merely to add a little spice to the situation."

"But not Trelawny?"

"No—for some reason, Desart was inclined to befriend Trelawny. I find it strange that Lord Byron's authority should be taken more seriously by La Tortue's pirates than that of King George, but the intricacies of British politics are far beyond my comprehension."

"How did this Desart contrive to intercept the *Belleville*?" Ned wanted to know. "According to Captain Argile, we made an unusually fast crossing. How could news of our arrival possibly have outdistanced us?"

"Ships leave Le Havre for the New World almost every day," she told him. "The *Belleville*'s cargo and passenger list were matters of common knowledge for a week before she sailed. Ships bound for Florida and New Orleans left within that week, making their first ports of call in the Bahamas. The news flew south from there. That, at least, required no magic."

Ned looked at her quizzically, trying to assemble all the information she had given to him into a coherent whole.

"You may ask me the question, if you wish," she said. "I shan't take offence."

Ned was wary of a trap, so he said: "What question?"

"Don't pretend to be more innocent than you are, Monsieur Knob. Short as you are, I know you're no child. I can believe that terms like *Tairo* and *zambo* are unfamiliar to you, but you must have heard talk of *vaudou*, and I know what associations the word must conjure up in your mind."

"Even so," Ned said, still exceedingly wary, "I'm unsure as to what question you expect me to raise."

"Don't you want to know," she said, "whether the secrets of which I claim custody include the secret of making *zombies*—of resurrecting the dead?"

Chapter Two
Answered Prayers

Ned Knob was, indeed, very curious to know whether Marie Laveau knew the secret of making zombies. It was, in fact, the secret of resurrecting the dead—in the proven manner practiced by Germain Patou rather than that of reputed *vaudou* magicians—that had brought him to the Caribbean region in search of the *Outremort* and the enigmatic General Mortdieu, but he was not yet ready to admit that to the pretty lady.

All he said, therefore, in response to her provocation, was: "Do you?"

"Of course I do," she replied, more than a trifle ironically. "Am I not the direct descendant and reincarnation of the Devil-Queen Anacaona, the supposed serpent in Christopher Columbus' Eden? Am I not the Anti-Christ of the *mestizos* and the mulattos, feared even by the Enlightened likes of Jean-Pierre Boyer, Henri Christophe and Alexandre Pétion? Am I not the Messiah of the *zambo*, destined to lead them back to dominion over the empire the Tairo lost, and to reign over it as their Queen?"

"If that is what you are," Ned said, judiciously, "then I'm very glad indeed to hear it. Not only does it imply that I might not die a wretched death as a castaway after all, but that I might have a more interesting future than I had imagined. As a servant of the English King, I offer you the kind regards of his people, O Queen."

She consented to smile at that. "You're a more amusing companion than I had expected," she said. "Do you need more water?"

"I'd be very grateful for another drop," he confessed, "but your need must be as great as mine, and I would not like to deprive you. I can do without for a while longer, if necessary. How long will it be until nightfall, do you think? The Sun still seems unpromisingly high in the sky to me, although it's surely past its zenith."

"At least four hours, alas," she said.

Ned scanned the circle of the horizon, but could not see the slightest sign of land—which seemed perversely frustrating, given that the maps he had studied had implied that the region where the Atlantic Ocean bordered the Caribbean Sea was replete with scattered islands. There were few reference-points available to him, save for the fins of the sharks circling the boat, but he guessed that there was no substantial current to move the boat along. If that were the case, the possibility of any land appearing on the horizon seemed remote. There was a wind blowing from the west—although it was little more than a breeze, for the moment—but the parasol, capacious though it was, could not provide much service as a sail.

"I don't suppose, your majesty," he said, "that your other secrets include the art of making rain?"

Marie Laveau looked up at the cloudless sky. "Even magic requires raw materials," she told him. "Given a cloud, I might be able to whip up a hurricane—but that might do us more harm than good, and in the absence of clouds, I can only confess my helplessness. What was your purpose in traveling to Port-au-Prince. Monsieur

Knob? Are you carrying some message to Boyer from the English King?"

"Radical as I am by conviction," Ned replied, attempting to match his interlocutor's mock-sorrowful tone, "I can't take the King's shilling and then betray his confidence. I'm sorry, Mademoiselle, but I can't tell you why I was dispatched to Port-au-Prince."

"Well," she said, "given that you're English, I can be reasonably sure that you're not working for the French, and that your employment of a French ship was determined by the simple fact that very few ships out of Liverpool or Southampton ever have ports of call in Haiti. You can't have any moral objection, though, to telling me why Monsieur Trelawny was—and still is—aboard the *Belleville*."

Ned considered that matter very carefully, but eventually decided that there might be more opportunity than hazard involved. In any case, the temptation was too strong to resist. "I believe that he's searching for a man named Germain Patou, in whom Lord Byron has a particular interest," he said.

"Ah!" she said, in what was presumably supposed to be a neutral tone.

"You might well have heard Patou's name before, Mademoiselle," Ned concluded. With calculated irony, he added: "You may ask me the question, if you wish—I shan't be offended."

She looked at him sharply then. "He too is reputed to make zombies," she said. "Better zombies than the *zambo*, or even the ancient Tairo: zombies capable of articulate speech, and action on their own initiative. I would very much like to meet such a man, if his reputation were justified. Do you think he's in Haiti, and that Trelawny will be able to find him?"

Having taken the gamble, Ned felt that he might as well increase the stakes. "Yes, Mademoiselle Laveau," he said. "I believe that Patou might have taken refuge somewhere on the island. I think Trelawny might be able to find him, since he's evidently clever enough and unscrupulous enough to deal diplomatically even with pirates. If they deliver him safely to Tortuga—La Tortue, as you call it—he'll likely be able to make his own arrangements for getting to the mainland and continuing his mission."

"And why should Desart help him?" the witch-queen asked.

"That, I don't know," Ned admitted. "Since you appear to be familiar with the pirate's reputation, your guess is probably better than mine. Monsieur Trelawny did, however, seem quite confident that Boyer's followers might help him, by virtue of Lord Byron's reputation as a friend to foreign revolutionaries. Byron is a vocal supporter of the Greeks in their rebellion against the Ottoman Turks. His friend Shelley once claimed that poets are the true legislators of the world. That's not true, alas—the true legislators of the world are, alas, the legislators—but it's a fine Romantic idea, and Byron is the perfect incarnation of adversarial Romanticism: a king and a redeemer in mythical terms, if not actual ones. His interest in Victor Frankenstein's technology of resurrection only adds to his reputation in that respect, setting him against the Roman Church as well as secular political authorities—to the extent that the Church has been prompted to revive the Inquisition in response to the perceived threat. It has commissioned a former Knight of Malta, Malo de Treguern, to hunt Frankenstein down."

"So this Trelawny is an ambassador, intent on establishing friendly relations with both Boyer and Patou—and, indeed, negotiating a pact between the two—in order that Byron and Frankenstein might make Haiti the base of their future operations?"

"That might well be his plan, or his hope," Ned confirmed.

"To which you, as an agent of the English King, are bound to be opposed?" she probed.

Ned found himself caught on the horns of a dilemma. There was a sense in which the pretty lady was correct, although he was also an agent of Patou's former collaborator Henri de Belcamp, in which capacity he had a very different set of priorities. Diplomatically, he said: "The English government has not yet made up its mind about the Haitian Republic or the potential of Frankenstein's technology. The Tories are diehard opponents of what they call 'Jacobin science'—which includes the advances in chemistry made by Joseph Priestley and Humphry Davy, and the advances in biology made by Erasmus Darwin as well as Frankenstein's discovery—but the Whigs, almost by virtue of an automatic reaction, take a very different view. We humble civil servants must be ready to serve any government voted into power, so we are not permitted to adopt firm positions of our own. As I said before, I'm not at liberty to discuss the specific terms of my commission—but I'm prepared to tell you that it's a matter of fact-finding rather than purposive action. I'd be extremely interested to discover Patou's whereabouts, but I have no hostile intention toward him, nor any hope of reconciling Boyer to his presence in Haiti. For what it might be worth, I think Trelawny's chances of achieving that goal are slim."

"Why?" she demanded, point-blank.

Ned hedged slightly. "I've met General Mortdieu, the most articulate of his Grey Men, and the true master of their company. He's only a little taller than I am, but he's a man of great prestige and determination. He's a warrior by inclination, by no means a natural diplomat—and the Republicans of Haiti are unlikely to consider him a welcome ally, or even a tolerable presence in their vicinity."

"I certainly can't imagine the blacks, mulattos or *mestizos* welcoming a zombie ally," Marie Laveau said, thoughtfully. "The *zambo*, on the other hand...Tell me, Monsieur Knob, is the name of Francis Drake well-known in England?"

Ned was taken aback by that question, which seemed to him exceedingly strange. "He's one of England's greatest heroes, your majesty," He said. "He's reputed to have saved England from invasion by the Spanish Armada, in the days of Elizabeth the Virgin Queen."

"Really?" she said. "He has a different reputation among the *maroons* of the Caribbean. He was the only white man ever to make effective common cause with *maroons*, in the days when they were universally hated. He gathered an army of *maroons* to fight the Spaniards on the mainland. I dare say that he did it for his own purposes, to further England's cause—but that army remained when he had sailed away, and its spirit spread throughout the islands. In *zambo vaudou*, Drake is a great hero, almost a *loa*."

"What's a *loa*?" Ned asked.

"The *loa* are intermediate between humans and gods. In varieties of *vaudou* that have absorbed elements of Christian faith—including those that flourish in New Orleans—they're somewhat akin to Catholic saints, helping to smooth the way to a quasi-Christian Heaven, but *zambo vaudou* isn't tainted in that fashion; although its African components include some of the same figures, its Tairo components assume a different relationship between life and afterlife, with a different notion of paradise."

"So you think that your own messianic cause might be greatly assisted if you could find a new Francis Drake?" Ned guessed. "And you think that Mortdieu, as an articulate zombie, might be better fitted to that role than an English buccaneer? You're certainly not lacking in ambition, your majesty."

"I'd rather you did not call me that, Monsieur Knob—especially in that sarcastic manner," the pretty woman said, in a tone whose neutrality veiled a hint of menace. "I owe you a debt of gratitude, but my tolerance isn't infinite." As if to soften her rebuke, however, she handed him the water-bottle, from which he sipped very gratefully before politely handing it back. He knew that once she had taken a few sips of her own, the bottle would be empty.

"I'm sorry, Mademoiselle," Ned said, rejoicing in the moistness in his mouth while it lasted. "I'm inclined to become bumptious when I feel that I'm in dire danger—and I must admit that our present situation seems exceedingly ominous. I'm no connoisseur of sea-shanties, but I've heard sailors in Sharper's singing *La Courte Paille* with gusto ever since I first learned to talk, and I know what horrors attend the fate of castaways."

Marie Laveau smiled wryly; she too was familiar with the words of *La Courte Paille*, which described in lurid detail the fate of castaways continually forced to draw straws to determine which of them would be next to be eaten by their comrades. There were versions of it in every European language, and it was presumably familiar in New Orleans. "I'm no cannibal, Monsieur Knob," she said, "although I'm grateful to know that your innate sense of decency would oblige you to sacrifice yourself before attempting to slit my throat and feast on my tender flesh...not, of course, that you could literally slit my throat, given that Desart was not sufficiently generous to leave us a knife."

Ned studied the woman's finely-chiseled features. "You really are confident, aren't you, that we shall be saved?" he said.

"Yes," she replied. "Help is on its way. It has a fair way to come and might not arrive before nightfall, but it will arrive in the end. All we have to do is wait."

Ned scanned the horizon yet again, but could not make out any dot. Then he looked at the circling sharks, which seemed equally confident that it was worth their while to wait. He was as skeptical in regard to the efficacy of magic as any devotee of Jacobin science, but he had no alternative in trusting Marie Laveau's witchery over the sharks' instinct. It was the only hope he had. In any case, her conviction that the *Belleville*'s arrival had been anticipated by virtue of news that had flown south from the Bahamas a day or two in advance of her arrival off the coast of Hispaniola presumably extended to confidence that it had even reached the zambo, who would have been even more delighted to hear it. "How can you be sure, Mademoiselle?" he asked, politely, interested to know how she would represent the matter.

"I'm sure that the *loas* will not desert me, if I plead for their intercession," she told him, wryly. "I also know that news travels with lightning-speed in La Tortue. The news that Desart set us adrift will reach *zambo* ears within minutes of the *Cayman* dropping anchor in the island's harbor—which it will do without delay, even if

Desart elects to keep the greater part of his crew aboard the *Belleville*—and those ears will already have been forewarned. Every *zambo* community on the north coast will send out searchers. The greatest danger we face is neither thirst nor the sharks, but the *mestizos* who will set out to sea in their turn."

"If you'll forgive me saying so, Mademoiselle," Ned observed, "the westerly wind won't have helped the pirate ship to reach Tortuga in a hurry. It might work more to the advantage of the rescuers you hope to see, but it isn't lively enough for my liking."

"The *zambo* are not sailors," she told him. "We prefer conditions of this sort."

"You're expecting your people to *paddle* to our rescue in *canoes*?" Ned exclaimed, in frank astonishment.

"I warned you that it would take time," she replied, serenely. "We'll be thirsty, I dare say, unless some cloud blows up, but we'll live—provided that wound on your head doesn't turn ugly and poison your blood...in which case, I would live but you wouldn't."

"Thank you for the reassurance, Mademoiselle Laveau," he said. "That, I suppose, would free you from your supposed obligation—but until then, we still have time to while away. Would you consent to tell me more about zombies?"

"I might," she said, "although, like you, I have secrets that I am obliged to keep as a matter of duty. Would you be willing to tell me more about the ones you've encountered?"

"In a spirit of fair exchange," he said, after a moment's hesitation "I'm not, alas, prey to Germain Patou's secret formulas. I saw him revive a dead man once, having immersed him in a chemical bath left over from one of James Graham's Temples of Health and Hygiene, designed to administer an electrical stimulus to living flesh. There were, I believe, other drugs involved, delivered into the corpse by means of a clyster and dissolved in the immersing fluid. The eventual effect is a metamorphosis of the body's substance, permitting it to renew the use of its own innate electrical pathways—the motor nerves, at least. Restoring the functions of thought to the brain is more difficult, but experiment had proved that it was not impossible, and Patou was trying hard to find efficient means of re-education. He had achieved some success in that direction too, especially with respect of an old friend of mine, Sawney Ross. Whether he's made any further progress in recent months, I don't know—but I suspect not, given the necessity of fleeing across the Atlantic and hunting for a safe haven."

He stopped, and waited patiently for her to honor her part in the bargain. After a brief hesitation, she said: "We use a combination of drugs, which we call *bokor*. They, too, have to be introduced into the bodies of the dead person by difficult means. We also employ immersion. What you say about the *electrical stimulus* is particularly interesting, however."

"Obviously, you have no means to deliver that," Ned said. He wondered, though, whether the "agricultural machinery" in the Belleville's hold might have contained Voltaic piles. There must, at any rate, be raw materials enough in a city like Port-au-Prince to make such piles. There was no reason why a 'Temple of Health and Hygiene' could not be erected and equipped in the tropics.

"To the *zambo*, however," Marie Laveau continued, "zombies are, essentially, creatures of the snake-god Damballah Wedo, and are subject to his will rather than their own. They can be controlled by magicians of both sexes, who are associated with the relevant *loas*, but priestesses of Damballah Wedo—especially those who consort with the god's favorite snakes—are most privileged in that regard. Most such priestesses, for obvious reasons, prefer to carry out their rituals in association with constrictors, which have no poison, but the greatest respect is always attached to those who deal with more dangerous creatures, especially those whose bite is reputedly deadly."

"I was assured that there are no poisonous snakes in Haiti," Ned said, warily.

"There are, indeed, no poisonous snakes *native* to Hispaniola," the young woman confirmed. "When Columbus arrived, it was entirely free of that sort of venom. Once slave-ships from Africa began to call on a regular basis, however, importation became possible, and perhaps inevitable. In the harbor at Port-au-Prince, such incomers are considered unwelcome and killed, but *vaudou* practitioners have a different view, and lavish the utmost care on their black mambas."

"And keeping close company with such deadly reptiles an essential part of the cost of being accepted as a descendant of Queen Anacaona and a potential savior of the *zambo*?" Ned concluded.

"Yes, it is," Marie Laveau confirmed, as a frown suddenly appeared on her face.

At first, Ned assumed that the frown had been occasioned by the thought of the poisonous snakes to which she might be introduced by the *zambo* of Haiti in order to fulfill her supposed destiny, and a quip about Anacaona being the serpent in Christopher Columbus' Eden was on the tip of his tongue before he realized that the young woman was looking at something.

38

He strangled the witty remark and turned his head. The horizon was no longer uniform; there was now a wisp of vapor visible upon it—slender, to be sure, but promising nevertheless.

"It's not much," he commented, "but as great oak trees grow from little acorns, perhaps it might provide the germ of a shower, if not a hurricane."

"It's no cloud," she said, a trifle anxiously.

"What is it then?" Ned asked—but then guessed the answer to his own question. He sat up bolt upright, placing his head in direct sunlight for the first time, and shielded his eyes with his hand. "Is it headed this way?" he asked.

"Yes it is," she replied, "but whether that's good news or bad, I have no idea. I had not thought that there were any steamships in these waters, although they're an increasingly familiar sight in New Orleans, and I saw several at close range while visiting France."

That reminded Ned that he had not thought to ask Marie Laveau how she had come to be aboard the *Belleville*, traveling to Port-au-Prince from Le Havre—but it was too late now, for there were more urgent matters to consider.

"I know of one," he said, "if rumor can be trusted."

She looked at him sharply. "Patou's ship?" she said, immediately.

"Not exactly Patou's," he replied. "It's Mortdieu's now. If that really is the *Outremort*..."

Marie Laveau's expression had changed completely, from one of fearful doubt to extravagant delight. "I was right to trust my magic!" she exclaimed, as if she had hardly dared believe it. "My *loas* have answered my prayers! They have guided me faithfully—even the pirates, unwittingly, have served their purpose! I truly am appointed by fate!"

She stood up in the dinghy, and lifted her green parasol so high into the air as she could—which was a good deal further than Ned's short arms would have been able to lift it.

Chapter Three
A Naval Engagement

When the ship came close enough to be identified, Ned saw that it was, indeed, the *Outremort*. He still could not believe that it was coincidence that had brought them into the same region of the western Atlantic at the same time, and Marie Laveau's similar conviction was increased by a further order of magnitude when she saw the crew of the launch put out by the ship, which consisted entirely of living men: men she unhesitatingly identified as *zambo*.

"My *loas* are, indeed, intent on protecting me," she told Ned, while they waited for the launch to cross the margin of sea still separating them from the steamship. "You're merely one of their instruments. Who would ever have thought that the *zambo* could take possession of a steamship in order to search for me? This is an excellent omen. The *loas* must have a powerful interest in the present course of Earthly events, else they would not interfere to this remarkable extent."

"Divinities are inclined to do that when there is messianic labor to be done," Ned murmured, covering his skepticism with an irony so gentle that it was hardly perceptible. "Even the Christian God—who had a long history of bullying his creations, if the Old Testament is to be believed—was prepared to grant incarnation to his son, before tiring of the game and forsaking him to crucifixion. You might read your lessons differently, Mademoiselle, but everything I know of gods suggests that they will always let you down in the end, having nothing but contempt for the Rights of Man."

When the *zambo* had drawn alongside, thought, the pretty woman was very quick to speak to them in a language that Ned did not understand. He was reasonably fluent in French, which was the native language of Haitian whites and blacks alike, but this must have been a form of Tairo. The *zambo* in the boat, however, did not immediately fall to their knees and bow down before their would-be Queen. Although they were clearly excited by what she told them, some of them seemed to be treating what she said with the utmost suspicion. The crewmen were clearly not united in their opinion, for they immediately fell to arguing among themselves. Marie Laveau continued to harangue them, and seemed to be gaining the upper hand—although it seemed to Ned that she was not best pleased by whatever information they were giving her. The quarrel faded away though, and their rescuers eventually seemed willing to accept whatever instructions she was giving them

While this parley was in progress, the *zambo* men looked at Ned with even greater suspicion, but their attitude changed thereafter. Their chief eventually turned to him and asked, in French: "What ship cast you adrift?"

Ned was not ready to assume that the sailor was merely checking up on what Marie Laveau had told him; he had not heard the words "*Belleville*" or "Desart" anywhere in her discourse, and thought it possible that she had deliberately left that part of the explanation for him to give. "We were passengers on the French vessel *Belleville*," Ned told him, "which was taken by pirates last night. I believe the pirate vessel was the *Cayman*, commanded by Amédée Desart."

This statement did, indeed, seem to be news to the *zambo*, and caused some consternation among them. Some of them muttered apparent curses in the tongue that Marie Laveau understood.

"They're angry," she whispered to Ned, in English. "They were after the *Belleville* themselves, and are annoyed to have been forestalled. They did not expect me, as I had hoped, but once I can offer them proof of who and what I am, they will follow me. You must help me."

Ned was not at all sure that he could see the necessity, but he was anxious not to offend anyone for the moment. "I'd never realized that agricultural machinery was of such passionate interest to pirates," he muttered, before raising his voice to say, in French: "Will you take us to General Mortdieu? I have information to impart that will interest him."

That cast a pall of silence over the *zambo*; they looked at him with new interest and even deeper suspicion. "What do you know of the zombie Mortdieu?" the man in charge of the launch asked.

"I met him once in London," Ned declared, airily. "We crossed swords, briefly, but parted on reasonably good terms. I believe that I saved him some trouble on the wharf at Greenhithe. It's to me, more than any other individual, that he owes his easy escape from England. He'll be interested to see Gentleman Ned Knob again, I'm sure."

Marie Laveau seemed to think that this particular stratagem was a poor answer to her demand that he must help her, but he took the liberty of touching her forearm. "Patience, Milady," he said, in English. "These crude fellows might be reluctant to recognize you for what you are, but if Mortdieu has a *zambo* crew, he must have made an alliance with your people. Once we're ashore, you'll have your chance to spread the word. Trust me to serve as your protector for a while longer, where Mortdieu is concerned, and I shall be glad for you to serve as mine when the time comes."

In the meantime the men from the launch had exchanged a few muttered comments in their own language, the upshot of which was that Marie Laveau and Ned Knob were welcomed aboard the launch and given a water-bottle from which to sip while the dinghy was taken in tow and they were rowed back to the steamship.

Once aboard the larger vessel, Marie and Ned were both hustled below decks to the chart-room, where Ned found himself face to face once again with the Grey General and would-be Emperor of the Resurrected Dead. Considering his condition, he looked well; the strange hue of his flesh gave him the appearance of a man of iron, further emphasized by the grey military greatcoat that he wore, despite the heat. His trousers were also grey, as was the scabbard of the ceremonial saber he wore at his belt. He had a manner to match his costume, and it was not surprising that the zambo were in awe of him—although, if Ned read their expressions correctly, familiarity had already begun to take the edge off that awe.

"I know you," the General said, in French, and in a manner that left much to be desired in terms of courtesy. He was staring at Ned.

Ned bowed, in a slightly florid manner. "You owe me a debt, Monsieur, it's true," he replied, also in French. "You may consider it discharged, for we might well have perished before any other help arrived. In truth, I'm glad to see you for other reasons, too. I have news of your most successful counterpart, Victor Frankenstein's first creation—the Adam of the new Grey race. You're more fortunate than you know in having found us, for this is Marie Laveau, a direct descendant of Queen Anacaona, and a custodian of the secret wisdom of the *zambo*. There's none more expert than she in the making of Grey Men, for she has been traveling in America and France, and has supplemented the knowledge of her tribe with further lore."

General Mortdieu was very different from the *zambo*. He seemed to take all this aboard with uncanny equanimity, but there was a strange gleam in his eyes—which no longer had any of the dullness of death about them. He was evidently intrigued—more so, perhaps, by Marie Laveau than by Ned.

"Sit down," the Grey Man growled, indicating two of the stools that were bolted to the floor beside the chart-table. Mortdieu evidently wanted to treat them as subordinates—perhaps even prisoners—but Ned judged that he was not entirely confident that he had sufficient autocratic authority, even aboard his own stolen ship.

Mortdieu turned to the *zambo* who had escorted the two castaways down from deck, and took one of them aside for a murmured conversation in French. This time, Ned did hear the words "*Belleville*" and "Desart" mentioned. Again, Mortdieu received the news without his grey face changing expression, and calmed his crewman with a few curt words. Then he raised his voice to issue the order to return to shore at full speed.

He returned to his own stool and sat down before addressing Ned, this time in English: "Tell me exactly how you came to be set adrift," he ordered, curtly.

Marie—evidently having seen Mortdieu's muted reaction to what Ned had said about her—immediately attempted to reassert her own authority. "I was traveling to Port-au-Prince aboard the *Belleville*, General," she said, imperiously, in French. "I had undertaken a mission to Paris on behalf of my people. The *Belleville* was intercepted by the *Cayman*, a buccaneer out of La Tortue, captained by Amédée Desart. He had been hired to capture her cargo of agricultural machinery, by someone intent on making sure that it did not reach Jean-Pierre Boyer—perhaps the French government, perhaps the Americans, perhaps even Bahamians intent on improving their own production. Two *mestizos* in his crew, evidently having been forewarned by the same agent of my presence aboard, took it upon themselves to murder me, having already stabbed my bodyguard to death on deck. Monsieur Knob was kind enough, and valiant enough, to cut them down like the dogs they were.

"Desart would probably have murdered us both, but there was another Enghlishman aboard, with whom he was inclined to come to some kind of arrangement, and his intercession led to the small concession of our being set adrift. I'm glad to learn that Desart was not the only man ambitious to capture the machinery, and that my own people knew its value. Ours is a rich land, if its plantations can be properly cultivated and managed, and the aftermath of the English war has increased the prices of tobacco and sugar very markedly. Can you pursue the *Belleville* successfully, do you think? She's tacking into the wind, and might not find it easy to double the Pointe du Cheval Blanc in order to come into the Golfe de la Gonâve."

Mortdieu shook his grey head, sadly. "I can operate in relative safety east of Tortuga," he said, "but west of the isle I'm in hostile waters, and tackling a pirate crew rather than the *Belleville*'s merchant seamen would make the task difficult even in safer waters. I can't risk the *Outremort* in a rash venture like that. News of the *Belle-*

ville's approach reached me too late, alas—she was almost 24 hours ahead of schedule, and Desart must have had the Devil's own luck to catch her. Next time, perhaps…but I have a consolation prize, have I not? A direct descendant of Queen Anacaona, and a skilled maker of zombies, will surely help cement my alliance with your people—which is, I readily confess, a trifle shaky at present, and will not be assisted by my failure to capture the *Belleville*."

"Forgive me for interrupting, General," said Ned, "But is Sawney Ross aboard, by any chance. I'd be very glad of the opportunity to see him again."

Mortdieu returned his attention to Ned. "No," he said, after a slight pause. "Monsieur Ross is not aboard. Nor is Germain Patou. There has been…a parting of the ways. Nothing irredeemable I'm sure."

But in the interim, Ned thought, *no wonder you're glad to meet a rival zombie-maker*. Aloud, he said: "I'm sorry to hear that, General, but not overly surprised. Something similar has happened in Europe, where Henri de Belcamp is endeavoring to make his own new alliances. Frankenstein is being hunted from pillar to post by the Church and various States alike, and his new Adam—who prefers the name of Lazarus—is having some difficulty in negotiating a reconciliation with his second parent. The prospective conquest of death remains a direly controversial subject, not much assisted by the fact that nature's Grey Men—the revenants popularly known as vampires—seem to be desirous of claiming the new secrets of resurrection for their own use and exploitation."

"You have actually seen this…Lazarus?" Mortdieu asked, cautiously.

"Yes, indeed. We've fought side by side against the forces of the Roman Church and the Tuscan Light Cavalry. I don't say that we emerged victorious, any more than you were truly victorious at Greenhithe, but we lived to fight another day. That's a triumph in itself, in today's world—and while we can continue our work, the spark of a brighter future remains alive."

"*Our* work?" the Grey Man echoed. "And what, exactly, is *our* work?"

"The logical extrapolation of Jacobin science and Tom Paine's politics," Ned told him, forthrightly. "The firm establishment, in an Age of True Reason, of technologies of resurrection, which will eventually offer all living men the hope of a second life, and all Grey Men the prospect of a rewarding existence, as free individuals fully entitled to pursue their own destiny, without fear of superstitious dread and the violence that is its invariable accompaniment."

Mortdieu's face remained virtually expressionless, with the exception of his eyes, but Ned observed that Marie Laveau was looking at him in frank surprise, clearly unsure as to whether what he had just said was an honest declaration or deceptive bluster.

"Perhaps I was wise to spare your life, when I might have killed you in Purfleet," Mortdieu observed— although that did not quite tally with Ned's memory of their brief encounter under arms. "At the very least, you might make a useful ambassador to Patou's party, just as your companion might be a useful intercessor with the *zambo*. Fate appears to have favored me, in commanding Captain Desart to subject you to trial by ordeal rather than committing brutal murder."

"Your lucky star is with you still, it seems," Ned muttered, half to himself, "Despite the eclipse that led to Waterloo."

Mortdieu stiffened noticeably, and his strange eyes flashed fire. "Patou told you that, did he?" he hissed.

"No, General," Ned replied. "I guessed. I've known Henri de Belcamp longer than you. I'm familiar with his obsessions—and his bloody-minded stubbornness. When he learns that you're here, he'll be eager to come to your aid. By that time, he might have a powerful society at his beck and call."

"Monsieur de Belcamp and I did not part on good terms," Mortdieu reminded him.

"Nothing irredeemable I'm sure," Ned remarked, silkily. He felt, rather than saw, Marie Laveau stiffen in her turn, and realized that she too had guessed what he meant, and who General Mortdieu had been while he was a living man. Given the Haitians' current attitude to the Emperor who had betrayed and toppled Toussaint L'Ouverture, that was bound to make her own task more difficult.

Mortdieu was interrupted then by his second-in-command, who came precipitately into the chart-room to make a report. Apparently, the way to shore was blocked by canoes, whose crews seemed to be intent on doing battle with one another.

"We've nothing to fear from canoes, Jeannot," Mortdieu declared, letting his irritation show. "We can maneuver around them."

His subordinate explained that the point was to help his own people—Mortdieu's *zambo* allies—against their would-be *mestizo* attackers. He did not threaten mutiny, in so many words, but it was obvious that this was one instance in which Mortdieu was expected to serve the interests of the *zambo* rather than the other way around.

"Very well," said the Grey Man, curtly, and then gave orders for the armory to be opened and guns issued to the crew's marksmen—although he issued stern warnings against the wasting of ammunition, which Ned deduced to be in exceedingly short supply.

As the *Outremort*'s engine roared more violently than before, the General turned back to his guests and beckoned to them, inviting them to follow him on to the bridge. "Are you familiar with the lie of the land in the north-eastern part of Saint-Domingue?" he demanded of Marie, as they ascended the stairway.

"No," she admitted. "I was born and raised in New Orleans; I've spent very little time in Haiti itself, and almost all of that in Port-au-Prince."

"That's a pity," said the Grey Man. "We're under siege, and someone with sophisticated local knowledge might be able to give useful advice as to how to lift it."

"*Mestizos*?" Marie asked.

"Yes—if it were Boyer's army we'd have been overwhelmed by now, but there were precious few *mestizos* with Jean-Jacques Dessalines at the battle of Vertières, and there's a schism within the troops that were there. The mulattos think that Boyer has betrayed them—they expected to be given full rights of citizenship immediately, in return for their support, but Boyer's dragging his feet, under pressure from the purist blacks. Boyer has more important things to think about than us—the fate of the Republic's hanging by a thread."

"As the fate of the French Republic was just a little while ago," Ned could not resist remarking. "Is Boyer strong enough to save it do you think—with or without proclaiming himself Emperor?"

Mortdieu stared at him again, but they were on the bridge now, and the Grey Man postponed his reply in order to take stock of the situation. The coastline of Hispaniola was no more than a thin line on the horizon, but the expanse of sea ahead was littered with canoes—Ned counted 30 before giving up, and he estimated the total at something over 100. Some of them, he presumed, might have set forth on the rescue mission that Marie Laveau had optimistically anticipated—but if so, they had been swiftly pursued. He could not tell the members of one hybrid race from another at such a long range, but he judged from the way that the canoes were maneuvering that the *mestizos* outnumbered the *zambo*. Mortdieu's muttered curses suggested that the General had come to the same conclusion, and would rather not have engaged such an enemy at present.

The Grey Man bellowed the expected orders nevertheless, instructing the *Outremort*'s helmsman to change course and head directly for the *mestizo* "fleet." Two musketeers took up positions in the bow, with four loaders in attendance, ready to maintain a relay of six weapons. A dozen spearmen ranged in support, but it seemed to Ned that their supply of javelins would run out even before the guns ran out of powder and shot. Any canoe rammed by the heavy vessel would be capsized or smashed, but Ned suspected that their paddlers might well be sufficiently skillful to avoid such disasters.

"Better hope that your *loas* are still on the alert, Mademoiselle," Ned muttered to Marie Laveau. "These pirates might prove more dangerous than the last lot, and less inclined to be merciful if they contrive to board us."

Mortdieu cursed again as he saw the reaction of the *mestizos*—which was not to scatter or turn tail, but rather

51

to close ranks and redirect their attention to the new foe. They intended to give battle to the steamship—and take her if they could.

"My people will not allow us to be captured," Marie replied, confidently—and made a megaphone of her hands in order to shout orders of her own, in her own language.

Mortdieu did not like that at all, and made as if to silence her—but Ned stepped between them.

"Let her be, General, I beg you," he murmured. "You need her more than she needs you, for the moment, and she might be the best hope you have of getting though this sticky patch."

One glance around the deck was sufficient to inform the General that his *zambo* crew were, indeed, reacting positively to the young woman's exhortations—especially Jeannot, his first mate, who seemed to have been converted to her cult. However suspicious the men on the launch had been, they had spread the word around the crew that they had a *vaudou* priestess aboard, who was ambitious to be their savior. They too believed in the *loas*, and that the *loas* would determine the outcome of the impending skirmish, if they cared to act.

One of the musketeers who had taken up a position in the bow discharged his weapon, far too soon—the *mestizo* canoes were still out of range. Mortdieu groaned wearily, as if he had half-expected such recklessness and did not care for what it portended. That gave Marie Laveau the chance to seize the initiative wholeheartedly.

The young woman screamed at the musketeers and bounded forward to join them. She seized the other ready weapon from the second sniper and barked orders to the loaders, who revised their formation. Then she took up a lone position in the bow of the ship, musket in hand, reminiscent of one of the proud figureheads that French and English warships often bore, carved into the form of imperiously beautiful woman.

Mortdieu groaned again.

"No, General!" Ned said. "She was born and brought up in North America—my guess is that she's a lot more familiar with guns than your islanders. If she's a good shot..." He trailed off. The distance between the *Outremort* and the leading *mestizo* canoes, which were heading straight toward one another, had declined so rapidly that the smaller vessels were now within range.

Marie Laveau put the first musket to her shoulder, took careful aim and fired. Without a second's pause, she passed it backwards and took the next. With practiced ease, she put that weapon to her shoulder, aimed, and fired again.

She was, indeed, a good shot. Her first two bullets hit the men standing in the prows of the two leading canoes, urging their comrades to row harder. Both stricken men fell into the sea, splashing loudly.

The effect on the crew of the *Outremort* was sensational—the shots evidently seemed to them to be near-miraculous. Led by Jeannot, they cheered wildly. Even Mortdieu, standing helplessly beside Ned Knob, could not restrain a small exclamation of surprise and exultation.

Marie Laveau was still shouting, pouring forth a torrent of speech. She was still shooting, too the electrified loaders were passing her the muskets as quickly as they could prepare them, and she was firing them in as fast a relay as Ned had ever witnessed. Some of the shots missed their targets, but it was the first two that had set an expectation, and the *zambo* behaved as if every one was striking home unerringly, guided by the *loas*. Nor was it only the *zambo* who were impressed. A significant fraction of the mestizos suddenly lost their appetite for engaging the *Outremort* and attempting to seize the vessel. Had all the paddlers stuck to their work with determination, they might have come through what was, objectively speaking, a very thin drizzle of gunfire and pressed home their attack, but it only required one in three to falter for the formation to break down and panic to ensue.

Suddenly, the canoes ceased to be forces attacking with skill and discipline, and became ready targets for the *Outremort*'s armored prow. The racing steamship rammed into them, catching no less than three amidships and toppling their entire crews into the water. Nor did the *mestizos'* troubles end there, for the *zambo* crews that they had been pursuing before they first caught sight of the *Outremort* had regrouped and come about, ready now to become aggressors in their turn.

Marie Laveau's shrill voice carried so well over the calm surface of the sea that the *zambo* in the canoes could hear her now, and they seemed less suspicious by far of whatever she was saying than the crewmen of the launch had been. They began to howl on their own account.

The panic in the *mestizo* ranks was now unstoppable. Had they retained sufficient discipline to flee in good order, nine out of ten would have escaped, but they were in hopeless disarray. The steamship veered this way and that as Mortdieu began to shout instructions to the helmsman, colliding with one canoe after another. The spearmen aboard the larger vessel began to hurl their weapons, with the confidence of men inspired. Marie Laveau continued firing, her bullets striking home more often than they missed, despite the fact that most of her targets were no longer heading straight toward her, and thus presenting obliging targets.

Ned was cheering too, caught up in the general fervor of excitement, alternating cries of "Montjoie Saint Denis!" with hurrahs addressed to Sir Francis Drake and the spirit of the British Navy, confident that the *zambo* would understand and appreciate both. Within minutes, the potential battle had become an utter rout, and the *zambo* in the smaller vessels were merciless in their mopping-up.

Ned could not begin to count the dead, and was too hard-headed a realist to believe for a moment that the sea was turning red with blood, but he was glad to take note that not a single one of the *Outremort*'s crew was injured, and estimated that *mestizo* casualties on the water must have outweighed *zambo* casualties by at least eight to one.

At last, the remaining *mestizo* canoes contrived to flee westwards, and the *zambo*, intent on killing swimmers, let them go.

Marie Laveau was still shouting orders, and Ned observed, with a slight thrill of alarm, that the canoeists had now begun hauling bodies out of the water, for the sake of preserving corpses rather than rescuing living men.

Finally, the young woman refused the next gun that was offered to her and strode back to the bridge, with a strutting gait that Ned thought quite magnificent. It was Ned that she looked at first, rather than the Grey General.

"Did I not tell you that my people would come?" she said, triumphantly.

"Yes, you did," he agreed. "And now, it seems, you have an army at your beck and call. Might I ask what you intend to do with it?"

"You shall see," she promised, looking at Mortdieu now rather than her erstwhile companion. "You shall see what the power of *vaudou* can achieve, once properly unleashed."

Chapter Four
Vaudou *in Action*

"Well," General Mortdieu muttered to Ned, as the *Out-remort* resumed her shoreward journey, her speed reduced so as not to outstrip the enthusiastic escort that now surrounded her. "What *will* she do?" The Grey Man was speaking through gritted teeth, although he had been allowed to maintain his position of nominal authority on the bridge while Marie Laveau was moving about the deck, consulting with her new disciples.

"How should I know?" Ned retorted. "I saved her life by accident, having not the slightest idea of what I might be unleashing. Can the *zambo* really take on Boyer, do you think? Could they really restore their own version of Tairo dominion to the island?"

"Never," was Mortdieu's expert judgment. "They're far too few, and too widely-despised. While Boyer is still weak, the consequent disorder can be exploited; the north country won't be pacified for some years. The best the *zambo* can hope for, though, is to hold off their enemies and establish a defensible enclave—and that would be best done discreetly. If they were to become so troublesome that the blacks and mulattos came to the support of the *mestizos*, in opposition to them, they'd be annihilated."

"Is there any hope of their finding allies outside Haiti?" Ned asked.

"The French, you mean?" the Grey Man replied. "None at all. France has every interest in keeping Boyer weak, but not at the expense of making any of his rivals strong."

"But the lady has recently been to France," Ned pointed out, "and has come back ready and eager to undertake her mission. The people of France might not be as drastically divided as the people of Hispaniola, but it's a troubled nation nevertheless, in which the enmity between Royalists, Republicans and Imperialists has by no means been laid to rest in the aftermath of military defeat."

Mortdieu's eyes glittered, but he had to concede the point. "You evidently know more about the present state of France than I do," he said. "Which of these forces do you think likely to support her, and how?"

When the question was put like that, Ned could not immediately think of any alliance the would-be Witch-Queen might have been able to forge. Indeed, he could only think of one man in the whole of France who might have been willing to pledge her anything. He racked his brains to recall whether he had mentioned Henri de Belcamp's name to her during their conversation in the dinghy, and concluded that he had not—any more than she had mentioned it to him. That thought caused him to glance at the young woman speculatively. To fill the silence, he said: "Has she any potential allies closer to home?"

Mortdieu shook his steely head. "Tortuga has become a pirate stronghold again, as it was the golden age of piracy 150 years ago," he said, "but the buccaneers are in no position to lend material aid to the *zambo*, even if they had any such desire. They're a sharp thorn in Boyer's side, because ships crossing the Atlantic invariably take the northern route along the line of the islands rather than taking long detours south to use the Guadeloupe Passage into the Caribbean Sea, but they're no more than that, and owe their persistence to the fact that he's reluctant to risk the depleted navy he seized from the French in an all-out attack on their heavily-fortified deep-water harbor. The *maroons* of Cuba feel no more kinship to the *zambo* than to the rival groups on their own island."

Ned shielded his eyes in order to study the rapidly-approaching coast. He guessed that the bay for which the *Outremort* was heading must lie to the east of Cap Haitien, almost due north of the Trou du Nord, not far from the notional border that separated Hispaniola into two indistinct halves. "Did Patou and Ross move further along the coast," he asked, "or did they head inland?"

Mortdieu only hesitated momentarily before saying; "Inland. The *mestizos* have cut them off, but they have *zambo* support too, so I doubt that they'll be slaughtered any time soon. My own company's in greater danger, for now—although I suppose I ought to hope that your friend's fine display might change that—because the *mestizos* would be just as happy to get their hands on a steamship as the *zambo* would be to have a some good steel tools and heavy ploughs to replace those the French took with them when they abandoned their holdings."

The Grey General raised his telescope to his eye in order to study the shore. The beach was already thronged with people, and more were emerging from the forest to the east of the inlet to watch the steamship's approach. Mortdieu scanned the distant company for a minute or more before saying: "They're in an ebullient mood. The fact that we've won a rare victory over the *mestizos* has raised their spirits enormously. Your friend is sure of an extravagant welcome—although it's likely that her performance will serve to stir the *mestizos* up like a nest of angry hornets. Can she really make zombies in profusion?" He had evidently taken note of the body-collection.

"I don't know," Ned said, "but she surely intends to try." His eyes flicked momentarily in the direction of the Sun, which was reddening as it descended toward the western horizon, but was still at least an hour away from setting. Then he adjusted his gaze downwards, and saw men moving along the western headland bordering the bay. He pointed them out to Mortdieu, and said; "*Mestizos*?"

Mortdieu aimed the telescope. "Yes," he said—but I doubt that there's any danger of an attack this evening. They want to keep an eye on what's happening, that's all—they'll need time to plan their next move." He did not seem entirely convinced, and Ned could not help recalling his earlier remark about angry hornets.

Ned saw that there were canoes off the point as well as scouts on land, but Mortdieu was right; they were not the advance guard of any attacking army, but merely scouts watching the *Outremort* return home.

The steamship headed for an inlet in the centre of the bay, where a substantial stream ran between tall trees—although the land to either side of the inlet had been partly cleared in order that crops might be planted. There was a wooden jetty at which the steamship could moor, and as dusk finally fell, Mortdieu—still conducting himself as befit the master of the vessel—led Ned and Marie over a makeshift gangplank on to dry land. Once they were ashore, however, the Grey Man made no objection to Marie Laveau taking the lead in order to address the considerable crowd that had gathered here, and was still swelling as she spoke.

Ned had no idea what she said to them, and he doubted that Mortdieu could make out more than the occasional word, but the crowd grew even more excited. Various individuals—females as well as males—began to peel off as they received specific orders of some kind, collecting others as they moved along the banks of the stream and into the forest. Some were armed with axes, machetes and spades, and Ned realized as he judged the quality of those implements why the people of Haiti had been so enthusiastic to renew the meager inheritance that they had acquired from the debris left behind by the fleeing French colonists.

"What is she sending them forth to do?" Mortdieu asked.

Again, Ned could only confess his ignorance, although he suspected that they might well be gathering the raw materials required for the manufacture of *bokor*. Then, however, he heard the name "Francis Drake" pronounced, and saw Marie Laveau gesturing in their direction.

"What is she doing now?" Mortdieu wanted to know.

"I think she's telling them that you're a reincarnation of Francis Drake, just as she's a reincarnation of Queen Anacaona," Ned replied, momentarily delighted that she had taken up his suggestion—and then he realized what the move implied. "That's where she intends to look for support, I think," he told the General, "not to the French or any of the other sectors of the population of Haiti, but to the *maroons* of the other islands. Her long-term ambition is to organize a Caribbean-wide movement, seeded here on Hispaniola."

"She's crazy!" opined the General.

"Yes, she is," Ned agreed. "But what a madness! If I were you, General, I'd accept her gift with gratitude, no matter how reluctant you might be to take the name of an Englishman. You must have gone to some trouble to conceal who you really are, and if someone in Patou's estranged company were to take it into his head to reveal the truth..." He stopped, as Mortdieu reached out and grabbed his arm.

"You have no idea who I really am, Monsieur Knob!" he hissed, with naked menace in his voice.

Ned had no wish to start an argument, so he bowed his head, released his arm gently, and said: "As you wish, General."

"No," Mortdieu persisted. "I mean exactly what I say: *you have no idea*."

Ned would have enquired further as to what the Grey Man meant, but the crowd parted then, and he became uncomfortably aware of the fact that hundreds of eyes were staring at the two of them, expectantly.

Marie Laveau stepped toward them, and spoke in a hushed tone, in English. "Please, gentlemen," she said, "trust me to do what is best, for now. I will preserve your hegemony, General, so that you might have a disciplined army to lead if and when the time comes, but we must work together if anything is to be achieved. I have a demonstration to make, and preparations to put in hand. Bear with me, I beg you—and go to your hut quietly, for now, to eat and rest. You will have pride of place at the demonstration, I promise you."

As was only to be expected, Mortdieu was not at all pleased to be so casually usurped in his own headquarters, but he recognized that matters were out of his hands. He consented to walk away, maintaining his dignity. Ned followed him, meekly, but not before whispering: "If he is to be the new Francis Drake, my lady, what am I?"

"Patience, Monsieur Knob," she said. "You'll be my ambassador to Germain Patou, of whose knowledge I might have desperate need within the week—but for now, rest and recover your strength. I have a long night still ahead of me, if I'm to strike while the iron is hot."

The evening heat was fierce as they moved through the village, seemingly more humid now that they were no longer out at sea. As Ned walked he was surrounded by a swarm of insects, which had emerged to frolic in the dwindling light. They filled the air above and along-side the creek—but they did not trouble General Mort-dieu, who walked among them as if surrounded by a magical *cordon sanitaire*.

There were a few more Grey Men among the crowd thronging the village, but not as many as Ned had ex-pected or hoped to see. All of them seemed to be slow-moving, and some had living companions to guide them, but they were treated with evident respect by the *zambo*, who made room for their progress and bowed their heads as they went by. Three came to meet Mortdieu, apparent-ly expecting to receive orders, but Mortdieu was content to dismiss them without specific instructions. It was ob-vious that the mixed company that had fled Europe had divided unevenly, the greater fraction of the self-aware and physically-capable Grey Men having elected to go with Patou, presumably for the sake of the care and edu-cation that he could offer. The *zambo* who had adopted Mortdieu as a military leader clearly had not been able to replenish the stock of his peers.

Mortdieu escorted his new ally to the largest hut in the village, which was built of the same coarse wood as all the others but showed some signs of architectural intelligence. Once they were safely inside, with the door closed behind them, Mortdieu took off his greatcoat and threw it aside gratefully, but retained his waistcoat and his saber. There was still something of the popinjay about him, even though he was no longer putting on a show for his ragged army.

Ned observed that the General had appointed his residence as well as he could with the aid of such treasures as the *Outremort* had brought from London, but had not contrived to gather much loot left behind by the French. The *Belleville* would have been a fine prize, had he contrived to catch it first and take it—but the more Ned saw of the village and its people, the less convinced he was that the *zambo* would have been able to take the prize, even with Mortdieu to plan their strategy and lead them into battle in a steamship. That the Grey Man had enjoyed a great deal of prestige here was indubitable, but he had obviously been working against the tide of circumstance.

"Eat," said Mortdieu, as he showed Ned to his dining-table—an uncommonly sturdy item cut from good English oak. "Then you ought to rest, as the lady says, for you're doubtless weary."

There were various fruits on the table, few of which Ned recognized, but there was no meat, and only poor bread made from maize. There was, however, a large pitcher of water and an earthenware cup, from which Ned drank gratefully before collapsing into a wicker chair and commencing a scrupulous investigation of the solid fare on offer.

"You were sent to find me, were you not, Monsieur Knob?" the Grey Man said.

"Strictly speaking," Ned said. "I was sent to find Germain Patou. He's the one with the valuable knowledge—unless you've persuaded him to make you party to all his discoveries."

"He knows less than you suppose," Mortdieu retorted. "I remain a mystery to him, although he's persuaded your old friend Ross to remember something of his former life, and the monster too."

"Monster?" Ned queried.

"The patchwork man—the one he put together when he and Belcamp still believed more of Walton's fantasy than was actually credible. The one whose brain was placed in a different body."

"The one he called John?" Ned queried, rhetorically. "I remember. Did the transplantation really work?"

"Better than most straightforward resurrections employing fresh and relatively undamaged corpses, although subsequent experiments along the same lines failed miserably. Patou understood it no better than I—but I, at least, have the privilege of personal experience. I know better than anyone what is involved in metamorphosis, mentally as well as physically."

"Metamorphosis?" Ned echoed, as he continued his experiments with the strange fruit. He raised his voice because a number of drums—perhaps as many as a dozen—had begun to beat outside, soon settling into a common but complex rhythm. "Is that why I have no idea who you are? Because you have undergone a metamorphosis that has made you a different person, no matter how many memories you retain of...your former self?"

"That is one of evolution's customary pathways, is it not?" Mortdieu said. "The Chevalier de Lamarck once presented my *former self* with a book on the subject. Worms discovered ways to transform themselves into all kinds of different creatures by means of their innate drive to perpetual improvement, just as the embryos of mammals learned how to become all manner of creatures by similar effort. Now, humans are beginning to master a new means of metamorphosis, in order to produce further imagoes...but few have begun to master the art, as yet, even with the right alchemical assistance."

"The most spectacular exception being yourself," Ned observed, "and you don't know how you performed the trick."

"No, I don't," Mortdieu admitted. "One thing I do know, though, is that it was not Patou's science that determined my transition, no matter how cleverly it assisted me. The urge to return, and the ability to make it happen, was already within me. The making of Grey Men is no mere mechanical process."

"That does seem to be the case," Ned agreed, thoughtfully. "Have you seen any *zambo* zombies as yet?"

"A mere handful," Mortdieu told him, "and all of them more stupid than the least of my erstwhile followers. Their existence proves, however, that return from death is not something new, and that Jacobin science cannot claim full credit for it."

"If what Guido told me about his vampire master is true," Ned murmured, "*vaudou* magic cannot claim full credit either, for such metamorphoses can happen without any kind of artificial intervention at all—and might be more common, were it not for customs dictating the burial or cremation of the dead. There are Societies for the Prevention of Premature Burial in Europe and America, which offer testimony to the fact that people thought dead do sometimes recover consciousness. Even so, artificial interventions of more than one kind obviously enhance the chances of the dead returning to a semblance of life. Do you know, perchance, what that drumming signifies?" The number of active drums had grown by now from a dozen to something of the order of 100, although most were more distant than those that had begun the concert.

"The *zambo* use drums in signaling as well as to regulate dancing," Mortdieu told him. "I suspect they're spreading news that will eventually be transmitted to every corner of the island—but not in any detail."

If the General was correct, then the drums served a dual purpose, for a Grey Man came into the hut then, with a *zambo* companion. The Grey Man greeted his commander formally, but it was the *zambo* who spoke thereafter, saying: "Anacaona invites you to witness the rite of Damballah Wedo, Monsieur Mortdieu."

"You won't have an opportunity to rest, after all, Monsieur Knob," the Grey General remarked, as he came to his feet. "We had best take some food and water with us. I've been witness to these native rituals before—it might be a long night."

Ned saw no objection to that. He stuffed fruit into his pockets and picked up the water-jug. He noticed that Mortdieu, as befit a great general, left that humble duty entirely to him, and permitted himself a slight sigh.

A huge bonfire had been lit some distance from the edge of the village, beside the stream that wound into the tangled forest. Ned saw that a number of shallow graves had been dug to either side of it, in the soft and glutinous soil of the stream's bank. When he was able to make a more accurate estimation, he counted two dozen of the pits, each containing several inches of muddy water, in which the bodies that lay within them were almost completely immersed. They were not so much graves, he realized, as baths. Each one contained a dead man harvested from the sea-battle—which implied, Ned supposed, that at least some of them must be dead *mestizos* rather than dead *zambo*, although the combination of firelight and shadow was not conducive to judging the identity of any particular body by the shade of its complexion.

Marie Laveau was about to attempt zombie resurrection on a scale that had probably never been attempted before among the *zambo*. She must, he presumed, have had teams of assistants working flat out to produce adequate quantities of *bokor*, according to the supposedly-secret recipe, for she had certainly not been able to bring anything with her from the *Belleville* when Desart had set her adrift.

The drums were still pounding, and many people in the crowd that had gathered in a broad arc around the fire were swaying to the rhythm, but there was no dancing as such. Drinking-bowls were being passed around, but Ned could not tell what they contained. Some of the seated drummers were chanting, but their words were meaningless to Ned and Mortdieu.

Mortdieu was conducted to a stool set up at the mid-point of the arc of human beings, but Ned was left to stand beside him, while the other Grey Man was positioned on his other side. Some time passed before Marie put in her appearance—perhaps, Ned thought, because she was allowing the tension of expectation to build up, in her guests as well as those she intended to become the loyal followers of her new cult.

The insects were not as troublesome now as before—not so much because the night was not completely dark, save for starlight, as because of the smoke from the fire, which was thick and aromatic. The wood and foliage that was burning was green and rich in sap, but the spitting and crackling of the conflagration was easily drowned out by the insistent drums.

Eventually, though, some invisible signal was given, and the tempo of the drums changed.

Marie Laveau then appeared, in her guise as Anacaona, the serpent in Columbus' Eden. There was, indeed a snake—a constrictor, Ned assumed—draped over her shoulders, with its tail coiled around her waist. She was not dancing, though. Instead, she was walking slowly, in a labored and awkward fashion occasioned by the fact that she had a heavy wooden pail in each hand, presumably full of water. Half a dozen nubile girls followed her, arranged in three pairs, also moving slightly awkwardly because they bore collections of huge palm-fronds in their arms.

Marie moved to the nearest of the pits, set the pails down, and reached into one of them, a trifle tentatively. She drew out something that might have been a fish, or a snake; it was difficulty to be sure, because it was wriggling so furiously. Handling it very carefully, she introduced it into the mud of the pit, beside the corpse's head. Then she began to cover the pit, neatly and carefully, with palm-fronds—a task completed by her acolytes.

"What is she doing?" Mortdieu hissed, in Ned's ear.

Ned was about to tell him that he had no idea, but then he guessed. "Dear Lord!" he murmured. "She's certainly not short of daring—or faith in her blessed *loas*."

"What kind of snakes are they?" Mortdieu demanded, as the reincarnation of Queen Anacaona laid another wriggling creature in the second pit.

"They're not snakes," Need replied, "although I dare say that they can pass for Damballah Wedo's creatures in the eyes of the zambo. If my guess is right, they're eels—electric eels. She must have had 50 fishermen chasing them up and down every stream in the region."

"Ah!" said Mortdieu, who knew well enough how Germain Patou carried out his own resurrections. "Surely it won't work?"

"Maybe not," Ned murmured, "but it can't hurt, so any effect it does chance to have is likely to be positive—and in any case, it's new. If it does contrive to increase the chances of zombie resurrection, it'll be proof positive, in the eyes of the *zambo* that she's exactly what she claims to be. Even if it doesn't, any success that she can achieve—and she's certainly giving herself plenty of chances—will work in her favor. It's a wild gamble, but it always was—the whole enterprise, that is. You have to give her credit for guts, even if she is a little crazy, and credit for listening too. I gave her that idea. I only helped to confirm the plan she's already made to use Drake's name, but this is a hasty improvisation occasioned by what I told her about Patou."

"You must be very proud," said Mortdieu, dryly.

It took time to place an electric eel in very pit, and then to cover each "grave" over with palm leaves, but Marie and her assistants completed the task, moving more elegantly now to the rhythm of the drums. Then she took up a position close to the fire—so close that Ned feared that she might be scalded or burned by the spitting conflagration. She unwound the constrictor from her body and handed it over to one of her female assistants. Then two men came forward, carrying two rush baskets in a very tentative manner.

"What now?" Mortdieu wondered. "Surely she can't…"

"I think she has to," Ned murmured. "The demonstration has to be complete."

From each of he two baskets, Marie took a snake—no constrictor, this time—holding each in one hand. Whether they were the "black mambas" that she had mentioned in the boat as having been imported to the island along with black slaves, Ned could not be sure, but their bodies were grey-green rather than black. Initially, the young woman held each one behind the head, in such a way that they could not possibly bite, but then she let their bodies coil around her outstretched arms, and released the heads, so that they hung down, suspended, free to strike at her body if they so desired.

The snakes apparently had no such desire. They were content to hang there, swaying slightly as if in time to the music.

They're torpid, Ned thought. *They've been numbed—not merely by the smoke and the rhythm of the drums, although that probably helps, but by some kind of drug. Deadly the might be, but there's no way that they're going to sink their fangs into her lovely breasts unless they're jerked out of their torpor by some sudden alarm. What a showman she is! An American through and through!*

Marie was swaying too, but only swaying, as if she too were benumbed. Her eyes were closed, but she was humming. The crowd took up the hum, until it grew into the sound of a vast insect-swarm: a hive of bees numbered in millions, or a host of locusts ready to devour everything in its path.

Then a single gunshot rang out, and the shock of the impact sent the would-be Witch-Queen reeling backwards.

For a moment, it looked as if the young woman might tumble into the fire, but the shot had not been mortal, and she contrived to avoid that disaster, falling on to her side in the margin between the roaring flames and the green-topped mock-graves.

Chapter Five
Pandemonium

Hundreds of the *zambo* seized makeshift weapons, and raced into the forest toward the place from which the *mestizo* sharpshooter had fired. There must have been other *mestizos* waiting in the trees, having used that cover to creep closer while their enemies' attention had been riveted on Marie Laveau. The sounds of conflict immediately flared into a chaotic cacophony of shots, shouts and screams. Dozens of gunshots initially rang out in near-unison, but the *mestizos* had only time enough to fire one concerted volley, which was quite impotent to stem the angry tide of vengeful *zambo*. The gunfire became sparse thereafter.

"The fools!" groaned Mortdieu. "For months I've been drilling them, teaching them discipline. I had a force that could at least defend its holdings, although it was not yet fit to mount an efficient attack—but they failed to set pickets, as I've taught them to do, and a single well-aimed bullet has taken them back to savagery at a stroke!"

We have two nests of angry hornets now, it seems, Ned thought.

He ran forward toward Marie as far as his short legs could carry him, leaping over several of the zombie-pits in order to get to her. As he went, he picked up a log intended to feed the fire, intending to take no chances with the snakes she had draped over her arms. It was as well he did; torpid as they had certainly been, the shock of the fall had revived them, and they were ready to strike. He killed one with a single blow, but had to dance backwards out of range of the other one, along a strip of ground that was by no means wide, with the blazing fire on one side and the treacherous pits on the other.

As soon as he was balanced again, Ned attacked the second snake with a will, and beat it to death in a matter of seconds. Marie, meanwhile, lay quite still.

The bullet had hit her upper arm—and might, with a little more luck, have struck the snake instead of her. Had it done so, the frightened snake would not have had the opportunity to bite her—which, alas, it had, a few inches below the ragged bullet-wound, close to the crook of the elbow.

Ned wasted no time, but picked the stricken woman up, and edged between the pits before breaking into a run. He carried her back into the village, to General Mortdieu's hut, where he laid her down on the General's own bed. Some 20 or 30 *zambo*—mostly women—followed him, anxiously, but were content to crowd around the door and windows of the hut, watching to see what he would do.

Ned judged that the bloody bullet-wound lessened the chances that the poison would be carried by the veins into her torso, back toward the heart, but the poison was still in her lower arm. "Give me a knife!" he screamed at Mortdieu—who was so astonished that he drew his saber and handed it over without a murmur.

Ned used the awkward but keenly-sharpened weapon to slit the flesh in the vicinity of the snakebite, and then set about trying to suck the poison out as best he could, spitting bloody fluid on to the floor of the hut in a series of violent expectorations. "Do you have any bandages?" he demanded of the Grey Man.

The General did have bandages, left over from the supplies the *Outremort* had taken aboard before her transatlantic voyage. Fortunately the bullet had gone straight through the flesh of the arm, so Ned was not required to attempt any further makeshift surgery in order to remove it. He continued spitting while he bound the wounds, fearful of swallowing venom himself. Finally satisfied with his work, he collapsed into a wicker chair that was positioned beside the bed.

"Will she live?" Mortdieu asked.

"How should I know?" Ned demanded, harshly. "Patou's the doctor, not I. Binding wounds was an element of Tom Paddock's course in villainy, but I could not guarantee the quality of the advice, and everything I know about snakebite comes from casual rumor. The *mestizos* must be exceedingly determined to murder her, to have found volunteers for a suicide mission like that."

"This is Haiti," Mortdieu told him. "Suicide is not as rare as it is in Paris—and tribal hatreds run very deep. She caused them a terrible loss of face this afternoon—as half-whites, they consider themselves much superior to the half-black *zambo*, and take defeats very ill."

"If she does recover," Ned muttered, "they'll pay for it in blood."

"They'll do that whether she recovers or not," Mortdieu judged. "This is out of anyone's control, now—all Hell has been let loose."

"Perhaps the *mestizos* dared not wait for the outcome of her experiment," Ned muttered. "If the zombies do rise from their muddy graves in due course...there might be more than Hell to pay."

"She was crazy," Mortdieu opined, again, as if talking to himself. "I knew that—but how could I stop her?

75

Any hope I had of maintaining a balance here is lost now."

"Can you get word to Patou?" Ned asked, abruptly. "The only chance we have of reasserting control over the situation is to make sure that Marie lives—and we'll stand a better chance of that if we have a trained doctor to help us. No matter what your differences are, you must summon him if you can."

The General only hesitated momentarily, and that was to wonder who he could possibly trust as an emissary. It only took a few seconds for him to decide. "I shall have to go myself," he said. "Nothing less than that will convince him. I'll take Jeannot and two more of the *Outremort*'s crewmen with me, if I can find two more who still have discipline enough to follow orders and respect enough for me to follow mine. Normally, it would be too dangerous, but I doubt that the *mestizo* siege is as tightly organized now as it was before. You stay here— care for her as best you can, and try to talk some sanity back into the *zambo* when daylight cools their heads again. Most of them—the men, at least—speak French as well as the old Tairo language."

"Agreed, General," said Ned, knowing that there was no other choice. "Go fetch Patou."

When the Grey Man had gone, the *zambo* keeping vigil outside the hut maintained their positions, patiently waiting to see what would happen. For some while, nothing did—but then the woman on the bed stirred, and opened her eyes. She tried to lift her arm, but could not, so she raised herself up on her other elbow and looked down at the bloody bandages. She was obviously in pain, but she was fighting to control it, and her mind did not seem to be wandering.

"Lie back," Ned advised her. "I'm glad to see you're awake, for you had a narrow escape. The bullet tore the flesh of your arm badly, but I was more afraid of the snakebite. I sucked out as much poison as I could, but I feared that I might have been too late."

She tried to stare at him, although she had difficulty focusing her eyes. "You really do seem determined to save my life, Monsieur Knob," she whispered, hoarsely. "I thank you—although the snakebite would not have killed me."

"Why not?" Ned asked, suddenly wondering whether the performance had been a trick, and the snakes harmless.

"Immunization," she murmured, letting her head fall back on the pillow. "A wise precaution. *Vaudou* priestesses in New Orleans keep mambas too. Tiny doses, over time…accustom the flesh."

But I have had no opportunity to immunize myself with tiny doses, Ned thought. *Still, I had to try to suck the poison out. I'm a gentleman, after all. If I continue in this vein much longer, I might yet qualify as a hero.* Aloud, he said: "I'm glad to hear it, your majesty. Even so, Mortdieu has gone to fetch Patou, if he can. It's pandemonium out there—you enraged the *mestizos* this afternoon, and now they've enraged the *zambo* in their turn. A patient siege has turned into an all-out war."

"The *zambo* will win," she murmured.

"I'm afraid that there's no guarantee of that, Mademoiselle. A more gradual approach might have served your experiment a little better, for it will take days—will it not?—for any of the dead that might rise again to emerge from their muddy holes like flies from their chrysalids. Do you really believe that electric eels might substitute for Patou's Voltaic piles?"

"Who knows?" she countered. "I have every faith in the *loas*—but they are never too proud to accept a little assistance. They will not let my wound fester, for I have work to do on their behalf."

"Even so," Ned observed, "they might appreciate a little assistance from Germain Patou, if Mortdieu can reach him and persuade him to come." Having ascertained that she was not about to slip back into unconsciousness, he gave her a drink of water, and he asked: "Who did you see in France, Mademoiselle? What alliance did you try to forge there?"

"I'm not at liberty to tell you that, Monsieur Knob," was her reply.

"Well," he said, "I suppose you think that's *for the best.*" He watched her eyes very carefully as he pronounced the final phrase. She did not react in the slightest. "Tell me," he went on, "have you ever heard of an organization that names itself *Civitas Solis*?"

This time, her eyes did narrow slightly. "I've heard talk of it in New Orleans," she admitted, cautiously. "The Society of Jesus played an important part in pioneering the southern states on North America, and is rumored to have other societies within it, or which overlap it."

"Wheels within wheels," Ned observed. "I only know them by rumor myself, although two of my dearest friends have had contact with them. Such are the complications of life, alas, that the two friends in question consider themselves mortal enemies, and it will take more than the humble endeavors of a man like me to bring about a reconciliation. One of them was born Comte Henri de Belcamp, although he uses many other names, including Tom Brown, James Davy, Percy Balcomb…and John Devil. Was the idea of representing

General Mortdieu as a reincarnation of Francis Drake, in the hope of uniting all the maroons in the Caribbean into an army of liberation, really your own, Mademoiselle? Was it even your own idea to represent yourself as a reincarnation of Queen Anacaona, in order to start that revolution in Haiti?"

She was almost too weak and weary to smile, but she contrived a faint grimace of amusement. She took advantage of her condition, however, to refuse an answer.

"You have been playing games with me, Mademoiselle," Ned said, suppressing his annoyance. "You knew who and what I was before you set foot on the *Belleville*. You had the advantage of me all along. Why did you not tell me that you knew him, and were working with him? Why, for that matter, did *he* not tell *me*?"

"You've taken the King's shilling, Monsieur Knob," she murmured. "You answer to Gregory Temple."

Ned sighed. The life of a double agent was never simple, especially for one who often did not know himself which side he was really on. He could hardly blame others for not trusting him, when he was not sure that he could trust himself.

"You do know, I suppose, that Henri's utterly and completely mad?" he said. "I might serve two masters, both with some reluctance and under some duress, but he has half a dozen masters competing for supremacy within himself. He's a genius of sorts, but his grand plans have a nasty habit of going awry—to an extent that makes even God seem reliable. Many men, so far as I've been able to observe, can easily qualify as their own worst enemy, but only in poor Henri's case does that amount to a veritable army ranged against him. He has exceedingly grandiose dreams, but he's never yet brought any of them close to fulfillment—and the manner of their failure makes him an exceedingly dangerous playfellow."

"This time," Marie Laveau insisted, "we will succeed. It needs an empire to change the world."

"And to reconcile the world to the pursuit of successful resurrection by Jacobin science," Ned supplied, "it will require an empire in which the reborn dead are honored, and welcome among the ranks of the living. I've heard the speech. That was doubtless the train of thought that brought the *Outremort* to Haiti, and directed the eyes of John Devil and Lord Byron to the same target—but Haiti has not responded as we could have wished, has it? Trelawny's chances of making a compact with Boyer are surely as remote as your chances of rousing the *zambo* to successful revolt—and the schemes cannot *both* succeed, can they?"

"And what is your plan, Monsieur Knob?" she demanded, adding: "There is, of course, no need to ask what Gregory Temple's plan might be."

Gregory Temple's plan, Ned knew—or, rather, his obsession—was to track down John Devil. Even the kidnapping of his grandson, which had forced him into temporary alliance with his arch-enemy, had not turned him aside from that quest. Temple kept Ned on a leash, even though he knew perfectly well that Ned was also reporting to Henri, precisely because that gave him a connection to monitor and follow. But what, indeed, was Ned's own plan for achieving the objective he had represented to General Mortdieu—and, incidentally to Marie Laveau—as *ours*? How did he indeed to bring about a world in which Jacobin science was free to seek and perfect a technology that would guarantee an opportunity for resurrection to everyone?

"I'm no grand strategist, Mademoiselle," Ned told her. "I just try to get by from day to day, lending a hand whenever and wherever I can, administering tiny pushes in the right direction."

She managed a slightly fuller smile. "For which I'm grateful, Monsieur Knob," she said. "I owe you more than one debt now."

The *zambo* drums, which had been silent since the furious *zambo* had launched themselves into an all-out attack on the *mestizos*, suddenly started up again. At first there were only a handful, whose sound seemed to be coming from the seaward side of the village, but their signal was taken up almost immediately by dozens more, and then by hundreds, as the message they were attempting to relay spread southwards and westwards, urgently and—if Ned was any judge of tempo—desperately.

"What's happening?" Marie demanded.

"I don't know," Ned told her, "but if I can judge the message by its tone, the battle hasn't gone well." He went to the door of the room and looked at the main door of the hut, where the *zambo* keeping vigil had already begun to melt away. "What does it mean?" he shouted, in French.

One of the *zambo*—presumably one of Mortdieu's crewmen—came into the hut. "We have no guns, Monsieur," he said. "We have no more than a handful of warriors to defend the village, and all in disarray. We must flee. You and the lady must come with us, else all is lost. We will protect you."

Ned could see that it was no time for argument. He nodded his head, and ran back to the bed. He picked Marie up, just as he had when she had fallen by the fire.

Short as he was, he had strong arms, and legs that could run for miles.

"Hold on to my neck, Mademoiselle," he said. "This might be a long chase."

He was wrong, though; he had hardly got to the threshold of the hut when gunfire blazed, and the man who was waiting there for him collapsed in a heap. To go outside would have been to risk instant death, and Ned had no alternative but to fall back to the table, which he overturned unceremoniously, in order that the tabletop might make a shield of sorts. He was careful, though, to snatch up the lantern from the tabletop before he tipped the table over, and set it down on the floor nearby, so that it could still illuminate the room. He deposited Marie behind the makeshift barricade, and then looked around for a weapon. Unfortunately, Mortdieu had returned his saber to its sheath before leaving, and the best he could find was a rusty machete.

"You must not let the *mestizos* take me," Marie said, urgently. "My people will defend me to the last man, but if it all comes to naught, and capture is inevitable, you must slit my throat yourself."

Ned glanced at the rusty blade of the machete, and knew that there would be nothing neat about any slit it made. The drums were already falling silent again, and he knew, too, that the pretty woman's romantic faith in the willingness of "her people" to give up their lives for her was wildly exaggerated. She did not really know them at all, and—more crucially—they did not know her. Even if her demonstration had not ended so abruptly, they would not have been ready yet to hail her as a messiah. Now, they were running for their lives, leaving her to whatever fate their enemies might have in store for her.

The guns continued to blaze: the enemy obviously had far more of them than the *zambo* would have been able to muster, even if their warriors had not been lured away to avenge the *mestizos'* surprise attack.

Ned calculated that he had a couple of minutes, at the most, to decide on a course of action. He decided that he would have to fight, futile as it was. He, at least, would have to give his life for his cause—and, under the dictatorship of circumstance, for the pretty lady. That would, at least, lend a tiny element of nobility to what would otherwise be an ignominious slaughter.

He set himself, therefore, to defend the upturned table to the death, ready to use his blade even if the first man through the door had a musket already raised.

In fact, the first man through the door did have a musket already raised—and the second one too—but the intruder was not so stupid as to charge forward thereafter. Both men stepped briskly aside, covering Ned with their weapons, while two other men stepped through the breach they left.

Both of the newcomers seemed to recognize Ned, although he only recognized one of them: Lord Byron's emissary, Edward Trelawny.

"What the Hell are *you* doing here?" Trelawny demanded. "Where's Mortdieu?"

Marie stood up beside her protector, towering over him by nine or ten inches, striking the attitude of a true queen. Trelawny's companion looked for an instant as if he had seen a ghost, but recovered very rapidly. "Damn it!" he said "The steamship must have picked them up."

Ned realized that the speaker must be Amédée Desart, and that the present attack on the village was not being carried out by *mestizos* at all, but by buccaneers from Tortuga, equally avid to possess the *Outremort*.

"*Byron* hired the mercenaries who attacked the *Belleville*?" Ned exclaimed, utterly astounded.

"Don't be ridiculous, Monsieur Knob," said Trelawny. "His Lordship would never have done any such thing. He understands full well that death is the currency of diplomacy, but that very understanding leads him to be miserly in his negotiations. Needs must when the Devil drives, however, and I have taken the opportunity to hire the cut-throats on His Lordship's behalf, on the grounds that it is better by far to have their firepower with us than against us. Again, *where are Mortdieu and Germain Patou?*"

"Safe," Ned replied, trying to contrive a sneer. "Out of *your* reach, at least. The only persons here who are capable of making contact with them now are Mademoiselle Laveau and myself—but I doubt that you'll find it easy to persuade us to help you, in the circumstances."

Chapter Six
Awkward Negotiations

"I'm not your enemy, Monsieur Knob," Trelawny said, coming forward to stand in front of the upturned table—though not quite within striking distance of Ned's machete. "I saved your life aboard the *Belleville*. Captain Desart wanted to slit your throats, but I persuaded him to let you go."

"Let us go!" Ned protested, utterly outraged. "Cast adrift in a dinghy, without oars—condemned to a slow death instead of a quick one."

"I knew that the *zambo* would come to your rescue, with or without the steamship," Trelawny said smoothly. "It was, at any rate, the only chance you had, and I obtained it for you."

The pirate captain seemed to feel that this discussion was a waste of time. "We have to go now," Desart said to Trelawny. "We have the steamship. If we linger, the *zambo* will try to take it back—or the *mestizos* will try to seize it. I'll be at full stretch as it is, having to split my crew three ways. I told you before the attack that it would have to be swift. We may have the guns, and all the powder we need, but they have the numbers and they're in an angry mood. Bring these two along, if you want to—although we'll only end up wasting a perfectly good dinghy casting them adrift again—but we have to go *now*."

"We came to get Mortdieu and Patou," Trelawny said.

"No," Desart corrected him. "*You* came to get Mortdieu and Patou. *I* came to get the steamship."

"But I'm paying you!" Trelawny protested.

"In promises," Desart said. "Your purse was already mine by right of capture, along with everything else you possess, including the clothes on your back. You promised me that your master would pay a handsome ransom for the talking zombie and the French physician, but they're not here, so you have nothing left to offer—not today, at any rate. If you want to come with us, you can—but if not, you can stay here. Time was only on our side for a matter of an hour or so, and that's run out."

Trelawny should not have been in the least surprised by this turn of events, in Ned's opinion—especially given the kinds of company that Byron had been keeping of late—but the Englishman was clearly at a loss. "Go with him," Ned advised him, jeeringly. "I'm sure that he'll have dinghies to spare now that he has the *Outremort* as well as the *Cayman* and the *Belleville*. He's surely too much of a gentleman simply to cut your throat."

Desart laughed at that, loudly enough to prove that he was not devoid of a sense of humor, while things were going well for him. "Last chance," he said to Byron's man, who made no move to turn and join him. Ned saw the pirate shrug his broad shoulders, and make the slightest of gestures toward his two musketeers—and then the three of them ran off into the night, doubtless enthusiastic to save their powder and shot for more urgent targets.

Ned was glad to know that he was no longer in immediate danger of death, or facing any necessity of cutting Marie Laveau's throat with a rusty blade, but he was not in a trusting mood. He pointed the tip of the machete at Edward Trelawny's breast, and said. "Give me that poniard you're wearing at your waist."

Trelawny still had the nerve to look hurt. "I'm not your enemy, Monsieur Knob," he said, again. "Did we not agree, during the crossing, that we're on the same side?"

"That was before you made a pact with a pirate," Ned pointed out.

"I had my own life to save, as well as yours," Trelawny protested.

"And you succeeded," Ned said. "Now, hand me that poniard, or I'll cut your treacherous heart out."

For a moment, it seemed as if Trelawny might jump backwards and draw his weapon, ready to engage Ned in a fencing match. Had he done so, he might well have won—but he was not prepared to take the chance. Meekly, he lifted the long dagger from its sheath, holding the hilt between his thumb and forefinger, and handed it to Ned—who promptly threw the rusty machete away.

"What now?" Trelawny asked.

"Now," said Ned, "we wait. If you behave yourself, I might refrain from telling Mortdieu and Patou that you tried to sell them to Desart, at least until Mortdieu recovers from his fury at discovering that he's lost the *Outremort*. Without the steamship, his fragile authority over the *zambo* will likely crumble away completely—but there's scope yet for a fruitful alliance between Mademoiselle Laveau and Germain Patou."

"But they're not here," Trelawny objected.

"They will be," Ned promised. "Not until midmorning, in all likelihood, and maybe not until midafternoon, but they'll be here. In the meantime, we'll just have to hope that the *zambo* have chased the *mestizos* away, or that they can defend the village successfully now that the pirates have gone."

Marie had become rather unsteady on her feet, but she managed to walk back into the bedroom with a substantial measure of dignity and lie down in a ladylike manner. Ned was glad to observe that the crowd around the hut was already beginning to thicken again, although the steamship's engine had only just roared into life, and the vessel could not yet be far from the jetty. There were no more gunshots sounding, and no more drumbeats echoing in the trees.

"Sit down," Ned said to Trelawny, having brought another chair from the outer room.

Byron's agent obeyed. Having regained his composure, he said: "Our arrival in these waters seems to have triggered quite a reaction."

"It's surprising what a hold full of agricultural machinery can move men to do," Ned replied. "That's evidence of the benefits of civilization, I think—worthier by far than squabbling over gold trinkets and silly jewels, as the pirates of old used to do. Don't you agree, Mademoiselle?"

"Entirely," said Marie Laveau—but her voice was tired, and she seemed already to be sinking back into sleep.

Ned felt quite exhausted himself, but he levered himself to his feet and went to the door of the hut, searching the night with his eyes for one of Mortdieu's crewmen. Eventually, he identified one, as much by the despairing expression provoked by the loss of the vessel as by any faint recognition of his features. He handed him Trelawny's poniard, and said: "The fellow that brought the pirates here is a mere dupe, but he needs to be watched. Can you do that, while I go to sleep? Mortdieu will return tomorrow—he and Patou will know what to do next. All we need to do is wait. Do you understand?"

"Yes, Monsieur," the *zambo* replied.

"Good," Ned said. "And try to keep those drums quiet for a while, will you? I really do need to sleep."

"Yes, Monsieur," Mortdieu's loyal crewmen replied, meekly—and was, it seemed, as good as his word, for Ned did not hear a single drumbeat before he woke up again, which he did not do until the Sun was almost at its zenith on the following day.

In fact, Ned did not awake until someone actually roused him by tugging at his shoulder, and even then was very sluggish in his reactions, although he ought to have been alert to the possibility of further trouble.

When he finally contrived to rub his eyes and force them open, however, he found that he was not confronting an enemy, but a friend that he had not expected to see again so soon. "Sawney?" he croaked, "Is that really you, Sawney?"

Ned had seen Sawney Ross as a Grey Man before, in Sharper's. Indeed, Sawney had been the first Grey Man he had ever seen, and he had recognized him then, even though he had had a great deal more astonishment to overcome. Time should not have changed the actor overmuch, now that he was dead, but the tropical climate seemed to have agreed with him. His eyes were much more alert with intelligence now than they had been before, and his face was by no means expressionless. In fact, Sawney Ross was smiling. "Ned," he said. "It's good to see you. How's the troupe?"

"Safe in the custody of Sam and Jeanie, I believe," Ned assured him, stretching his limbs and writhing to remove the inevitably discomforts to which he had been subject by virtue of sleeping in a wicker chair.

The reunion was cut short by General Mortdieu, who elbowed his fellow Grey Man aside in order to say: "You've lost my ship, damn you!"

This accusation seemed distinctly unfair to Ned, even though Mortdieu had made the token gesture of leaving him in charge while he went to search for Germain Patou. On glancing around the room, he saw that Patou had, indeed, been found, and had been prompt to attend to his patient—although Marie Laveau, who was sitting up in bed, seemed surprisingly well for someone who had been shot and bitten by a venomous snake within the space of half a minute.

Patou turned round before Ned could improvise an answer to the unjust accusation, and barked orders to no one in particular. "I need water that has been boiled and is still hot," he said. "I need fresh bandages, too, and I need space in which to work. Trelawny—you can stay to assist me. The rest of you get out."

These orders seemed a trifle unjust too, given that Trelawny had been a prisoner rather than a collaborator, and given what Ned and Marie had already gone through together, but Ned remembered that he had never contrived to give Patou any strong reason to like him, and decided, in any case, that he would rather have a chat with Sawney. While Mortdieu stalked off to relay the doctor's orders and take stock of his deleted army, therefore, Ned took his old friend by the arm and led him through the village beside the bank of the stream, all the way to the beach. There they found shelter beneath a palm-tree, armed with a water-bottle and a basket of fruit, and sat down to make a late breakfast.

"How have you been, Sawney?" Ned wanted to know.

"I was ill for a long time," the old man told him. "Not myself at all. Hanging can do that to a man, I suppose—and I'm doubly glad, now, that I made something of a career saving men from such a fate. Do you remember what fun it was coaching witnesses for the defense? What actors we had—and how assiduously we searched out fresh chickens! And the performances too! Great days, Ned!"

"Good days," Ned agreed, with conscientious modesty. "So you're back to your old self, now?"

The Grey Man looked at him, with a strange expression that Ned could not read at all. "No, Ned," he said, gravely, "not my old self. You can't go back to your old self, no matter how much you remember. That's not the way it works. I'm a new man now. I've crossed the great divide. This is the Underworld, for all that the Sun shines as brightly on me as it does on you."

"But it's not Hell?" Ned queried, anxiously. "You're not suffering?" *You have no idea*, Mortdieu had said to him, and indeed he had not.

"Oh, no!" Sawney replied. "Not that we're incapable of suffering, you understand, but...no, I'm content with my lot. It's good to be....whatever I am, instead of alive. I'm different now, though. I'm not a shadow of my former self. I've moved on. John can explain it far better than I, but he stayed behind to look after our people. We're in constant danger here."

"John's the one that Mortdieu calls the patchwork man?" Ned said, checking to make sure. "The man whose brain was transplanted into another body?"

"That's right," Sawney told him. "He was once a poet, you know, as frail as frail can be—but he's a colossus now. The *zambo* love him. We haven't been able to bring others back from the dead, though—not enough equipment. What we salvaged from Purfleet wasn't enough. We have no electricity supply, and no way of replenishing our chemicals. We've been studying the native methods, hoping to find some adequate means of improvisation, but they're so sorely harassed that they're at the end of their tether."

"I've noticed that," Ned confirmed. "I'm not sure that Mortdieu will be able to command their allegiance, now that the *Outremort* is gone, and Marie Laveau has arrived too late in the day to turn things around, in spite of the sheer bravado of Henri de Belcamp's new grand plan."

"Henri de Belcamp?" Sawney queried. "I remember him, just about. He and Mortdieu quarreled. Then Mortdieu and Germain made peace. Then they quarreled too. Here, the *mestizos* are trying to exterminate the *zambo*, the mulattos hate the *mestizos*, and the blacks hate everyone. We live in a very quarrelsome world, Ned—it makes one yearn for the peace and merriment of Sharper's."

"Relative peace and occasional merriment," Ned said, favoring honest modesty again. "Patou's company is deep in trouble too, then?"

"Very much so. He's appealed to President Boyer for help, offering the Republic his services as a physician and potential ambassador to France, but Boyer considers him an outlaw, little or no better than Desart, and his association with us makes everyone wary. If Mortdieu is willing to forgive and forget, we'll likely move our people back here, so that we can at least put up a united front against the *mestizos*, until they wear us down."

"I doubt that you'll get any objection from Mortdieu, proud as he is," Ned remarked. "How's your eye-
sight now that you're dead, Sawney?"

"Not bad," said Sawney. "Why?"

"Can you see what's happening out there, on the
horizon?" Ned asked, pointing north-eastwards beyond
the tip of the headland, where a ragged cluster of dots
was silhouetted against the pale cloud that was massing
in that direction, obscuring the blue of the sky.

"Three ships, heading south-east, for the coast
beyond the border," Sawney said. "I think one of them's
a steamer."

"You're right," Ned confirmed. "The *Outremort*
should have been safe in Tortuga by now...but if that's
her, she's on the run! Perhaps Desart's overplayed his
hand! Boyer must have been enraged when he heard that
the *Belleville* had been intercepted. He might be reluctant to risk his fleet in an attack on Tortuga, but catching
her at sea's a different matter. Desart wasn't able make it
back to Tortuga after last night's raid, and now he's
looking for somewhere to hide. The *Belleville* and the
Outremort haven't got a single cannon between them.
With the westerly wind blowing so briskly, the *Outremort* might have difficulty outrunning a warship, even if
she has sufficient fuel—which she probably hasn't. Desart must have unloaded the *Belleville*'s cargo, so she
might have the speed to outdistance pursuers, but I don't
know about the *Cayman*. They must be trying to find
shelter, beyond Haiti's border—but surely that's *zambo*
territory too."

"Is this good news?" Sawney asked. "Will Boyer
return the *Outremort* to us, if he captures it?"

"I'd certainly be glad to hear that Desart had been
clapped in irons and sentenced to hang," Ned remarked,

"but I don't know about the *Outremort*. Have Boyer's men ever come after her before?"

"He poses as a man of law, respectful of private property," the actor said, "in the hope of making a treaty with the French—but now the *Outremort*'s been captured by Desart, different rules might apply."

Ned was straining his eyes, trying to make out more detail of what was happening out to sea, but it was hopeless without the aid of a telescope, and even with such aid, he would not have been able to make out any details of real significance. He had already deduced all that there was to deduce, and the ships were passing on now, disappearing beyond the spur of the headland. Two more sails were, however, emerging into visibility on the northern horizon.

"How ominous is that cloud, Sawney?" Ned asked, then, turning his attention to the backcloth against which the desultory drama had been displayed.

"Cloud's always ominous, in these parts," the Grey Man told him. "Storms blow up very suddenly—but the wind's taking the cloud south-eastwards; we should be safe from a storm, unless it changes to a southerly, although it's likely we'll get some rain." He paused, and when Ned said nothing more, he added: "What news is there of England, Ned?"

"The powers-that-be have hanged a great many more good men since they called it quits with you. There's been no evolution, nor even a change of government. What more is there to know?"

"What of Temple?" Sawney wanted to know. "Are you still in his employ?"

"Yes," Ned admitted, "and relatively honest in that employ, to tell you the truth. I keep the Belcamps informed—Jeanne's company at the château as well as the

Marquis-who-never-was, but Temple knows that, and tolerates it. Little by little, he's becoming fascinated by the possibility of a second life, as befits an old warhorse who wants nothing more than to continue the fight that old age is sapping from his limbs. He was on his way to Paris when I left, to interview an old friend of Patou's and investigate rumors of a vampire at large there."

Sawney nodded slowly. "Patou's always alert for rumors of vampires," he admitted, "but I've never encountered one. They're shy—and who can blame them? We thought that men like me might be more welcome in a land accustomed to zombies...but it doesn't seem to work like that."

"If you get the chance," Ned advised, "head for New Orleans, and then westwards. There's a great deal of scope in North America for all kinds of new things. There, if anywhere, you'll find a safe haven."

"Not *we*, Ned? This is just a flying visit, then?"

"I don't know," Ned muttered. "I just take one day at a time, trying to stay alive. It's not easy to make plans beyond that. I'll try to reach some kind of agreement with Patou, if we can get out of this death-trap—but so will Trelawny, and to be perfectly honest, Byron probably has more to offer him at present than I do. As figureheads go, Byron can easily compare with Francis Drake and Queen Anacaona, even in Haiti, let alone in Europe."

"Patou had Napoleon himself once," Sawney said, wryly, "but that didn't work out either. The trouble with figureheads is that they don't like dragging Ships of Fools in their wake. They have their own ideas."

"Of which the likes of us poor mortals apparently have none," Ned remarked.

"None at all," his old friend confirmed, serenely.

Chapter Seven
Changing Fortunes

There had, it transpired, been a reason why Germain Patou had asked Edward Trelawny to stay and assist him while he changed Marie Laveau's wounds—a reason more substantial than the gentleman's social status and relatively clean clothes. By the time Ned and Sawney Ross got back to Mortdieu's hut—from which the General was still conspicuously absent—the pact between them had already been negotiated and sealed. Nor were the two parties to the agreement ready to explain its terms to Ned, although their churlishness was amply repaid when Marie Laveau sent them away, saying that she wanted to talk to Ned in private.

"Trelawny has offered to go to Boyer to negotiate a settlement," Marie told him. "If Boyer will send a ship to the bay, Patou will embark his own Grey Men thereon—he speaks for all of them, it seems, except Mortdieu and a handful of stupid companions, and he seems confident that they will capitulate. Trelawny is sure that Boyer will be glad to get rid of the Grey Men, even if their expulsion were not the cost of Lord Byron's public friendship and propagandistic support."

"But where will Trelawny take them?" Ned wanted to know.

"He would not say, exactly, but he claims to have a safe location in mind somewhere in the Americas, to which Byron will bring Frankenstein, Shelley and enough equipment for the research to start again in earnest. Patou has had enough of his tribulations here—and I cannot see that Mortdieu has any alternative but to rejoin him, now that the steamship is lost."

"If I were in Patou's shoes, I'd take the deal," Ned admitted. "But I'm not so sure that I'd grant it, if I were in Boyer's."

"I think he will," Marie told him. "Byron is highly esteemed among certain factions in France. Boyer is desperate to find some effective advocacy in Paris, and the overt support of the Republicans would be worth a lot, even though they're not in the political ascendancy. They're mostly businessmen, after all, and it's business that Boyer wants to do."

"And what about you?" Ned asked. "What will you do, if the plan works out? You have an interest in the renewal of research too."

"I'll stay here," she replied, "if I can."

"If?" Ned queried.

"Boyer might well want to be rid of me, just as he wants to be rid of Mortdieu and Patou. My expulsion might be part of the deal—but they'll have to find me first. Despite last night's fiasco, this is *zambo* territory, and I'm a *zambo*."

"You haven't given up on Henri's crazy plan, then?"

"It's *my* plan," she told him, flatly.

"And where do I fit into it?"

"That's up to you, if you want to fit into it at all. The more relevant point, so far as you're concerned, is that you don't fit into Trelawny's. He doesn't want an agent of King George in his company—and neither does Patou. Your old acquaintance won't be able to talk him round, no matter how firmly you've renewed your friendship."

"I see." Ned frowned. Inspiration seemed to have deserted him, for the moment; he could not see any obvious way to make capital out of the situation as it was now defined. If Boyer agreed to Trelawny's terms, then the ship taking the Grey Men away from Haiti would sail without him, and he would have no alternative but to return to Gregory Temple with a very ignominious report to offer—one that Henri de Belcamp would not like any better. On the other hand, the idea of staying behind to fight for the revolutionary cause with Marie Laveau did not seem particularly attractive—even if Marie could avoid deportation herself."

"Damn Trelawny," Ned muttered. "The fellow has spoiled everything. I almost wish I'd cut his throat last night, when I had the chance. I expect Desart thinks the same, now that he's running for his life from Boyer's makeshift navy."

"What's that?" the young woman demanded.

Ned explained what he had seen—or, rather, what he had inferred from the little he had seen.

"There's nowhere he can go!" Marie exclaimed. "I can feel the wind freshening—there's a storm brewing. It will probably track to the north-east of the island, leaving us the rain on its fringe, but it'll cut the ocean off as a potential avenue of escape, and if he hugs the shore too closely, the Dominicans might well join the chase—they don't like the pirates of La Tortue any more than Boyer does. Desart surely can't put into any harbor on the mainland without finding enemies eager to slay him. There's justice for you."

"It doesn't help us," Ned pointed out. He stood up and turned toward the door.

"Where are you going?" asked Marie.

"To find Mortdieu," Ned said. "He's the man most likely to put a spike in Trelawny's scheme, if anyone can."

He was not given a chance to do that, however. Germain Patou and Edward Trelawny were waiting for him at the door of the hut, with smiles on their faces. "Monsieur Knob," said Patou, extending a hand to be shaken. "It's good to see you again. The resemblance between us is even more striking than it was before, I believe." It was not much of a compliment, given that Patou had to be 20 years older than Ned, and looked it.

"I have been mistaken for you in a dim light," Ned admitted, graciously. "I've come a long way to find you, on behalf of your former partner."

"Really?" Patou said, without losing his smile. "I understood that you were now working for His Britannic Majesty's Government."

"Gregory Temple is not your enemy, Monsieur Patou," Ned said, swiftly, "but I was John Devil's man long before I was Temple's—and once a man's affiliated to John Devil, he does not change his allegiance, no matter what colors he might run up his mast."

"Very honorable, I'm sure," Patou said, "after your own fashion. But that's of little consequence. Monsieur Trelawny and I have a proposition to put to you."

"Really?" Ned said, in his turn, trying to put on a smile to match the physician's. "What's that?"

"We want you to join us on an expedition to Port-au-Prince. We want to petition President Boyer for the use of a ship to take us to another island, and we think that your powers of persuasion, added to our own, might tip the balance in our favor."

Ned was reminded of the old proverb, which counseled keeping one's friends close and one's enemies closer. Trelawny apparently did not want to leave him alone, as a loose canon rolling around the deck of his newly-improvised scheme. "Mademoiselle Laveau has just told me that you do not want to take me with you to you new safe haven," he said, coldly.

"That's true," Patou said, with perfect serenity. "What we need you to do is to serve as one of the English government's ambassadors in Port-au-Prince—and, if you feel that the two roles are compatible, as Lord Byron's ambassador too. We anticipate that diplomatic relations between Lord Byron, England and Haiti might well improve in the near future. We would be very glad to know that you are here—and so, I think, will President Boyer."

"You intend to leave me here as a *hostage!*" Ned exclaimed.

"Certainly not," Patou was swift to retort. "For better or worse, you're the only man here who's acquainted with all the interested parties—including Mademoiselle Laveau, who will presumably elect to stay. You'll be invaluable to President Boyer and it will be very useful to everyone else to have such a contact within the Presidential Palace. This is a great opportunity for you, Monsieur Knob."

From one point of view, Ned could see, it *was* a great opportunity, offering unprecedented prestige. Indeed, he could not quite comprehend why his gut reaction was so bluntly antagonistic to it. Nevertheless, he did not want to remain in Port-au-Prince, even if it offered him an opportunity to play Francis Drake in Marie Laveau's insane plan for a Caribbean-wide *maroon* revolution. What he said aloud, by contrast, was: "In that case, gentlemen, it will be a pleasure and a privilege to accompany you both to Port-au-Prince, and assist in your negotiations with the President and his government."

"Excellent," said Trelawny—whose poniard was back in its sheath, Ned observed.

"Mademoiselle Laveau is not as poorly as we had been led to expect," Patou said. "You must have done an excellent job of sucking the snake-venom out of her wound, although I had always suspected that to be a dangerous and ineffective stratagem. At any rate, there's no reason why we should not set out immediately—as soon as you can be ready."

"I have no bags to pack, alas," Ned remarked, wryly. "I'll be at your service, gentlemen, as soon as I've thanked General Mortdieu for his hospitality."

"There's no need," Trelawny said. "General Mortdieu has agreed to accompany us. We shall be a four-man delegation."

Ned was taken aback by that, but tried not to show it. "Where is Mortdieu?" he said, stalling for the sake of a moment to think.

"He had some business to transact with his *zambo* allies," Patou told him. "I believe he's on the shore somewhere—but he has already agreed to our terms. He and I have had our differences in the past, but nothing irredeemable, and he's a reasonable man. We're both of one mind now as to the best course to take."

Privately, Ned doubted that, but he doubted that Mortdieu would confide in him, if he were secretly harboring a different scheme of his own. "Have you considered the possibility," he asked, warily, "that if you deliver the General into Boyer's custody, along with yourselves, he might think it prudent to take us *all* as hostages?"

"Nonsense," said Trelawny, serenely. "He's the President of the world's youngest nation, and a man of honor. He has far too much need of new friends to risk making any new enemies. What on Earth are those fellows getting so excited about?"

The "fellows" to whom Byron's agent had referred were *zambo* warriors, who were running back and forth to seize weapons, and rouse their exhausted companions to action. The drums had also started up again, beating furiously and calling forth echoes from the east—or perhaps answering signals coming from that direction.

There was no sign of Mortdieu, but Ned was sure that whatever was happening would not have caught him napping. Automatically, he moved toward the shore, craning his neck to see what was happening there.

For a moment or two, Ned thought that the *mestizos* must be returning to the attack—but the attention of the men responding to the alarm did not seem to be directed westwards at all. They all seemed to be gazing in the opposite direction.

Ned had to take a dozen more paces to find a position from which he could look out along the shallows in an eastward direction, at the shore of the headland. In spite of the trees growing on the spur, he could see the topsails of a medium-sized vessel tacking landwards in a labored fashion, trying to make headway toward the west.

Behind the fluttering sails, the cloud-mass now filled more than half the sky, although its bulk was still moving south-eastwards. The sailing-ship was forced to tack very awkwardly in order to make progress, but she was a sleek vessel, apparently capable of running closer to the shore than the captain of a larger and more heavily-laden ship would have dared to do.

"What ship is that?" Patou asked, sharply. "Where on Earth is she headed?"

"It's the *Cayman*," said Trelawny, who had seen the vessel before. "She must be running for Tortuga—but whoever's in command, it can't be Desart. She'll never make it. Look at all those blessed canoes!"

Ned saw that the *zambo* were, in fact, taking to the sea in droves—and finally, he saw Mortdieu, urging the warriors on from the strand as he took up a position in the prow of a canoe himself, carrying a brace of muskets. Evidently, the Grey General had not yet given up hope of obtaining a ship of his own, and he was prepared to settle for a pirate sloop if his steamship had gone for good.

"We've got to stop him!" was Trelawny's reflexive reaction—although it must have been as obvious to him as it was to Ned that the bird had already flown.

"I think the vessel's master is prepared to face up to spearmen canoes," Patou said, "rather than head into open water. To do that would only make it easier for *her*." He pointed further east beyond the headland, at a larger vessel, further out to sea, which appeared to be tracking the *Cayman*'s course in the same labored fashion, zigzagging ponderously in order to catch the unfavorable wind."

"That's no hunter trying to give chase," said Trelawny, mournfully, having seen that vessel before as well. "That's the *Belleville*. That's Desart's too, now. They're coming to attack us—and I doubt that those canoes can defend us!"

The truth, Ned, realized, was that *both* vessels were in flight from an as-yet-invisible enemy, and he had no doubt that if the trees on the headland had not been blocking his view, he would have seen more sails in the distance. Desart really had overplayed his hand in making his bid for the *Outremort*.

Was it possible, Ned wondered, that the *Cayman*'s master could find no alternative harbor to Mortdieu's bay, and really believed that he could fend off the *zambo*? If so, the fool was sadly mistaken. The ship undoubtedly had guns, but it would be direly difficult to target canoes with cannon. And where was the *Outremort*? Perhaps the pirate was attempting to use the steamship to slow down Boyer's pursuers, taking advantage of the fact that it was much more maneuverable against the wind. Unable to outrun the naval vessels while the latter had the wind in their favor, and trapped beneath the hostile land and the storm-swept ocean, Desart might well have decided that he had no alternative but to make a run along the shore for Tortuga, even though the odds were clearly against him.

Ned did not believe that the *zambo* could possibly capture both the *Cayman* and the *Belleville*, and would have to endure a bloody battle if they attacked only one—but the wind was in their favor, at present, and the *Cayman* would not want to be delayed, for at least one of Boyer's vessels would surely be able to escape whatever delaying tactics the *Outremort* might adopt.

"Damn him!" Patou muttered, presumably meaning Mortdieu. "Well then, let's allow him to play his own game. We don't need him. There's no reason for us to wait. The faster we three can get to Boyer, the better."

"You can't be serious!" Ned protested. "We need to know how this turns out!"

"He's right," said Trelawny, reluctantly. "We don't have to care—but we do need to *know*. We can go to Boyer without Mortdieu, if necessary, but not without knowing what has become of him."

The *Cayman* doubled the eastward headland, but did not head for the inlet. Instead, it continued to make what headway it could toward the western headland.

"Desart's hoping that the *mestizos* will attack the *zambo* again," Ned guessed. "He's desperate to find any allies he can, and he thinks that they'll take heart from the cover his cannon can provide—but he has no idea what the effects of last night's battle were. If the *mestizos* have been driven far enough back..." He left it there, because that was obviously the case. No second fleet of canoes had taken to the water to engage the *zambo*, whose light vessels were already maneuvering to surround the laboring ailing-ship. A storm of gunfire erupted from the *Cayman*'s deck, including several cannon-blasts, but the *zambo* did not take many casualties, and there were simply too many canoes, moving too rapidly.

A nest of angry hornets, Ned thought. *The pirate's trapped—nowhere to go, nothing to be done. The* Belleville *'s her only hope now.*

The *Belleville*'s master, however—who was doubtless armed with a telescope—had a clear view now of what was befalling the *Cayman*. Had she had better wind to aid her, the *Belleville* might have been able to join the battle swiftly and turn the tide, but Desart had divided his crew three ways, and had obviously been reluctant to take on too many new men in Tortuga, so both the ships now in trouble were undermanned. The *Belleville* did not come to the *Cayman*'s aid at all; her master tried instead to sail across the mouth of the bay to round the western headland. The pursuing vessels, however—there were two, not one—were now clearly visible.

"They're going to put into shore on the far side of the headland," Trelawny judged. "They'll have to abandon the ship and make a run for it inland. If they'd stuck together…but they're pirates, after all, not navy men."

Patou was still watching the *Cayman*, which was now trying to come about. Her decks were shrouded by a pall of gunpowder smoke, but there were fewer gunshots now; the muskets and cannon could not be loaded swiftly enough. The canoes were all around her, and the boarding-parties were already swarming up her sides.

"Like an ox run down by a pack of wolves," the physician muttered. "She's delivered herself to Mortdieu like a sacrifice. Her master got everything wrong—far more enemies than he hoped to find, and no help at all."

"It won't work to our disadvantage," said the ever-inventive Trelawny. "The capture of a pirate vessel is a major event in these parts, and it will delight Boyer, who must be desperate for a victory over the buccaneers after the interception of the *Belleville*. If we can deliver the *Cayman* to him, even without Desart…"

"But *we* don't have the *Cayman*," Patou pointed out. "Mortdieu dies—or will have, within the hour. The question is, what will *he* do with her?"

"He's already agreed to our terms," Trelawny said, with some asperity—but Byron's man had to know as well as Patou did that any agreement Mortdieu had made before would be null and void if the Grey General captured the pirate vessel intact.

"You might not need to make an agreement with Boyer at all," Ned pointed out. "If the *Cayman* remains seaworthy, Mortdieu might be willing and able to take you to your new safe haven without the need for further diplomacy."

Patou seemed far from delighted by this prospect, and Trelawny scowled—but both men shook their heads in denial. Even if Ned were right, that would have put

Mortdieu back in control, which neither of them wanted. They knew, however, that there was little or no possibility of Mortdieu taking permanent control of his prize. The warships sent to hunt the *Cayman* down had hunted her down, and Boyer's captains would not allow Mortdieu to keep her simply because his pack had brought the quarry down in advance of their arrival

The three of them stood together and watched the battle, which was fast and furious, although it almost seemed to Ned to be happening in slow motion, so impatient was he to discover its outcome. The guns were no longer blazing—the combat was hand to hand. The pirates were undoubtedly hardened fighting-men, but the *zambo* had experience of their own in that respect, and the weight of numbers soon swung in their favor as more and more warriors clambered on to the deck.

Ned saw Mortdieu climb aboard in his turn, and could actually hear the sound of the General's voice carrying over the water, as he shouted demands for the *Cayman*'s crew to surrender.

Apparently the pirates could see the inevitability of the situation as clearly as everyone else. Everything went quiet as they laid down their arms.

The *Belleville* was out of sight now behind the western headland, and the two pursuing vessels were heading toward the bay at a good clip, cleverly catching the wind to sustain their course.

Ned had expected Mortdieu's men to bring the captured *Cayman* to the jetty where the *Outremort* had long been moored, in the expectation of a rapturous welcome, but that was not what happened. As soon as the sails were under control again, the ship came around and began to tack in the other direction, heading out to sea, albeit at a snail's pace.

"He's raising a white flag!" Trelawny exclaimed. "He's surrendering to Boyer's ships!"

"Wise man," Patou muttered. "If the warship had caught up with him while he was still in the bay, trying to make for the jetty, its master might well have given the order to open fire on him. Boyer's men will take the ship anyway, in the end—better by far to make him a present of it meekly."

They watched the distance between the two vessels decline by degrees, and then saw the *Cayman* put out a launch. The Grey General was clearly visible in its bow.

"He's making a ceremony of his delivery," Patou observed—but there was a slight edge of anxiety in his voice. He was obviously anxious as to what diplomatic overtures Mortdieu might be able to make, now that he had established himself as an enemy of the pirates and, in consequence of the situation, an ally of the Republic.

"There's nothing more to see here," Trelawny said. "Should we make our way westwards, to see what has become of the *Belleville*?"

"Best not," Patou opined. "The *mestizos* might be in dire disarray, but any step beyond the limits of the village might be dangerous, and the westward headland's theirs. We have no alternative but to wait for news from the General—which I'm sure he'll be only too eager to send, now that he seems to have the upper hand again."

"But he doesn't!" Trelawny protested. "I'm the only one who can negotiate with Boyer on Byron's behalf."

Patou touched him on the arm then, suggesting that he turn around. Ned turned too, and saw that they had not been alone in watching the battle. Gathered behind them was a silent crowd, in which a dozen Grey Men were attended by as many as 200 *zambo*, almost all of them women. Now that the battle was over, the vast majority were staring at the three Europeans. Marie Laveau was making her way through the crowd, which parted reverently as she passed. Her injured right arm was obviously still painful, but she was walking proudly, as regally as she could. Ned realized that everyone in the crowd knew that she had been bitten by the mamba as well as shot, but here she was, utterly undaunted. Mortdieu was not the only one whose temporarily-dented prestige had now been restored.

"Be careful, Monsieur Trelawny," Patou murmured. "You have made enemies here as well as friends.

As if taking her cue from this remark, Marie Laveau spoke in her own tongue to two of the remaining *zambo* warriors, who immediately stepped forward to take Trelawny by the arms. The action was more symbolic than aggressive, but its meaning was clear. Trelawny was a prisoner again.

"Now, Monsieur Patou," the Witch-Queen said. "Let us discuss *my* terms for the return of your company to the bay, and the future of our mutual campaign."

Although he had not been taken prisoner, even in symbolic terms, Ned was extremely annoyed to be excluded from the subsequent discussion in Mortdieu's hut, in what seemed to him to be a monumentally unfair fashion. Once again, he had no alternative but to kick his heels and wait to see what others decided.

"What will happen now?" Sawney Ross asked him, having sidled up to him while he indulged his chagrin.

"Who can tell?" Ned replied. "Marie is ever anxious to strike while irons are hot, and is evidently unprepared to wait for Mortdieu's return to set her own plans in motion again—and we cannot even know for sure whether Mortdieu will return. If the captain of the warship is not inclined to bargain with a zombie, he might well decide to clap him in irons and take him back to Port-au-Prince. On the other hand, Mortdieu's *zambo* might conceivably be clever enough to capture the warship as well as the *Cayman*, if that is what he's ordered them to do. By the time the second warship can capture the *Belleville* and take her in tow, Mortdieu might be in a position to challenge that one too. If he has trained enough *zambo* to be sailors, he might then set off in pursuit of the *Outremort*. He was a bold commander in life, and death does not seem to have mellowed him at all."

The first possibility he had mentioned was by far the more likely, in Ned's estimation, but he was almost prepared to believe anything, now.

Chapter Eight
Doubtful Conclusions

"How do you want all this to come out, Sawney?" Ned asked, as the two of them sat idly on the jetty, while the sunset turned the lingering remnants of cloud blood red. The heaviest rain-clouds had, as predicted, passed the island by, shedding their burden out to sea in copious deluges whose distant atmospheric effects had been visible on the horizon. There had been no more than a shower in the bay, which was now deserted, and Ned had followed the example of the zambo in emerging from shelter again as soon as the rain had stopped. The *Cayman* and the ship to which Mortdieu had surrendered it had both sailed eastwards, tacking as best they could against the oblique wind. The canoes that had returned to shore had brought no news of Mortdieu's negotiations or his ultimate fate. Marie Laveau was now firmly in control of the little colony.

"I don't know," the Grey Man replied. "I don't know what sort of possibilities the future might hold. When I was a living child, I was surrounded by adults, who provided maps of what might befall me as I grew up, and what I might endeavor to achieve, but now that I'm a child of sorts again, I have no such guidance. The Lazarus you've mentioned might be the one true Adam of the new race, but there's a sense in which we're all Adams: John, Mortdieu, me...none of us knows how long we might endure, or of what our new bodies might be capable, under the guidance of our new minds. The zombies made by the *zambo* in the past were as poor as the worst of Patou's disasters, and we have no way of knowing, as yet, whether what is rumored in regard to vampires is anything more than mere folklore. Who knows what our being might amount to, if ever we find the freedom to *be*? Who knows what it might be possible to desire, and what it might require to satisfy the kinds of desire we might entertain? I don't. Mortdieu has his obsession, and John is trying to recover his poetry, but I'm just an old stager, who spent his entire life playing parts before going to the gallows. Thus far, in my new life, I've been at the beck and call of circumstance, hoping to get by from one day to the next and little more."

"We can all say that," Ned murmured, "but I see what you mean. I, at least, have some notion of the potential scope of human desire, and its available rewards. I have some notion, too, of historical ambition, although I never stated it clearly until I felt forced to justify myself to Mortdieu. I *am* working toward a goal, no matter how trivial a contribution I can make to its fulfillment: a world in which Frankenstein's discovery has been perfected, in which every second life is as fruitful of intelligence as yours, and in which even common men like me might have an acknowledged right to live again. Do you think that's possible, Sawney? Do you think that a world like that might be a better one than ours? Do you think that the resurrected dead might put the further accumulation of their wisdom and experience to good use, in making a society at peace, where the Rights of Man hold sway?"

"How can I tell?" Sawney replied. "From what I've experienced so far, though, I doubt that any such Utopia can come about smoothly. If individuals of my strange kind are not summarily exterminated, as our tentative kin have been throughout history, we shall likely have to fight for any freedom we can win—and not only against the savage likes of aristocrats, Churchmen and *mestizos*. If I have any vision of the future at all, it's one in which zombie armies clash incessantly, as human armies always have, in the dark night of ignorance and fear. That's my nightmare, Ned—that resurrection will, in the end, turn out to be nothing more than a renewal of the ceaseless war of all against all, with nothing but the heavy hand of despotic states to hold it temporarily in check. My hope, to be sure, is that it might be otherwise—that people of my kind, if they're allowed to survive and thrive, might think and act differently, with the aid of a new sanity...but that has yet to be proven, and that proof will likely be an exacting trial by ordeal."

Ned would have replied to that, but a *zambo* canoe glided into the jetty at that moment, and the paddlers gripped the pillars supporting the platform, in order to hold it steady, while their leader stood up and addressed Ned. Ned recognized him as the former first mate of the *Outremort*.

"Monsieur Knob," Jeannot said, "General Mortdieu sends greetings. He has a message for Mademoiselle Laveau."

Ned was not about to admit that he was not in Mademoiselle Laveau's confidence at present, and was glad of the apparent opportunity to get back into it. "Thank you kindly," he said. "Tell me what it is, and I'll see that she gets it immediately."

"He says that he will return before dawn, if all goes well, with the *Outremort* and President Boyer's guarantee to support the *zambo* in their conflict with the *mestizos*. We have a task to perform, in order to seal the bargain, but he believes that we can do it—but she must keep Patou and Trelawny here, for now, and maintain the situation until he returns."

"Where is he?" Ned wanted to know.

"Lying on the far side of the western headland, aboard the *Cayman*," Jeannot replied. "Now that the Sun has set and the wind has changed, though, he will set sail within the hour. I must return to join him."

Ned observed that the wind had indeed swung round as the bad weather had moved on, and was now blowing lightly from the south-east rather than the north-west. It would doubtless intensify as the island cooled more rapidly that the sea after dark, and added a land breeze.

"Sawney," Ned said, on a sudden impulse. "Relay the message to Mademoiselle Laveau—although she hardly needs to hear it, having already taken that initiative herself. I'm going with Mortdieu."

"To do what?" Sawney asked.

"I have no idea," Ned admitted, "but whatever it is, that's where the future is being made—and that's where a bold and dutiful spy needs to be." Without asking Jeannot's permission, he hopped down into the canoe. The *zambo* made no objection, but simply signaled to his men to turn the little vessel around and head out into the bay again.

By the time the canoe reached the *Cayman*, the ship was ready to sail again. Ned was surprised to find her lying quietly at anchor on the far side of the headland, with the *Belleville* and both Republican ships moored alongside her, the whole company surrounded by a fleet of *zambo* canoes. There was no sign of any *mestizo* activity on the shore, and Ned concluded that they had retreated westwards, beaten back by the *zambo* attack and fearful of returning while the ships and canoes were there.

Mortdieu was on the *Cayman*'s bridge, handing down orders to his *zambo* crewmen and evidently delighting in his recovered authority. He looked at Ned with more suspicion than surprise. "What do you want, Monsieur Knob?" he asked. "We're setting sail immediately—we won't be back until dawn, if we come back at all."

"What's your plan?" Ned asked.

Mortdieu studied him briefly, and then said: "Do you intend to come with us?"

"Why not?" Ned retorted. "I'm not such a good marksman as Marie, but I have my uses."

The Grey Man's expression did not change. He shrugged his shoulders. "You're a fool, Monsieur Knob," was all that he said before he returned to the business in hand, giving further orders to his crew. Ned could not see any of the *Cayman*'s former sailors, and assumed that they had been transferred to the Republican warships. He observed however, that the *Cayman* was lying lower in the water than she had been when her master had unwisely sought sanctuary in the bay, and concluded that she had taken on cargo of some sort, either from the ships lying alongside or from the shore.

Ned tried to persist with his questioning, but Mortdieu was too busy to look at him, let alone provide answers, and he had no alternative but to settle meekly into a corner of the bridge, to wait with as much patience as he could muster.

The *Cayman*'s sails caught the wind without difficulty, and she glided away, setting an eastward course, escorted by 50 of the canoes.

"Where are we going?" Ned asked, when they had been under way for 20 minutes or so, and Mortdieu had finally found an opportunity to pause for rest.

"Tortuga," Mortdieu told him, curtly.

"The pirates' lair?"

"That's right. It's a difficult harbor to get into, apparently, for ships that aren't recognized. The fortresses built by the French before the Revolution to defend the entrance to the port are manned by friends of the buccaneers now, with sufficient firepower to make its recapture direly difficult."

"You hope to find safe haven there?" Ned asked, deeply puzzled.

"By no means," Mortdieu told him. "But I hope to get in without difficulty, given that the *Cayman* will be recognized, and its former master has been persuaded to surrender the secret of the appropriate signals—which I trust, for he'll be hanged if the information turns out to be false, but set free if it proves correct. I hope to get out again alive, if my lucky star is still shining. You'd best stay as close to me as you can, and be ready to fight for your life. Can you swim well?"

"Yes."

"Good—if you couldn't, I'd have to put you in one of the canoes, and you'd miss the greater part of the excitement." And with this cryptic observation, Mortdieu put his telescope to his eye, and began scanning the starlit sea in front of them, presumably searching the expanse for shadows that might be ships.

The journey to Tortuga was not a long one, and the *Cayman* might have completed it in less than three hours had she not been attended by the fleet of canoes, but Mortdieu saw to it that their progress was moderate and that the convoy remained in formation.

Ned asked him again what his plan was, but the only reply Mortdieu was prepared to offer as he strode back and forth along his bridge, like a grotesque parody of some ghostly admiral, was that he intended to slip past the forts into the harbor, and then escape with his life, if he could.

A full five hours went by, without any incident whatsoever, before the coast of the island loomed up ahead of the ship. The *Cayman* steered to port in order to skirt the southern coast, headed for the sheltered deepwater harbor where the 17th century pirates of the Caribbean had established a thriving criminal colony, from which the navies of Spain, France and England had had considerable difficulty uprooting them.

As the vessel drew close to the harbor entrance, which was fortified to either side, Mortdieu's *zambo* crewmen began clambering over the side and leaping into the accompanying canoes. At least half the ship's company had abandoned the vessel before the canoes dropped back and peeled away, leaving the *Cayman* to make her final approach unescorted. Jeannot was at the helm, and the sailors handling the sails had been reduced to a mere handful.

It was only when the ship was hailed from the nearer fort, and the challenge had been successfully answered, that Mortdieu condescended to make a more detailed explanation to Ned, with a certain dry amusement in his voice.

"Desart did not unload all of the *Belleville*'s cargo in the port," the Grey Man said. "There was a part of it he took care to keep aboard, and would not leave behind in Tortuga even when he set out to take the *Outremort*. His miserly attitude got the better of him, you see—his

117

grasping nature, and the fact that he could not trust his fellow buccaneers not to steal his prize if he let it out of sight. Had he even taken on enough men to make up the crews of his little fleet, once he had captured the steamship, he might have fared better against the adverse wind—but he over-reached himself, and came to grief. I seized the *Cayman*, while Boyer's men secured the *Belleville*—intact, mercifully.

"It wasn't easy persuading Boyer's captains to agree to my bargain—you might almost have thought that they believed themselves to be making a pact with the Devil himself—but I have a certain reputation in these parts now. They allowed me to transfer the remainder of the *Belleville*'s cargo to the *Cayman*'s holds, in order to make use of an opportunity that might not present itself again very soon, and would require more courage and better seamanship than Boyer's makeshift navy could supply. In the meantime, my *zambo* warriors raided the abandoned *mestizo* camps on the shore. There were supplies of palm-oil there, carefully harvested and barreled for trade along the coast.

"The Republicans have the ships the French lost, but not the expert crews to man them, so they've never dared risk them in an all-out attack on Tortuga, preferring to suffer the depredations of the pirates—at least until Desart took a step too far in seizing the *Belleville*. When I explained to them how I might be of service to them, given the unique circumstances, they were prepared to take the risk of making a diabolical pact. So here we are, making war against the resurrected Tortuga, helping to make the Caribbean sea-lanes safe once again for civilized traffic."

At the dead of night, there was not much to be seen in the harbor that was host to the pirates' lair; the lights on shore seemed feeble and distant, and the ships moored along the quay were no more than hulking shadows, having no need to obey conventional regulations regarding the lighting of ships in port. Mortdieu called out a few further orders, raising his voice just enough to be clearly heard on deck.

"I don't understand," Ned said. "What cargo did Desart feel obliged to keep aboard the *Belleville*, rather than risk its theft by his own fellows? Wasn't she carrying agricultural machinery, to enable Boyer to renew the productivity of the plantations that the French abandoned."

"Yes, she was," Mortdieu confirmed. "But what Desart's followers were able to tell us, once they had surrendered the *Cayman* to me and had been offered a choice between execution and co-operation, was that she was also carrying a considerable quantity of barrels filled with black powder—a fact that they had not noised about, for fear of alarming the so-called first-class passengers. Gunpowder is one of the few substances worth its weight in gold in these parts, at least for the present. You will remember of course, that Mademoiselle Laveau wanted to represent me as a reincarnation of Sir Francis Drake—well, who am I to dispute her judgment in such matters?"

The night was warm—so warm that Mortdieu had forsaken his grey greatcoat—but Ned felt a sudden chill run down his spine. "You're going to use the *Cayman* as a *fireship*?" he said, incredulously. "You've promised Boyer's captains that you'll destroy the pirate fleet?"

"Even Drake only managed to singe the King of Spain's beard," Mortdieu pointed out. "It would be optimistic to think that I could destroy more than half of the buccaneers' vessels, even with luck on my side—but yes, the *zambo* have been laboring all day to turn the *Cayman* into a floating torch, with an explosive heart. You might want to join me in abandoning ship, now. The wheel's lashed, and it only remains to light the fuse."

So saying, the Grey Man took out a tinder-box, and struck a flame, which he used to light a trio of oil-lanterns neatly lined up on the rail of the bridge. Then, one by one, he picked them up and threw them down on to the deck, simultaneously shouting an imperious warning—for which the remaining crewmen had obviously been waiting. There was a series of splashes as they jumped into the water.

Ned felt a pang of regret with respect to his claim that he was a good swimmer—which was only half-true. The better option, it seemed to him, would have been to let himself be transferred to the canoes before the Cayman ran the gauntlet of the forts, in order that he might watch events from a safer distance, as a clever and cautious spy ought to have done. He had no choice now though, but to follow the advice he had been given, and stay close to the General.

Without any hesitation, he leapt over the bulwark in the Grey Man's wake.

By the time the two of them had swum clear of the hull, the *Cayman* was ablaze, with her carefully-disposed sails still catching the wind and drawing her inexorably toward the ships clustered along the quay.

Mortdieu patiently trod water, watching her progress, even though the sentries on the fortresses to either side of the harbor entrance, who had let Amédée Desart's ship pass without a second glance, once they had identified her, had opened fire with their muskets. They were not actually firing *at* anything, Ned realized, but merely wanted to be seen to be doing *something*, however belated and futile. The bullets plopped harmlessly into the water.

Ned trod water too, still sticking close to Mortdieu—and also to Jeannot, who had come to join his captain. Ned spread out his arms, and contrived to stay afloat as he watched the burning ship move toward its fatal encounter, with a seemingly-supernatural grace. He knew, of course, that the vessel was going to blow up—but knowing it could not prepare him for the violence of the explosion, which deafened him and sent a shock wave through his body that caused him to draw in his arms reflexively. His head dipped below the surface, but he closed his eyes and mouth, and contrived to float back up to the surface again—just in time to catch the violent wave that the explosion had sent forth across the harbor. The wave submerged him again, and caused such chaos in the water that he floundered helplessly for a full minute, holding his breath desperately.

By the time he had fought his way back to the surface again, shards of burning wood were still flying in every direction from the place where the sinking remnant of the *Cayman* was brightly ablaze. The shards were peppering the other vessels, whose huddled silhouettes stood out in the half-light much more clearly than before, but the greater danger to the anchored ships was the pall of burning oil that was spreading out over the quiet water of the harbor, licking at a dozen hulls.

Death is the currency of diplomacy, Ned thought—and remembered Sawney Ross's nightmare of the future, in which entire armies of the reborn dead might clash in battle, in blind and stupid continuation of that endless dark night of warfare, by which means common humankind still preferred to settle its affairs.

As the water became a little calmer, it became easi-er to swim, but Ned could feel the numbness of exhaus-tion creeping into his limbs. He had eaten but poorly of late, and had not slept peacefully in quite some time. He was not sure that he could swim all the way through the harbor-neck in order to rejoin the canoes—especially if the sporadic musket-fire from the forts continued.

Fire was climbing the flanks of a second vessel now, and a third. Watchmen had been left aboard both ships, and they had supplies of water, but they had not been ready for any such eventuality as this. Ned watched them racing around like crazed ants, with little more ef-fect. Military discipline and practice gained in fire-drills might have saved them, but they had neither. The flames took hold of both vessels, and continued to spread as the layer of burning oil was carried further afield.

Then there was a new explosion; Captain Desart was not the only pirate to have hoarded his powder sup-plies aboard his vessel. The shock-wave was not nearly as great this time, but Ned had to grit his teeth to steel himself against its various effects. The explosion was more fizz than bang, though, and he was not deafened again. Indeed, he heard Mortdieu say, with grim relish: "My guess is that every captain in Tortuga has stock-piled powder in fear of a famine, just as Desart did. It only requires one more substantial arsenal to ignite, to set off a chain reaction. We'd best be going, though—if the canoes are sighted they're sure to be bombarded, and we need them to stay as close as possible to the harbor mouth."

Jeannot took this speech as permission to set off, and did so, his long and powerful arms carrying him through the water without any seeming effort. Mortdieu, being much shorter, found the task less easy—but he was a metamorphosite, and his undead body seemed to be free of at least some of the constraints affecting Ned's all-too-human flesh. Both his companions soon outdistanced him, and he scolded himself yet again for his careless half-truth.

I'll never make it, he thought. *I've doomed myself with a silly boast.*

He had no alternative, though, to take his swimming one stroke at a time, and make what headway he could in spite of his weariness and inefficiency.

Behind him, there was another loud detonation, as another cargo of powder was ignited by the rampant blaze. As Mortdieu had judged, that was enough to set off a chain reaction. Ned could not resist the temptation to take one last glance behind him, and it seemed to him then that the entire crescent-shaped quay had been turned into an arc of fire, as the hungry flames devoured the wreckage of 25 or 30 pirate ships. Mortdieu had done more than singe the buccaneers' beards; he had almost single-handedly put an end to the Tortugan Renaissance—and he was escaping with his life, plowing though the water like a squat shark.

There was no cannon-fire from the forts; the garrisons there had obviously found more urgent occupations. Ned knew that the *zambo* in the canoes would be edging closer, searching the turbulent water for their comrades and their admiral. Even so, he was convinced that he could not stay above water for another minute. He seemed to have been swimming for an eternity.

He did not go down without a fight, but he did feel himself going down, and was certain that he was done for—before strong arms grabbed him and lifted him up again, and held his head out of the water until more arms reached down to haul him into a canoe and pull him aboard. Jeannot, who had held him up, followed a moment later. Afterwards, he lay supine in the bottom of the vessel, utterly helpless, for what seemed to be a very long time.

In the distance, he heard a sporadic sequence of further explosions: *Boom! Boom! Boom!*

Such is the fate of empires, great and petty, he thought. *Even those restored after an interval of exile are bound, in the end, to meet their Waterloo.*

Eventually, Ned was able to sit up, and to seek out Mortdieu, who was already sitting proudly in the prow of the canoe, with Jeannot sprawled behind him. The Grey General made room for Ned to sit beside him.

"You might have warned me," Ned observed. "I almost drowned."

"You had the option of being placed in a canoe," Mortdieu reminded him. "But had you taken it, you'd have robbed yourself of a fine tale to tell—or at least, the opportunity of representing yourself as one of its heroes. I did tell you that you were a fool—but you're a mortal man, with a poor understanding of the threat of death."

"You risked as much as I did," Ned pointed out. "The experience of death does not seem to have armored you against taking mortal risks."

"I have my obligations to my cause," Mortdieu retorted.

"*Our* cause," Ned corrected him. "It *is* ours, whether you like it or not. And don't tell me that I have no idea what the world is like, from the viewpoint of a Grey Man—I intend to form an idea, as best I can."

"Perhaps it is *our* cause," Mortdieu admitted, not entirely ungraciously.

"Do you really expect to get the *Outremort* back in exchange for what you've just done?" Ned queried. "Do you really think that Boyer's captains will keep their word? Do you think Boyer will let them?"

"Yes, I think so," Mortdieu said. "The President has more than enough enemies already. He can't be too selective in the matter of new friends. He'll honor the bargain, I imagine—even to the extent of sending military support to relieve the *mestizo* siege of our small colony."

"You intend to stay in Haiti, then, and refuse Lord Byron's offer of a safer haven?"

"Better the haven you've earned than the haven you haven't," Mortdieu said, grimly. "If Byron wants a stake in our affairs he can come to us—and Boyer will still have the opportunity to bargain with him, on terms no worse than before. This is a new dawn for the undead, my friend. You *are* my friend, are you not, Monsieur Knob?"

"Oh yes," said Ned, pretending not to hear the dull note of threat in the other's voice. "You can rely on me. So long as we're working in the same great cause, you and I—and Patou too, now that we have the means to talk him round—are true brothers-in-arms. It's a new dawn for the undead, as you say. For you and for Sawney, for John the poet... and for all the zombies that will emerge from Marie Laveau's fresh graves, if her *loas* really are on her side."

"The gods help those who help themselves, in my experience—recent as well as former," General Mortdieu informed him.

"Empires are not built in a day," Ned countered, matching him cliché for cliché, although he was swift to add: "but they *can* by built, by men such as you."

125

Chapter Nine
Epilogue

Marie Laveau's acute sense of theater ensured that what she called the ceremony of awakening would take place in the wake of yet another blood-red sunset, as the brief subtropical twilight gave way to a velvety darkness lit by torches, lanterns and bonfires. The *zambo* had come by the thousand from the entire northland, paying no heed to the national border separating the Republic of Haiti from the eastern half of the island.

The sense of expectation was palpable.

Ned knew that there was still abundant risk in the prospective display—that the Witch-Queen's trial by ordeal was not yet over—but he also knew that she and Germain Patou had checked the two dozen covered pits very carefully several times over during the last few ways, and had improvised as best they could with the use of the electric eels still captive in the pits, most of which had contrived to survive thus far.

Ned was seated beside Germain Patou, on a stool that was noticeably less status-worthy than Patou's wicker chair, although the latter was by no means as grand as the twin thrones that had been carved for the use of the now-undisputed rulers of the Land of the Reborn Dead: Mortdieu, the new incarnation of Sir Francis Drake, and Marie Laveau, the new incarnation of Anacaona, Queen of the Tairo. Edward Trelawny had been kindly allowed to squat on the ground, between Sawney Ross and the "patchwork man"—who had arrived the day before, along with the remainder of Germain Patou's company of Grey Men, from the Trou du Nord.

"How many zombies will rise from the depths, do you think, when she summons them from their rest?" Ned asked the physician.

Patou did not reply to Ned's question immediately, probably because he could do no more than guess, but eventually, he said: "She will need eight, at least, if she is to cement her reputation. "Twelve would be better, but four would be a disappointment. It will not matter much that they are idiots, if that is to be their fate, as long as they can stand up. That will be a sound beginning. Any more will be a gift from the gods."

"From the *loas*," Ned corrected him. "We are followers of *vaudou* now, my friend—you more than I, for you must play the priest as well as the physician from now on, if we're really to build an empire."

"For a good Radical, you seem to have the word *empire* on your lips a great deal of late," Patou observed, dryly. "You've been too often in Mortdieu's close company, and he has infected you with his disease."

"Perhaps so," said Ned, accepting the rebuke. "Empires do not generally end well, I know—but they're a powerful instrument of historical change, and I'm now convinced that nothing less than a profound historical change will serve our purposes. You have Boyer's protection now, and Lord Byron will have to bring Frankenstein to you if he wants to maximize his own chances of playing a hand in the game of destiny. Henri de Belcamp will not be far behind, if I'm not mistaken, and I'm certain that he will not come without strong support."

"We're still a minuscule enclave on a tiny island," Patou reminded him, soberly. "France still holds Jean-Pierre Boyer's destiny in her hands, and France is a fickle jade, no matter how assiduously her parliamentarians seek the *juste milieu*. She will not like the name of Francis Drake being bandied about so freely here, any more than that of Queen Anacaona. Once Frankenstein is here, our work will doubtless make more rapid progress—but whether it will be rapid enough to defy the enmity of half the world, with only a divided island and a fragile Republic to insulate us from its fury, remains to be seen."

He fell silent then, as Marie Laveau began her circuit of the zombie-pits, with a constrictor snake draped over her shoulders and four handmaidens in close attendance, moving rhythmically to the cadence of the *zambo* drums.

Ned held his breath as the handmaidens stripped away the palm fronds covering the first pit, and the Witch-Queen knelt down, extending her hand to the seeming corpse that lay within, half-immersed in viscous mud. She gripped the hand of the supine figure, and drew it upwards, tugging very gently. She could not possibly have lifted the dead weight of the body in that manner, but she did not have to do that. The zombie responded to her touch and to her summons, and came slowly to its feet.

The first hurdle was overcome. The relief within the crowd was palpable in the rumor of excitement that ran through it, extending back from one rank to the next and vanishing into the trees surrounding the resurrection site.

While the first zombie stood quietly erect, and men came forward with pails full of water and sponges, to clean the mud from his grey flesh, Marie Laveau moved forward to the next, and repeated the ritual.

The second zombie also rose from his grave, and so did the third. The fourth did not, but the pattern was set.

By the time she had visited the entire two dozen, 15 zombies had been brought back from the dead, at least to a form of half-life. There was no way to tell, by their present appearance now, which had been dark-skinned *zambo* in life, and which had been light-skinned *mestizos*.

"If even five are educable," Patou murmured, "then this is more than a symbolic dawn. If even three reach a consciousness as full as John's or Ross's, then the new era is begun."

"All you'll need," Ned remarked, sarcastically, "is an endless supply of corpses, preferably slain in the prime of life and the full flush of health, ready-equipped with the kind of determination with which men like Bonaparte are born. You might count yourself fortunate to live in a very obliging world, on the former score, but the latter element might be in much shorter supply."

"You have been party to the deaths of a great many men yourself, Monsieur Knob," Patou retorted. "You have no moral high ground to stand on, in that respect."

Ned accepted that rebuke too. "Perhaps not," he agreed, "but I, like you, am working for the resurrection of all—and when I'm given the choice, I almost always run away rather than attempting massacre."

The ceremony, Ned judged, was already a success: the zombies were able to stand—and as they were washed clean of the clay that had helped to give them birth, a few of them began to sway to the rhythm of the drums, which they could evidently hear, or feel. Their eyes were open, and one or two looked up at the starry sky, almost as if they recognized its promise, before they were led away by their appointed companions. They walked steadily, as meekly as any of the anticipated multitude to whom the inheritance of the Earth had been promised.

That was more than mere success. That was a triumph.

As Marie Laveau returned to her throne she paused by Ned's chair, and said: "I believe that the trial by ordeal is over now, and that we have come through it successfully."

"We're no longer adrift, it's true," Ned replied. "We have a means to steer and a star to steer by...but the trial will never be over. The ultimate triumph will require more lives than ours, and a greater thirst than two mere mortals could ever muster...but Monsieur Patou is right—the new era *is* begun."

PART TWO:
THE NECROMANCERS OF LONDON

Chapter One
Waiting for the Night Mail

November 1823 had turned out to be unseasonably cold, and the members of the thin crowd awaiting the arrival of the evening mail coach from Dover were all huddled in the coffee-shop next door to the Post Office, sitting as close as possible to one or other of its two black-leaded stoves. One man, however, had stationed himself slightly apart from the two clusters, alone at a table. He was muffled by a greatcoat, a scarf and a capacious felt hat, with a coffee-pot and a white china cup before him. The dregs had long since gone cold.

The coach was late—unsurprisingly, given that the chill of the night must have frosted all the ruts and potholes in the road into jarring solidity, and that a freezing fog had settled that must be even worse in open country than the streets of London, though not quite as smoke-laden.

When a slender but not unmuscular individual came over to the table where the lone man was sitting, carrying a fresh coffee-pot and a clean cup, the latter looked up gratefully, although he did not allow the concealing scarf to fall from the lower part of his face. The gratitude vanished from his eyes, though, and he scowled behind the scarf. The benevolent newcomer was not a waiter.

"Good evening, Mr. Temple," the newcomer said, politely. "Or should I say 'good morning,' given that it's past midnight? Do you remember me?"

Gregory Temple cursed the mention of his name, although it had been spoken in tone so soft and silky that he doubted that any other members of the patient crowd had heard it. "I remember all the hirelings who bore false witness against Richard Thompson, with the intention of sending him to the gallows for a crime committed by John Devil," he said. "Given the chance, I'd bring them all to their due reckoning—and be sure to keep them from the kind of evasion accomplished by Sawney Ross. You have a damnable nerve approaching me, Mr. Hopkey."

"You can call me Sam," the actor said, as he sat down and poured out two cups of coffee for himself and the secret policeman. "And I'll freely admit that I was never comfortable with that affair. I've been to the Old Bailey half a dozen times in all, but always to secure an acquittal, save for that once. John Devil took care to snatch Thompson away from the noose, though—for which you might be a little grateful. You've forgiven Ned Knob, after all, and taken him into your service."

"I've forgiven no one," Temple growled, although he picked up the full cup readily enough, and put the hot brim to his lips gratefully, "and I know full well that Knob didn't send you, for he's still in the Caribbean with your old master, trying to play the diplomat in the founding of a zombie empire."

"Might I ask how that work is going?" Sam Hopkey said, with the ghost of a smile on his lips.

"None too well, as you doubtless have your own means of knowing," Temple retorted. "Limehouse is swarming with sailors returned from the Americas, and they all turn up at Sharper's eventually, although many must be disappointed to find it metamorphosed into Jenny Paddock's Cabaret Theater. I hear that your slut has pretensions now to be a tragedienne, although I doubt that she was playing Phaedra tonight."

"You have no right to call Jeanie a slut, sir," Sam Hopkey replied, with a certain dignity. "We might not have solemnized our union in church, but we're as faithful a couple as you'd find at one of the Duchess of Devonshire's affairs, and far more so than any you'd find in jolly George's rotten court."

There was no scope for denying that, so Temple merely said: "What do you want, Mr. Hopkey? Best hurry—the coach will be here at any minute."

"Not a chance, Mr. Temple," the wiry man replied. "It'll be another half-hour at least, on a night like this. As you must have guessed, I'm here on Tom's behalf."

Temple had guessed, but he was still intrigued. He had lately had some slight contact with a representative of *Civitas Solis*—the man who styled himself Giuseppe Balsamo—and the fact that Tom Brown, alias Henri de Belcamp, thought it necessary to make separate contact suggested that the latter's plan to become an influential figure in that shadowy organization was faring no better than Germain Patou's plan to secure a haven in Haiti where he could resume his necromantic vocation with all possible fervor and efficiency.

"John Devil and I might have forged a brief alliance in the recent past," Temple said, "but we are not friends. Any information you give me, I am likely to use against him. I'm even more eager to send him to the gallows than you and your doxy."

"Tom told me that you would be gruff and surly," Sam replied, calmly, "but he told me not to take any notice, because you know as well as he does, in your heart of hearts, that you're both on the same side now, facing the same adversaries with the same heroic spirit. He says that no matter what you might say aloud, you're no more committed to the King and Parliament than Ned Knob is."

"He has a damned cheek, then," Temple opined, wrathfully. "I'm loyal to my country—and Parliament has not yet made up its mind. Canning used to be the most ardent of the enemies of Jacobin science, but now he's in charge of the nation's destiny, he knows better than to play the bigot."

Although Lord Liverpool was the Prime Minister, everyone knew that George Canning was the man in charge of the Tory party and the government. Sam merely smiled at the mention of the name, though. "I've played the bigot myself, on stage," he said, "and the opposite too. Mr. Canning's a fine actor, but I know the art too well to trust anything he says. If you think that his Commission of Inquiry intends to make a fair report of the affair at Fyne Court, you're a greater optimist than I took you for."

Temple scowled, although he knew that if Tom Brown were now in London—as he surely must be, if Sam Hopkey had come here on his behalf—then he had ample means of finding out what was going on, even in the wilds of the Quantocks. He would know, just as Balsamo had, that Victor Frankenstein, whom Lord Byron had hoped to escort to the Americas, had instead accepted an invitation from Andrew Crosse and Michael Faraday, the most prominent English pioneers of electric research now that Humphry Davy was dead, to stage a demonstration at Crosse's home in Somerset—and that Canning had set up a commission to investigate the claims that Frankenstein had made regarding the resurrection of the dead, in which selected parliamentarians would associate themselves with members of the Royal Society. Temple was due to take charge of the escort that would accompany the commission's members to Fyne Court in less than 36 hours time.

"That's none of your business, Mr. Hopkey," Temple growled, "nor of John Devil's."

"It's everyone's business, Mr. Temple," Hopkey replied, flatly. "If the world is to be turned upside-down, there's not a man, woman or child within it who doesn't have an interest at stake. This is the 19th century, Mr. Temple—what you call common people are no longer prepared to let their fate be decided by aristocrats and mill-owners, especially in matters of life and death. I didn't come to quarrel with you, though, or to issue challenges. I came to give you information that you direly need to know. For one thing, Szandor and Addhema are in England, probably in London."

Temple knew that Addhema was another name by which Countess Marcian Gregoryi was known in what was assumed to be her native land—or the native land of the person she had once been. He had not known, however, that the vampire and his minion were in England, and Sam was right to judge that it was information of which he and his superiors were in need.

"It was only to be expected," he said, ungraciously. "They're as eager to take possession of Frankenstein and his secrets as Byron and *Civitas Solis* are."

"Not to mention half the governments in Europe, now that credulity is beginning to dawn," Sam said. "It's not just Limehouse that's swarming with sailors returned from the Caribbean. Patou may still be in trouble, but Marie Laveau's publicity has spread. If Canning were to prove willing, in spite of pressure from the Church, England might steal a useful march on her rivals. It's not just Frankenstein that Szandor might be after, though, according to Tom. He sent me to warn you that you may well be in danger yourself."

"I doubt that," Temple said. "The vampire had the opportunity to kill me in Miremont, and refrained."

"It's not the vulgar peril of assassination that threatens you," Sam Hopkey told him. "The vampire might have intended to capture you as well as the Colonel at the Grafina von Boehm's château—and Szandor's probably not the only new enemy whose attention you've attracted."

"It was Byron that Szandor intended to capture," Temple corrected him. "The rest of us were merely bystanders."

"That's possible," Sam insisted. "Tom believes, however, that it was Byron he intended to *seduce*, along with the Grafina. The man he probably intended to *capture* was Colonel Bozzo-Corona—he presumably believed that he already had you, having hobbled you and set you aside for later collection."

"Why would the vampire want to capture the Colonel?" Temple could not help asking, genuinely curious. "Surely not because of his wealth, if he had Sarah von Boehm in his sights."

"According to Tom," Sam said, "the Colonel is considerably richer than the Grafina, although his fortune is much better defended. It wasn't the Colonel's money that interested Szandor, but his antiquity—and Tom believes that Szandor's interest might well have aroused the Colonel's in its turn. It's not your influence as a secret policeman, which seems to be almost annihilated, that interests other parties now, in Tom's opinion—merely your stubbornness in having lived so long, while giving no sign of any conspicuous loss of your mental and physical prowess."

Temple was genuinely puzzled. He had had cause to wonder himself at the remarkable fashion in which the aged Jean-Pierre Séverin had conserved his skill and acumen, but he had not thought to include himself in the same category. It was Séverin that he had come to meet from the Dover coach, although he did not know yet why the Frenchman had asked him to be there. "I thought that Szandor was interested in means to secure and prolong life-after-death, and regarded the living as mere prey," he said.

"That was not what he told you when you met him," Sam said, so confidently that Temple knew that he or his master must have had an eye-witness report of the encounter. That could only have come from one person.

"Is Lazarus in England too, then?" Temple asked. He had lost track of Frankenstein's first Grey Man after the affair at Miremont, and had had no news of him since. "Is he the one you're warning me against?"

"No—he still seems intent on forging a reconciliation with his maker. The people of whom Tom commissioned me to warn you to beware are Balsamo and Sarah von Boehm."

"In other words, *Civitas Solis* and the remnant of the *vehm* that took up arms against them when they kidnapped Jeanne and Sarah's children. I can understand why it might be in John Devil's interest to make me wary of both, if he's engaged in some sort of power-struggle with Balsamo—but I've had no indication of hostility from either party." He did not think it politic to add that he had received overtures of friendship from one—and he knew, in any case, that overtures of friendship from a man like Balsamo might easily conceal intentions of a very different sort.

"The proposed demonstration at Fyne Court has become a significant focus of interest, Mr. Temple," the actor told him, with an expansive flourish of his right arm. "The attention of all those working in the cause of Enlightenment, as well as all those working against it, is focused upon it for the moment. If Faraday returns to the Royal Institution suitably enthused and duly licensed to begin his own experiments, London will become the Necromantic capital of the world, with material and intellectual resources that far outstrip anything that Germain Patou and Marie Laveau might contrive in Haiti, let alone those that *Civitas Solis* can presently call upon, given its current state of disarray. Frankenstein's technique is not, however, the only topic of interest whose urgency has been revived by recent events, especially in the ranks of the older Secret Orders. There is more than one kind of potential immortality, Mr. Temple, and more than one way to approach their investigation. You already know that the Commission you will be escorting will include several individuals with secret agendas. Tom advises you to be wary, and to be exceedingly careful in deciding who your friends are."

"I always am," Temple said. "As I've already told you, I certainly don't count John Devil among them. Lazarus, on the other hand..."

"...Has his own ambitions, and makes his alliances in accordance with his own ends."

Temple recalled that the Grey Men's New Adam had admitted something of the sort, but it was hardly necessary. As with Szandor, Lazarus' first priority had to be the interests of the dead-alive, not the living. To the extent that the two sets of interests coincided, he seemed as reliable an ally as any, but if ever there was a conflict, he might be as redoubtable an adversary as any…except, perhaps, Szandor, who was certainly gifted with uncanny powers of delusion and apparently possessed what Temple had decided to call "dividuality:" the ability to divide his person into two. Balsamo, Sarah von Boehm and Colonel Bozzo-Corona, on the other hand, were bound to be interested, first and foremost, in means of prolonging life rather than surviving death; if the methods of modern science were to replace those of the ancient alchemists in that search, that would be the principal focus of their attention—but modern science required empirical observation and experimentation, which would require subjects: living ones, in this instance, rather than dead ones.

Temple still could not believe that he might be as interesting, in that context, as Séverin, or the Colonel—or Balsamo himself, if he were more than a mere impostor—but what Sam was saying was certainly worthy of some thought…unless, of course, John Devil were extending this lure to him precisely in order to deflect him from other concerns and paths of Inquiry. That, he knew, was perfectly possible.

"We all make alliances according to our own ends," Temple told his unwelcome companion, brusquely. "Which is why I will make none with you or your master. Since you've brought me a message from him, I'll give you one to take back: while I still have duties to perform, I shall carry them out to the best of my ability, but if and when I am free once again of immediate obligations to crown and country—which might be very soon, if my superiors' patience runs out—then I shall resume the hunt for John Devil, and pursue it doggedly."

"Alone?" Sam queried.

"If necessary," Temple stated—but he knew that he was being disingenuous. He would not be alone; he had been promised all possible support by the Comtesse de Belcamp, with the sole provision that he did not pursue his chase to the death. Jeanne was interested in capture, not annihilation.

"Tom asked whether you would consent to meet with him," Sam Hopkey continued, after a slight pause. He was obviously not hopeful that his offer would be accepted.

Temple was, in fact, hesitating over the wisdom of uttering the refusal that leapt to his lips, and wondering whether it might be more profitable to accept, when there was a rumble of wheels outside, and the night-coach from Dover was heard racing into the Post Office forecourt.

The waiting crowd rose as one man, and not merely because they had been waiting for so long. The postillion was sounding his horn, and the blast was an alarm signal, intended to summon help. Something was amiss.

Having longer legs than Sam Hopkey, Gregory Temple reached the door first, three or four strides ahead of any of the people who had been huddling closer to the stoves. He bounded out into the street and set off across the courtyard as the coach pulled up, the four hoses steaming and the wheels squealing like souls in torment as the brakes were applied.

Uniformed employees were already emerging from the Post Office itself, and one of them shouted: "What's wrong?"

"Wounded man inside!" cried the coachman. "We were attacked!"

"Highwaymen?" queried a second official. "In 1823! On the Dover Road! Impossible!"

Temple's heat was already sinking, however. He knew that the word "impossible" had virtually lost all meaning, precisely because it was 1823. For the moment, he was far less concerned with the plausibility of highwaymen attacking a mail coach on the Dover road than with the identity of the wounded man. Jean-Pierre Sévérin, he knew, was not a man to submit meekly to any kind of attack—but even a man reputed to have been the best swordsman in pre-Revolutionary France could not be expected to be able to defend a mail coach against bandits armed with pistols. It was easy enough to image the ex-morgue-keeper responding chivalrously to a challenge and being shot down in consequence.

The first official reached the flank of the coach ahead of Temple, and pulled open the door. There were only three passengers inside, one of whom was sprawled on the floor between the benches while the other two pored over him with evident concern. There was blood on the floor and on the stricken man's clothing.

None of the three, however, was Jean-Pierre Sévérin. The man lying on the floor, having been bloodily slashed on his upper right arm, not far from the shoulder, was Malo de Treguern, Knight of the Order of St. John Hospitaller—another ancient who would inevitably have responded with violent chivalry to any demand to "stand and deliver!"

Temple shoved the Post Office official out of the way, and forced the two concerned passengers to sit down. "Monsieur de Treguern!" he said, urgently. "What happened? Was Sévérin with you? What has become of him?"

Malo de Treguern opened his eyes, as if slightly surprised to discover that the coach had reached its destination. "Mr. Temple!" he said. "Thank God you're here! You must summon reinforcements immediately. We were stopped on the road. Séverin and I tried to fight. We expected to take them by surprise, but they were ready for us. They took him, Mr. Temple—the cowards led him on, then dropped a net on him. They dared not face him, even though he only had a stick, and not a blade. I too had a staff, but…"

Temple had been examining the wound. "You've lost a lot of blood, Monsieur de Treguern," he said, "but you'll live, with luck and God's favor. We'll have you in St. Thomas's in no time." As he spoke, he looked at the official, who nodded. A stretcher was already being brought out, and its bearers were well used to sprinting to the hospital. Highwaymen were exceedingly rare nowadays, but traffic accidents were becoming increasing common, as if by way of compensation. The number of people run down by coaches and carriages in the London streets was dizzying to contemplate.

"Why are you here, Monsieur?" Temple asked, as practiced hands transferred the injured man from the floor of the church to the stretcher.

"Séverin is not to blame," Treguern stated, in a hushed but determined voice. "I insisted on accompanying him. We have not become firm friends since our adventure at Miremont, I admit—but once two men have fought as comrades against monsters, there is a bond between them. He was coming to warn you that Comtesse Marcian Gregoryi has crossed the channel, doubtless to pursue her evil schemes in London. He has information about her master, gleaned in Paris…as have I. He saw the virtue of our traveling together—not virtue enough, alas!"

By the time this speech was finished, Temple was trotting alongside the stretcher as it was being carried through the bitterly cold streets in the direction of St. Thomas's Hospital. He could see Tower Bridge in the distance, its candle-lit towers looming out of the mist as if suspended in mid-air.

"I will come to see you tomorrow," Temple promised, relenting in his pace, and then turning back. The coachman, he knew, would be able to tell him exactly where the attack had taken place, and the Post Office would be glad to lend him a horse once he made his identity known. The Postmaster would summon constables and guardsmen to take up the chase I his wake, but he wanted to make a start as soon as humanly possible, before any tracks that the coach's attackers had left behind could be obscured.

Sam Hopkey was waiting by the carriage.

"Don't go, Mr. Temple," said the actor, obviously having guessed his intention. "It might be a trap—they may want you too, remember, whoever they are."

"Séverin is my friend," said Temple. "He's also a foreign national on English soil; I'm honor bound to protect him from harm, and to pursue anyone who seeks to injure him." To the Postmaster he said: "I'm Gregory Temple, late of Scotland Yard. I need your best horse."

"He's being saddled as we speak, Mr. Temple," the official said, along with half a dozen others. "Should my men go with you, or should I save the horses for yours?" Temple's name was obviously not unfamiliar to him, although it might have been if he had been a younger man, and he was obviously not to be deterred from offering full assistance by rumors of madness.

"Save the horses for the constables," Temple said. "The guardsmen will bring their own, when they come." He turned to the coachman, who was still catching his breath. "Where?" he growled, tersely.

"Between Blackfen and Crayford," the driver replied, "not far from Hall Place. There were at least six, perhaps ten—not common blackguards, but skilled swordsmen. They might have killed the warrior monk, if they'd wanted to, but were content to put him out of the fight. He said as much himself."

"They'll be differently inclined toward you, Mr. Temple," Sam Hopkey said. "If you go charging in without a dozen men at your back, you'll likely meet the same fate as the Frenchman."

"Only if they're expecting me," Temple said, as the saddled horse was brought forward. "I'll travel faster alone, and might have to wait ten minutes and more for any reinforcements at all, let alone a dozen men. If your master turns out to be behind this caper…"

"He's not, sir," the actor protested, vehemently. "This is far more likely to be Balsamo's doing."

So there's definitely a rift in the Civitas Solis *lute*, Temple thought, as he climbed on to the horse's back. *Henri has not mastered that organization as easily as he mastered the Deliverance—which is doubtless why he has taken on the mantle of Tom Brown again, to muster the raggle-taggle army of the London Underworld.*

He urged the horse forward. He was not wearing spurs, but the animal was a veteran post horse, loyal and willing. It set off at a fast trot, and accelerated to a gallop within a dozen strides. Temple headed for Bermondsey at top speed. The coach had covered nine-tenths of its journey before being attacked, practically on the outskirts of the capital. That meant that its assailants had had time already to have fled into one or other of the city's rookeries—but would they have done that? Would they have dared, if they were indeed adversaries, rather than hirelings, of John Devil? More likely they had gone to Dartford, in order to make use of the river to reach a more distant destination.

Temple knew that he was being something of a fool in leading the pursuit on is own, but he had been inactive for some time, and had not forgotten that Jean-Pierre Sévérin had saved his bacon in Miremont, when he had done more harm than good himself by unwittingly taking the vampire into the new château. He had a debt to repay, to himself as well as to the Frenchman.

The horse was a magnificent specimen, perhaps not one of the fastest in the world but certainly one of the sturdiest. Its stamina did not flag as it covered the miles of the Dover road, passing through Greenwich and Eltham like a cannonball, swathed in the fog as if by a cloud. Beyond Eltham there were no more street-lights, and the three-quarter Moon was only visible at present as a pale glow lighting the mist, but the horse had been this way many times before; it knew the road, and was confident of its footing, even on the frost-ridged carriageway.

The mist began to crystallize out and sink to earth as frost while Temple made progress. The Moon became more distinct by the minute, and the stars began to peep through; the sky above the fog was almost free of high cloud. Temple knew that dawn would be a long time coming, given the season, but there was light enough to let him see, and the layer of sparkling white frost covering the highway and the objects to either side of it assisted him in that task.

By the time he reached the place where the mail coach had been attacked, there was no danger of him missing the residual evidence of the assault, which showed almost as clearly as it would have done on freshly-fallen snow. Temple was convinced that he could pick out Jean-Pierre Séverin's footprints, and those of Malo de Treguern, left when they leapt down from the vehicle, armed with a cane and a staff, to battle the marauders. He dismounted and tethered the post horse to a bush, then swiftly located the spot where the Hospitaller had been interrupted and wounded, but did not pause to examine the blood-stains flecking the thin layer of rime. He pressed on, following Séverin's footprints to the point where they too reached a confused terminus, beneath the overlapping boughs of two venerable trees.

He looked up then, to see where the net that Treguern had mentioned might have fallen from—and realized his mistake.

The trap had been re-set, and his detective skill had led him straight into it.

The net fell again, and caught him in its toils. He struggled hard to throw it off, and might have succeeded had he had a minute longer—but the bandits had not left their trap to do its work unaided. Shadowy forms emerged from the pools of darkness beneath the trees, and reached out to grapple with him. One, at least, was armed with a wad of German tinder steeped in some sweet-smelling substance.

Realizing what the substance must be intended to do, Temple held his breath and tried to continue the fight—but he was outnumbered by at least four to one, and would have succumbed within a matter of seconds had the contest not turned into a brawl, in which his immediate assailants seemed to be fending off an attack by another party.

The battle took place in silence; no one barked any orders or expressed surprise in curses. The whole affair had a supernatural feel to it, as if none of the combatants, save for Temple himself, was fully human—but that was probably an illusion, caused by the fact that his exertions had forced him to take a tainted breath.

He struggled to retain consciousness, but his mind became dizzy and it seemed that the world began to spin around him.

His one regret, as he fell into unconsciousness, was that he had not been able to obtain a single useful clue as to who had tried to capture him, or who had tried to stop them, or who was likely to triumph in the ensuing conflict.

Chapter Two
Beyond the Dover Road

Gregory Temple had fallen unconscious in the course of his investigations on several previous occasions, and had even been the victim of chemical narcotics more than once. When he began to come round, therefore, his first lucid thought was that he ought to conceal his condition, to feign unconsciousness in the hope of overhearing something that might be to his advantage.

He could hear someone moving about—more than one person, if the discrimination of his hearing could be trusted—but no words were spoken. After a little while, the evidence of one of the movers faded away; the individual had either left the scene or become very still.

As to what "the scene" might be, Temple was only able to make a few deductions. He was lying on a dusty wooden floor, too stable to be the deck of a boat—although the sound of water lapping could be heard not far away. If he was in a dwelling or storehouse of some kind, it had to be on a shore, probably that of the Thames. He was lying under a thick blanket, but his hands and feet were not bound, so there was a possibility of mounting a swift and effective action against his captors if he could work out where they were positioned. He began to tense and flex his muscles, but without stretching his limbs in a fashion that might disturb the blanket in a revealing fashion.

He decided, in the end, that the second individual that he had heard moving had indeed gone away, even though he had not heard any door opening or closing, and that the other was situated to his right, some three or four feet away, in a wooden-legged chair of some sort. There was no evidence, so far as his closed eyes could tell, that the place in which he was being held was brightly lit, but he assumed that there must be at least one candle burning close at hand, in order that he might be watched.

When the time seemed ripe, he tried to cast off the blanket and rise to his feet with a single fluid movement, and began reaching out toward his mysterious watcher even before he opened his eyes. The sound he emitted thereafter, however, was not a snarl as he launched himself forward aggressively, but a groan, as a reflex educated by long habit made him pause, forbidding his arms to act aggressively against the woman who was seated in an armchair beside an unpolished table—which did indeed bear a candle, positioned so that its light would fall upon a supine body in the location he had just escaped.

He groaned because he thought that the reflex had betrayed him: that what he saw was not really a woman at all. He recognized her, having seen her twice during his most recent excursion to Paris and its environs. It was the individual who called herself Countess Marcian Gregoryi, alias Addhema—the vampire's minion.

Had she been carrying a weapon, she could easily have shot or stabbed him while he hesitated, but she was not, and obviously had no such intention. Her hands were holding an open book, which descended slowly to her lap as she looked up at him, mildly.

He tried not to meet her eyes, knowing what magic there was in them, and how completely he had been deceived by her master's mesmeric art at Miremont, but it was not easy. In that matter too there was a reflex at work—a reflex guided by an innate capacity for lust that he had not entirely put away, in spite of his advanced age.

The pretended Countess—or Comtesse, or Grafina, according to her arena of operations—was very beautiful. "Do you intend to strike me, Mr. Temple?" she asked, in perfect English. "That seems a trifle ungrateful, given that my men saved you from…well, doubtless not a fate wore than death, but a fate that would surely have proved inconvenient to you."

Temple's reflexive pause became a frozen hesitation—and he realized that he was, indeed, very cold, although there was a stove next to the table, whose coals were still bright. The space was not easy to heat, for it was some kind of warehouse, capacious enough to defy the stove's efforts even if its rear door not been standing open, letting in the pale light of dawn.

Countess Marcian Gregoryi did not appear to be feeling the cold, however; she was clad in a think woolen coat and a fur wrap, but even that might have been a disguise. Did vampires feel cold at all?

"Pick up your blanket, Mr. Temple," said the Countess. "Keep warm—the daylight does not promise much relief to the frozen world."

Recognizing the wisdom of the advice, Temple did as he as told. "You claim that you saved me from the trap that was set for me?" he said. "Who, then, disposed the net for a second time?"

"I don't know," she said. "The men who drugged you were mere hirelings, of course, and did not know themselves who issued the order, else I'd have got the information with very little effort. I do know that they took your friend Séverin to Purfleet, with instructions to deliver him to a barge. I've sent Guido after them, with instructions to follow the barge to its destination, if he can. They're playing a dangerous game, whoever they are, because they'll be heading into the heart of Tom Brown's territory if they go upriver, and I can't imagine that they'll head for the marshes."

Having swathed himself carefully in the blanket, Temple said: "And why did you save me—if indeed you did?"

"I can hardly blame you for your mistrust," Addhema said, "after that fiasco in Miremont—but we have nothing against you on that score. If you were not a hunter in the pay of the state, we would have nothing against you at all, but you understand now, I think, what kinds of prejudice we have faced in the past, and still face, in our fight for survival."

"You might not be a literal blood-drinker," Temple retorted, "but if there is any truth at all in what Séverin has told me, you are certainly a killer."

"I don't deny it," she told him, equably, "but I plead self-defense. Do you imagine that men have not tried to murder me, in spite of my camouflage? But you have made alliances with murderers before, under the pressure of circumstances. Tom Brown has certainly contrived as many deaths as I have."

"My grandson and his son were threatened by the same malefactors," Temple said, dully. "It was a rare circumstance, in which the enemy of my enemy became my principal hope of attaining my goal—but we are not and never will be friends, and I consider you in the same light, even if some of your present enemies are also ill-disposed toward me. I do not make alliances with vampires."

"You were willing to make an alliance with Frankenstein's first Grey Man," Addhema pointed out, "and your employee Ned Knob seemed actually to like him, if

Guido is to be believed. Now that you know that Szandor and I are merely Grey Men created by the hazards of nature, why should you be unduly troubled by the reputation that legend and superstition have foisted upon us? Szandor took advantage of you in Miremont, it's true—but can you really blame him? He took care not to hurt you. Indeed, when your friends attacked us, we were content to slip away without hurting anyone, rather than make a fight of it. The *vehmgerichte* have been after us ever since, and Colonel Bozzo-Corona has begun inquiries of his own that might prove equally inconvenient. Our hopes of making common cause with Lord Byron have been dashed, for the moment. We were tempted to take ship for Haiti to seek out Marie Laveau, but Faraday and his self-styled Necromancers of London are closer at hand. Faraday is the real prize in the game as it presently stands—there's a man who can easily put the likes of Germain Patou and Balsamo's antique alchemists in the shade! What a triple alliance might be forged between him, Frankenstein and Szandor!"

"If a triple alliance is formed," Temple opined, "Andrew Crosse will be the third member. He, after all, is brokering the potential friendship between Faraday and Frankenstein. Darwin is dead, alas, and the Lunar Society little more than a memory, but England has enough great men of science not to need your master—or you, his second self."

"Second self? We're not quite as closely allied as that, Mr. Temple—although you'd doubtless find the terms of our relationship interesting, if you were to open your mind to the Inquiry."

"Is that why you've taken me captive?" Temple demanded.

"Captive?" she echoed, mockingly. "Why, Mr. Temple, we haven't taken you captive, but merely freed you from potential captivity in someone else's hands. You're as free as a bird. You're not bound, and the door stands open not 15 meters away. No one will attempt to inhibit your movements—unless you surrender to the violent impulse that overtook you while you were still lying down, feigning unconsciousness. For the time being, you and I are on the same side, whether we make any formal alliance or not. We both want the parliamentary commission to reach Fyne Court safely, and to be dazzled by a successful demonstration of Frankenstein's technique. You might not be as fully committed, as yet, to the cause of the dead-alive as your associate Mr. Knob and your mercurial adversary John Devil, but you're a man of reason, a champion of deductive logic who does not stoop to using rhetoric as a means of sustaining belief when the evidence becomes challenging."

"What are you looking for in London, Addhema?" Temple demanded.

"What we have long been looking for everywhere else," the beautiful countess replied. "The secret of immortality...or, if you prefer, of eternal undeath. We are presently working on the assumption that the secret we need is not the same secret for which *Civitas Solis* and the Bavarian Illuminati have long been searching. Although there would be a certain esthetic symmetry in the discovery that an effective method of maintaining God-given life were also effective in maintaining the second life that some individuals achieve, naturally or artificially, *after* death, we have no reason to expect that to be the case."

"God-given life?" Temple echoed. "Do you believe in God, then?"

"Not in the kind of God that would declare us an abomination, a blasphemy against His dictates—but who knows what plans the divine mind might have for the future progress of humankind, if there is indeed a God?"

"Malo de Treguern believes that information to be contained in the revelation of the scriptures," Temple said.

"But you doubt it, Mr. Temple," Addhema countered. "Scriptures tend to rush to judgment, which is why they are always being augmented, reinterpreted and replaced. Even so, Treguern's scriptures are not averse to the idea that the dead might rise from their graves, in the flesh, in order to build a Millennial Kingdom on the Earth."

Temple's gaze went to the book resting on her lap, but it was not a Bible. Nor was it a copy of the anonymous *Frankenstein*. It was printed in Gothic script, apparently in German, but it seemed to be a recent text, more likely a philosophical treatise by some follower of Leibniz or Kant than some romance by Ludwig Tieck or the Baron de la Motte Fouqué.

"Show me your true form," Temple whispered, forcing his voice so that she would be able to hear him. "Show me what lies behind your *camouflage*."

Countess Marcian Gregoryi laughed lightly. "Do you still believe that I am a skeletal monster, like the one that Séverin thought he saw, on the night that his daughter killed herself, or the one that René de Kervoz thought he saw when he believed that he had shot me in the head? Do you think that I am a mere husk, more dust than flesh, and that what you see before your eyes is but glamour? You have no idea, Mr. Temple, what Grey Men and Grey Women might be capable of making of themselves, given time and education…just as you have no idea what living men and women might make of themselves, given the same resources. You are on the brink of discovering something of your own inner resources, just as Colonel Bozzo-Corona appears to be…but you are still blinded, as he is, by your preconceptions, by ideas that you have long taken for granted, although the only basis they have is the strength of your conviction. We are more alike than you imagine, Mr. Temple—but I am older than you are, although appearances are deceptive. Szandor is older still….and there may be Grey Men even older, who have greater skill in concealing themselves, just as there are may be living men even older than Saint-Germain and the Jew, unhampered by the superstitions that have shackled those two. Szandor does not like that idea overmuch, but he has always had a tendency to vainglory. I find it intriguing, don't you?"

Temple had heard of the Comte de Saint-Germain and the Wandering Jew, just as he had heard of Giuseppe Balsamo before the man currently using that name had introduced himself, but he had never believed in either and suspected that Addhema was teasing him. All he said aloud, however, was: "I am not a supernatural being. I am merely a living man who happens to have grown old."

"I am not a supernatural being either," the vampire countess retorted, "but merely a woman returned to life after death, who appears not to have grown old. I wish you well, Mr. Temple—for the moment, at least, we have the same enemies. Be careful, I beg you. Keep Frankenstein and Faraday safe, if you can." She stood up as she was speaking, and gathered her fur wrap more tightly around her shoulders and neck, as if she were indeed fearful of catching a chill. "The Sun is up, as you can see," she continued, "and vampires prefer the dark. I must bid you farewell."

For a moment or two, Temple wondered whether he ought to arrest her, or at least make the attempt—but he had no charge to bring against her that could possibly be proven in a court of law and he was, in any case, more than half-inclined to believe her when she said that it had been her men who had saved him from the predators who had sought to trap him in the same net that had trapped his friend. For that reason, he simply let her walk out of the door and move off into the gathering but still-gloomy light of day.

After a short pause, he followed her, eager to know where she might be headed—but when he arrived in the doorway and peered out, she was nowhere to be seen. He had to wonder whether he had been the victim of mesmerism, at least to the extent that he had allowed her to make her escape, but there was no use crying over spilled milk.

He set off to walk along the shore of the river, heading westwards. At the first possible opportunity, he hailed a boatman who was steering his skiff toward the port. He still had money in his pouch—at least Addhema was no cutpurse—and he paid for passage to Tower Bridge.

"Has there been any unusual traffic on the river of late?" he asked the boatman.

"Not that I've noticed, sir," the boatman replied, "but this is the Thames, after all, where the usual is a broad church. Were you thinking in terms of conspirators or ghosts?"

"Conspirators," Temple said, firmly. "Germans, in particular, or other Eastern Europeans."

"No, sir," said the boatman. "I've seen nothing of that sort."

"And what of John Devil the Quaker?" Temple asked. "Is he up to his old tricks again?"

"The rallying cry is said to have been broadcast in Jenny Paddock's," the boatman admitted, "but I never go to such places myself—I'm an honest man, sir."

Every thief and scoundrel in London declared himself to be an honest man, Temple knew—and many of them, he suspected, actually believed it, being far readier to see the motes in their neighbors' eyes than the beams in their own—but he judged by the boatman's weary tone that he, at least, was an ignorant individual who preferred to nurture his ignorance rather than take the risk of knowing too much.

From Tower Bridge, Temple set off in the direction of St. Thomas's Hospital, where he found Malo de Treguern abed, evidently weak but fully conscious.

"What did you find out, Mr. Temple?" the Knight of St. John enquired. "Do you know what has become of Jean-Pierre?"

"No, alas," Temple confessed. "I nearly fell into the same trap myself—and I must confess to some slight surprise that you were spared."

"Spared?" Treguern queried, looking down at his bandaged arm. "They could have killed me had they wanted to, I suppose, but they certainly did not spare me. I've sustained worse wounds, in the days before the revolution, and lived to tell the tale, as I certainly hope to do again, but I'm no longer a young man."

"That," said Temple, "is exactly why they might have taken you—but they were bravos acting under orders, and probably knew no more than I did that you would be accompanying Séverin. Why were you with him?"

"I heard that he was coming to England, with information relating to the vampire. I had information of my own, from the Church's informants. Like him, I thought you should be apprised of it. Szandor and Addhema are in England. Byron having departed from Europe, their attention is now directed toward Victor Frankenstein again. Whether they intend to harm him, I cannot tell, but I am certain that they want to know his secret, and that they would use it if they could."

"I believe they would," Temple agreed. "And you would go to any lengths to prevent that, I assume?"

"I am sworn to uphold God's law," the warrior monk stated, proudly, "as you are sworn to uphold the law of England. Neither, I think, extends any tolerance to vampires or necromancers."

Temple frowned. "For the moment," he said, "Victor Frankenstein is under the protection of His Majesty's Government. Whether he will remain so depends on the outcome of an official Commission of Inquiry. I ought to remind you, Brother Malo, that the Roman Church has no authority on English soil."

"In this instance," Treguern relied, "the Roman Church and the Church of England are in perfect agreement. Even your dissenters have no truck with necromancy. There is a Bishop on the Commission of Inquiry, is there not?"

Temple nodded, unsurprised that the information in question had been communicated to the Knight of St. John. "The Bishop of Salisbury," he confirmed. "Along with three members of the House of Commons, Robert Hastings, Stephen Southborne and John Medstead—two Tories and a Whig—and three men of science: Thomas

Young, Peter Barlow and William Snow Harris. Michael Faraday would undoubtedly have been included had he not already involved himself with Crosse's trial as an enthusiastic supporter. I do not know how many of them, apart from the Bishop, have strong religious convictions of one sort or another, but I suspect that God's acknowledged servants might be in a majority"

Malo de Treguern expressed his satisfaction with this judgment with a mere nod.

"That might not be of any great consequence," Temple added. "The genie is out of the bottle. Grey Men are being manufactured by the score, if not by the hundred, in Haiti, and it is only a matter of time before the practice spreads to Cuba and New Orleans. If the information transmitted by our diplomats is reliable, experiments are being conducted in Paris, Leipzig, St. Petersburg and Constantinople. This is the 19th century—religious objections tend to be set aside once the prospect of profit puts in an appearance, and governments have scented potential advantages in labor and in war. The only prospect worse than failing to seize an advantage in such matters is that of seeing others seize and exploit it instead. The competition has already been joined; the only question now is who will win; I believe that the parliamentarians will have been apprised of that, and that their scientific colleagues would not require any such formal instruction. The commission's report will not be as reflexively negative as you might hope."

"Do not be so sure, Mr. Temple," the knight said. "In any case, the commission's report might be a minor matter of provocation. God has intervened before, with flood and fire, when blasphemy and corruption threatened His plan."

"There are many who would agree with you that London is the new Sodom, and Paris the new Gomorrah," Temple conceded, "but the world is larger now than it was once imagined to be, and it would require a vast volcanic eruption to consume them both, and other dens of iniquity besides. Men of your kind are ever avid to preach that the world's doom is imminent, but they have never been correct before. To make matters worse, from your point of view, *Civitas Solis* might gain the upper hand even within the Church, if its reignited research into the principles of longevity bears fruit."

Treguern looked at him long and hard, despite his evident weariness. "Have you been in recent contact with the man who calls himself Giuseppe Balsamo?" he asked, shrewdly.

"Yes, less than a week ago," Temple replied. "We are not friends, though. His associates arranged the kidnap of my grandson, in the course of a plot to capture Henri de Belcamp, alias Tom Brown—Germain Patou's one-time collaborator."

"Balsamo and his associates are dangerous heretics," said the warrior monk, "but the Vatican has their measure. They did capture the man you call John Devil, if the information transmitted by *our* diplomats is reliable, but he gave them the slip not long afterwards. They're searching for him high and low—low being the more likely eventuality."

"He has friends in many strata of society," Temple observed. "He undoubtedly has the ear of the Duchess of Devonshire as well as that of Jenny Paddock, and has probably doffed his Quaker hat to King George more than once. His mother taught him well, but she betrayed him in the end, although he swears that she was mistaken, and that he never intended to leave her for dead. On the last point, at least, I believe him—he did love his mother, and valued what she and Thomas Paddock taught him far more than the formal education for which his father paid."

That was not the information for which Malo de Treguern was fishing. "Was it his agents who attacked the mail coach, do you think?" he asked.

"Unlikely," said Temple, although he did not want to tell the Churchman about Sam Hopkey's warning. "If I had to bet, my money would be on the Grafina von Boehm's *vehmgerichte*. They're the most aggressive of all the interested parties—although it would smack of ingratitude, after you and Séverin came to their rescue at the new château in Miremont. Their resurgence is rumored to be due to the active involvement of the Bavarian Illuminati—who originated, I believe, as a splinter-group of *Civitas Solis*."

Treguern's brow was furrowed and he was biting his lip. "I could imagine them pinking me, but scrupulously leaving me alive," he said. "They have a peculiar notion of chivalry, more Romantic than Roman—but Séverin is cut from different cloth. They'll get nothing out of him."

"I doubt that information is what they want," said Temple, thoughtfully. "They might well be interested in his experiences as a morgue-keeper, but it's his own apparent possession of an innate elixir of long life that intrigues them far more. While they can't lay their hands on Saint-Germain or the Jew..." He trailed off, provocatively.

Treguern's eyes narrowed, testifying to the fact that the names were not unknown to him, and their mention in connection with the present affair not entirely unexpected, but he rose no further to the bait than that. Like so many other players in the game, he did not regard Gregory Temple as an enemy, but nor did he regard him as a wholly trustworthy ally. "On that score," the monk said, "they might have done better to take me as well, if they could; Sévérin and I are much the same age. How old are you, Mr. Temple?"

"Old enough for my name to have become legendary, in certain circles," Temple admitted, "but I do not drink the blood of virgins, or feed gluttonously on the life-force of young men, else I'd have sucked the likes of Ned Knob and Sam Hopkey dry some years ago—and Tom Brown too, had I ever laid hands on him long enough to do it."

"You must not speak like that, Mr. Temple," the Churchman told him. "Even jests can be blasphemous. I beg you to keep the Bishop safe when you escort your charges to Somerset, and not to be blinded yourself by whatever you see at Fyne Court. I would go with you if I could, and will follow when I can."

"I would rather you did not, Monsieur de Treguern," Temple said. "My duty is complicated enough as it is."

"No, Mr. Temple," Treguern retorted. "Your duty is perfectly clear and perfectly simple—it is your doubts that are clouding your judgment."

Chapter Three
Fyne Court

The next day, Temple and four agents of Lord Liverpool's secret police met the members of the Parliamentary Commission at Paddington Green, from which westward-bound coaches set off at regular intervals, mostly bound for Bath or Bristol. The convoy that was to carry the expedition would take the Bath Road, and then depart from that city in a south-westward direction, heading for Taunton, and ultimately for Broomfield, the site of the ancestral home in which Andrew Crosse had installed the finest electrical laboratory in England.

The commissioners, along with their servants and other companions—Hastings and Medstead were traveling with young women who were not their wives, as MPs far from their constituencies sometimes did when on official business—were divided into four carriages. One of Temple's agents was instructed to ride with each carriage, seated next to the coachman. Temple rode a horse, sometimes at the head of the column and sometimes at the rear. The party changed horses twice before making its first substantial stop in Reading, and four times more before eventually reaching Bath, where it made an overnight stop.

Temple was perfectly sure that *Civitas Solis* and at least one other organization must have spies among the women and the servants accompanying the commissioners, and perhaps among the commissioners themselves, but there was no way to identify them. His own men took care to eavesdrop on as many conversations as possible, and to report their substance back to him, but he did not expect anything to come of that, save for an estimate of the likely temper of the discussion that would follow Frankenstein's demonstration, if it were to prove successful.

At least three of the seven commissioners appeared to be convinced that it would not be successful, and that the whole affair would prove to be nothing but a hoax, but those who took the possibility seriously seemed direly suspicious of the whole business. The Bishop, in particular, freely expressed the opinion that if an appearance of life were to be returned to a corpse after death, the only possible cause would be its possession by a demon. He declared himself ready, materially and spiritually, to perform an exorcism if necessary, both to prove the point and rid the world of the demon in question.

So far as Temple could judge from snatches of overheard conversation, it was the parliamentarians rather than the scientists who were most prepared to approach the question with open minds, ready to weight up the evidence presented to them. Whether or not the scientists were sincere Christians, their commitment of faith to the science they knew seemed unwavering, and two of them—the aging Young and the much younger Barlow—seemed to take it for granted that death was irreversible, and that whatever they saw when the demonstration was mounted would most probably be a hoax of some sort, achieved by means of trickery. Temple heard Young opine that the trickery would likely be mesmeric in kind, but Barlow would not even admit the honesty of mesmerism as a technique or an art.

At dinner that evening, in Bath's finest coaching inn, the Bishop addressed the whole company on the subject of the Devil's wiles, and the possibility of an all-out assault by the legions of Hell on the human world, which had fallen too far into apostasy, thanks to the blasphemous ravages of Jacobin science. Temple noted, however, that although most of those present nodded politely, the men of science were definitely opposed to the Bishop's views and the members of parliament seemed distinctly dubious. There was no talk of mesmerism while the company of travelers was at table, but there was a good deal of skeptical talk about progress, with Medstead the Whig seeming only a little less doleful in that regard than the two Tories.

Material progress, according to Medstead, might well be linked to the progress of mores, but that did not mean that it was an unalloyed virtue in itself. Like most Whigs, he maintained mental balance-sheets whose accounts were scrupulously made up in terms of utilitarian calculations of arithmetically-expressed pros and cons. Not surprisingly, however, his remarks made no inroads in the Tories' assumption, as voiced by Hastings, that technological progress was a mere fad, which served to deflect attention away from the moral progress that was humankind's collective vocation, and that the moral progress in question had to be based in a sound understanding of humankind's past and a ready appreciation of the causes of human folly.

The scientists, not unnaturally, saw things differently. Young, in particular, agreed with the Bishop that progress in morals had reached its terminus in the teachings of Christ, which would have improved human society long ago had the mass of men ever been inclined to follow them, but contended that great strides had yet to be taken in the matter of progress in knowledge and the understanding of the natural world. All three of the men of science professed belief in natural theology: the doctrine that the proper study of mankind was God's creation, and that every discovery of new phenomena and the laws controlling them brought the minds of men closer to the mind of the God who had designed and ordained those phenomena.

But if I read the Book of Genesis right, Temple thought, *death was no part of God's original plan, at least so far as sentient and willful beings were concerned. It was a punishment that he inflicted on Adam and Eve for disobeying His instruction not to eat of the Tree of Knowledge. Perhaps it was always His plan—or His hope, at least—that knowledge would eventually lead humans back to a remedy for the plight, by one means or another. And perhaps God took care to ensure that there would be a choice of such means, in order that humans would have to take responsibility for the architecture of their own fate.*

He said none of that aloud, though; it was not his place. He contented himself with listening carefully to as many of the discussions taking place around the table as he could. There was little profit to be gained by such eavesdropping, however, from an intellectual as well as a political point of view. Eventually, as his overloaded head began to swim, he cursed himself for his insatiable curiosity. A wiser man, he thought, might have abandoned all philosophizing about progress long ago, having discovered that it did not lead anywhere but around in circles

On the following day, the expedition's own progress—construed in a purely practical sense—became much slower, the roads leading westwards from Bath having not been maintained as well as the highway connecting that city to the capital. It was by no means unknown for such roads to become quite impassable between late December and early March, but the cold snap that had descended upon the country in the last few days had arrived in the wake of a relatively dry and balmy spell, and the frost did not linger long in the ground once the Sun came up. The gradual ascent into the Mendip Hills posed difficulties, but the four carriages were the sturdiest that government money could hire, and there were no major mishaps apart from the customary instances of lameness among the 16 horses, which did not slow them down overmuch in site of the relative infrequency of relay stations.

Temple maintained his vigilance, in spite of a near-total recent lack of natural sleep, but there seemed to be no sign of danger, and the commission's members seemed quite safe in their apparent relaxation. Their relaxation was manifest—a tendency Temple had often observed in London-dwellers when they left the capital for the country. It was as if they were making a crossing from one world to another, where time slowed in its pace and the inert mass of the past reasserted its dominance over the seductive magnetism of the future.

If the conversations of the scientists and parliamentarians ever took on a sinister edge, it happened while Temple was out of earshot; he saw and heard nothing but everyday pleasantries and friendly banter. He continued nevertheless to watch the road like a hawk, and to listen in on the conversations going on inside the carriages, even though both exercises had come to seem like wasted effort. Nothing was said that might have betrayed an individual who was not what he claimed to be, and there were no armed confrontations, even on the minor roads taken by the carriages in order to avoid the city of Bath entirely, its temporary and permanent inhabitants having been reduced to penury and crime, wittingly or not, by dire and stubborn circumstance.

Even though no attempt was made to interfere with the convoy, Temple was heartily glad to see the rooftops of Fyne Court appear. The house was said to have been built during the reign of Charles I, but had obviously been extensively modernized, Andrew Crosse's taste for the contemporary obviously extending far beyond his scientific adventures. Crosse had the local reputation of being a wizard rather than a man of science, intent on mocking God by aping His creation of a human being out of common clay, but Temple knew how easily gaudily-clad rumor may outstrip dull reality in the eyes and memories of men; for that reason, Temple supposed that Crosse was merely a rich man who had taken up electrical science as a hobby, much as his ancestors might have taken up the study of astrology or alchemy, and that he was much misunderstood by his neighbors.

The arrival was inevitably hectic, with trunks being transported from the carriages into various quarters of the house according to the instructions of Crosse's butler, a typical domestic tyrant named Caddick. Temple and his men were, of course, given rooms in the servants' quarters, although Temple was immediately summoned to meet Andrew Crosse and his guests in the library.

Temple found four men gathered there. He recognized Michael Faraday, and had no doubt which of the four was Victor Frankenstein. Crosse, in his capacity as host, was the first to address him. "Your reputation precedes you, Mr. Temple," he said, "and we're very glad to have you here. With such a famous detective on hand, no one will be able to suspect us of any trickery. Welcome to the inaugural gathering of the Necromancers of

London—for we hope to move our endeavors to a town house soon enough, where we shall find it much easier to obtain the equipment we need."

Not to mention a much readier supply of corpses, Temple thought, as he bowed.

Crosse introduced his companions then; the man Temple did not know was identified as an old friend whom Crosse had not seen for some years, but whose presence was exceedingly welcome: George Singer.

"Singer's passion for electrical science was even greater than mine at the outset," Crosse explained. "It was he who first introduced me to Mr. Faraday, ten years ago, and Faraday, in his turn, who arranged for me to give a lecture in London in 1814, where I met Percy Shelley and his wife-to-be. It was through Shelley, of course, that I initially made the acquaintance of Dr. Frankenstein. We have been correspondents for some years, although I am not the avid traveler my father was—he frequented the court of Louis XVI for a while, where he made the acquaintance of Ben Franklin."

Temple shook hands with all four men, gravely. Faraday, a young and slender man, seemed to be bubbling over with excitement and enthusiasm—so much so, in fact, that he barely devoted a second of his time to Temple before returning to his interrupted conversation with Crosse. Crosse was older—almost forty, to judge by appearances—but more aristocratic in his bearing, seemingly able to look down tolerantly upon his less well-born companion, even though he was a full inch shorter. Singer, who seemed a little older than Crosse, was more reserved and somehow less conspicuous; for the moment, he seemed to have been slightly edged out of the conversation, and his attempts to strike up a dialogue with Frankenstein appeared to have been inhibited by the latter's morose anxiety.

"I believe that you have met an employee of mine," Temple said to Frankenstein, for want of any more profitable subject. "Edward Knob."

Frankenstein did not seem to recognize the name immediately, but it eventually struck a chord in his memory. "The young man who came to Shelley's aid in San Terenzo," he said, nodding glumly. "Shelley took quite a shine to him, as I remember—he recognized him as having attended at least one of Davy's lectures, although Mr. Crosse's performance must have been before his time. Was he a policeman, then?"

"Not exactly," Temple replied, "but he has his uses. He is in Haiti now, with Germain Patou and Marie Laveau, but I am expecting him to return in the new year."

"With exciting news, I hope," Singer put in. "Rumor always exaggerates, I know, but if the tales regarding Mademoiselle Laveau have any truth in them at all, she must have access to a useful traditional wisdom of which we know nothing. Given that Patou has already obtained a measure of success comparable to Victor's, there is reason to hope that he might be making further progress."

"Indeed," Temple agreed. "If you'll forgive the impertinence, Dr. Frankenstein, might I ask whether you have had any contact since you were in Spezia with the product of your own success, who now goes by the name of Lazarus."

"There has been some communication between us," Frankenstein reported, warily. "Why do you ask?"

"Is he expected to arrive here in order to witness the demonstration?"

Frankenstein frowned. "He expressed a desire to be here in a letter," he admitted. "I replied that I did not think it wise—but he has become so headstrong that I cannot imagine that he will pay much heed to my opinion."

"To be perfectly frank," Temple said, "I would not have been displeased to find him here. I have talked with him briefly, in Paris, and I believe that he would help to protect you if he could. There are, alas, other parties from whom you might need protection."

"The mysterious Count Szandor?" Frankenstein asked, probably having obtained the name from Lazarus.

"Possibly," Temple conceded, "but I am more anxious, for the present, about members of two secret societies: *Civitas Solis* and a Bavarian *vehm*. Both have agents in London as we speak, and almost certainly have spies here. My men and I will do our utmost to prevent them taking any hostile action, and they may well be here only to observe and report, but I must ask the four of you to be careful of your own security. Much might hang on the outcome of your demonstration. Are all the preparations well in hand?"

Crosse smiled at the delicacy of that question. "We have three dead bodies, obtained by legal means with the consent of the next of kin, which have been immersed in the baths," he said. "The first should be ripe for revival tomorrow. As to what mental condition they might be in, if the resurrections are successful, I cannot tell—but if we are fortunate, one at least will be capable of speech."

"Yes indeed," Singer agreed, "but I fear that we cannot answer for what they might say, if one or more of them turns out to be loquacious." Temple glanced at him briefly, trying to fathom the wry smile that played upon his lips, but immediately returned his attention to the

Swiss scientist, who seemed to be eager to address another question to him.

"I believe, Mr. Temple," Frankenstein said, "that you met some of Patou's Grey Men before he fled Purfleet. Did they include the self-styled General Mortdieu?"

"Yes," said Temple. "Ned Knob had more contact with him than I, as he had with his old friend Sawney Ross, sufficient to form a strong impression of the General's ambitions, but not form any elaborate notion of his intended plan of action."

"What else did he learn?" Faraday asked, curiously.

"He claims that he watched a demonstration very similar to the one you intend to mount, which was half-successful. The body returned to life, and was able to remember a name—but nothing more than that, alas."

"I'd settle for that, if need be," said Faraday. "Once the principle is firmly established, before a host of unimpeachable witnesses..."

Temple was not at all sure that the seven men he had escorted from London were "unimpeachable," but he would not have dreamed of saying so. "Has there been any untoward or unusual occurrence in the vicinity of the house in the last few days, sir?" he asked, addressing Crosse.

"There have been poachers on the estate," Crosse reported, "but that's not unusual, considering that the cold weather has arrived. The village is abuzz with gossip, of course, much of it hostile—but I have not been confronted directly, and I don't expect any trouble. There have been a number of burglaries in local country houses, but we have been spared. Ghosts have been seen, but that's not unusual either, in view of the prevailing tension—servants are very amenable to hysteria."

"Ghosts?" Temple queried—although he knew that the remark about burglaries was more likely to be symptomatic of the presence of hostile forces.

"Oh yes—all country houses of any antiquity have their contingent of ghosts, whether or not they've been modernized. The house was built in 1634, but all the descendants of Odo de Sante Croce, who came to England with William the Conqueror, are supposed by the superstitious to have taken up residence along with my nearer ancestors, including the Sante Croce who was killed at Agincourt. Ghosts of knightly ancestors are inherently more exciting, are they not, than those of 18th century scholars and travelers? I've never seen any ghost myself, of course, and nor has Cornelia, my wife—we have servants to do that for us. Even Caddick has never seen one, although Cook has, and you'd be hard-pressed to find a serving-maid who hasn't."

Temple frowned. "Sometimes," he said, "living men can be mistaken for ghosts, especially if they pose as such. Please tell me if any further sightings are reported by your servants."

"I will," Crosse promised. "Shall we go down to dinner now?" he was addressing his guests, not Temple, who was not dining with the commissioners in the main hall but with the servants in the kitchens.

The ex-detective recognized the question as a tacit dismissal and withdrew. He expected, at any rate, to pick up more in the way of interesting gossip in the servants' quarters and he was not mistaken. Caddick was on duty upstairs, so there was no one to suppress the servants' natural garrulousness; Temple sat quietly to one side, listening to as many overlapping voices as he could. The situation was further confused by the fact that servants were coming in and out all the while, having carried out

173

missions upstairs, and were eager to report on events in the principal dining-room. Apparently, the Bishop as not on his best behavior, and had already undertaken to lock horns with the Devil, in the form of sententious speeches that Crosse and Faraday had greeted with more mockery than alarm. The rules of hospitality, however, forbade host and guests alike to go too far in the matter of giving offense, so the banter had apparently retained a surface of good humor.

As usual, the servants' dinner lasted even longer than the one upstairs, because the servants on duty had to eat in shifts. Temple had to answer the call of duty three times himself, to check in with his men, who had been set to work shifts at various sentry posts. Every time he had to leave he made a brief tour of the surrounds himself but once dark had fallen the visibility outside became very poor.

As in London, there was a freezing mist, but this time there was a cloud layer above it, which maintained the humidity and opacity of the atmosphere. Beyond the area dimly illuminated by the light filtering out of the windows of the house, the gloom was impenetrable. That made Temple feel very uneasy, although he certainly did not envy the lot of any spy posted to watch the house in such inhospitable conditions.

On three occasions Temple bumped into servants in unlit corridors and vestibules inside the house. On the first two occasions, the individuals with whom he collided were maids, who were full of apologies as soon as they realized that he was not one of their customary colleagues, but on the third and last occasion, it was a man who bumped into him, who made no apology at all but made haste to be gone. He must have known the layout of the house, for he had vanished as if into thin air by the time that Temple reacted to the fact that a folded piece of paper had been thrust into his hand.

After two minutes of futile pursuit, the detective paused by a lantern in one of the principal corridors in order to unfold the note and read it. It was, inevitably, unsigned, but its contents were as disturbing as they were enigmatic.

The note read: *SINGER DIED IN 1817.*

Any other recipient of such a note might immediately have thought in terms of ghosts, but Temple had had experience of circumstances that he immediately likened to the present ones.

"Szandor!" he whispered, biting his lip anxiously. "Is he here already, and already as close to Frankenstein as can be? If so, no wonder his minion was at such pains to persuade me that he is not my enemy."

Chapter Four
Interview with the Vampire

It did not take Temple long to find a pattern in the responses he received to his questions about George Singer. The older retainers remembered him well enough from the time when he and Crosse had been fast friends and collaborators in experimentation, but their memories became strangely vague when they were asked about the circumstances that had parted the two men, or what Singer had been doing since 1817.

When Temple explicitly suggested to Caddick that rumor had reached London of Singer's death, Caddick immediately agreed that some such rumor had gone around the neighborhood, and had caused "the young master" some grief, but hastened to add that the sorrow had been more than counterbalanced by the universal joy at discovering the rumor to have been untrue.

"I will not liken his return to that of the prodigal son, sir," said Caddick, sententiously, "for that would verge on blasphemy, but I can guarantee that if Cook had had a fatted calf to hand, its throat would have been cut without delay."

"I see," Temple said—but the hour was very late by then, and he thought it best to retire to the tiny attic room he had been given, in order to sleep before deciding what action to take. As was his habit, he placed a loaded pistol beneath his pillow before lying down.

He fell asleep as soon as his had hit the pillow, or so it seemed, and his sleep was deep enough for him to have not the slightest idea how long he had been unconscious when he was suddenly awakened by a cold touch.

His first instinct was to reach for the pistol, but he found it gone. There was an abrupt crack as a flint was struck, and a wisp of German tinder ignited, which was immediately touched by an expert hand to the wick of a wax candle.

The light was held in such a position as to illuminate George Singer's face from below.

"Count Szandor," Temple said, immediately, in an attempt to surprise the other. "Have you come to drink my blood, or merely to spill it?"

"You know perfectly well that I wish you no harm, my friend," the so-called vampire said. "I removed the gun for my own protection, not because I have any intention of using it. Did you recognize me, or were you warned?"

"I was handed a note," Temple admitted, reluctant to lie because the alternative claim would have been a facile boast. "I was not quick enough to identify the person who gave it to me."

"Tom Brown's man, I assume," the other replied. "The others would take pride in leaving you completely in the dark—which is, I admit, one of the reasons why I would rather enlighten you. I give you my word that my only purpose here is to aid Frdankenstein's demonstration as fully as I can. If it succeeds, then I intend to maintain the identity of George Singer, and to become a member of the company that Faraday is already calling the Necromancers of London. Crosse has been so delighted to have his old friend returned that it would be impossible to convince him, now, that I am not the man he believes me to be, while Faraday and Frankenstein are avid for all the support they can obtain. Your gaze, I knew, would be much harder to deceive in the long term."

"You might count yourself fortunate, then," Temple said, pensively, "that Jean-Pierre Sévérin is not here…nor Malo de Treguern."

"I bear Sévérin no ill-will for what happened at Miremont," Szandor-as-Singer said, "and might have cause to be grateful to him for the reminder of my limitations. Treguern will, I suppose, always be my enemy, but even he might be more amenable to reason than he thinks, when his faith finally begins to crumble under the unbearable stress of reality. The immediate point is, however, to convince you that you should let my plan proceed—and, indeed, that you do your best to support it if the clowns of *Civitas Solis* or the Prussian dolts take it into their heads to interfere."

Temple did not challenge the vampire's reference to the hirelings of the *vehm* as Prussians rather than Bavarians; he was aware of the intricacies of middle-European exploitation. All he said was: "I might take a deal of convincing."

"A good deal more than Lord Byron, no doubt," the other conceded, as he settled himself comfortably into the wooden chair set beside Temple's meager dressing-table, having placed the pistol on the table-top. "Alas, His Lordship is out of reach at present, as is his loyal ally Shelley—who is still alive, by the way, not yet a Grey Man like his dear friend Keats. Even so, Mr. Temple, you are not without a hint of the Romantic about you—as befits the adversary of John Devil. The latter would be an easier recruit to my cause, I suppose, but my ambition now is to emerge from the Underworld to which I have been too long confined. I do not simply want to masquerade as George Singer for the duration of a festival—I want to become George Singer, in order to take up the cause of electrical science where he was forced to leave off by a stupid aneurism. I want to work with Faraday and Crosse, as well as with Frankenstein, for I believe that there is no quadrumvirate in all the world that could make faster and further progress in this revolution."

"And you want my help to do that?" Temple said, skeptically.

"If possible, yes—or at least your agreement not to interfere. You represent His Majesty's secret police, and I would far rather work within their protective cordon than without it. I have been a fugitive for far too long, regarded by the living as a deadly enemy and obtaining neither succor nor support from my own sad kind. In time, I fully intend to take Faraday, Frankenstein and Crosse into my confidence, in order that they might profit from my accumulated knowledge as I might profit from theirs, but I judged it better not to complicate this week's demonstrations unnecessarily. The last thing I want, however, is to be unmasked in inconvenient circumstances—and that is why I am coming to you beforehand. I readily confess that I fear your skill and enterprise, and hence your opposition. Clearly, I was right to do so, even though you appear to have needed a nudge from your arch-enemy to put you on the track. I do not come empty-handed; not only have I information to offer in return for your co-operation, but the services of an agent with far greater expertise in espionage than anyone else in your employ."

"The Countess," Temple guessed.

"Exactly so. She has played the spy before, of course—she was as useful to Bonaparte, in her own way, as the legendary Fouché."

179

"But she is merely you puppet, is she not?—an extension of yourself rather than an independent individual. Can she really work for me as a spy while you play Singer's part at the heart of Faraday's necromantic adventure?"

"She is certainly my apprentice," Szandor replied, "more the creation of my mesmeric powers than her own will. Initially, I set out to shape her as a companion in my loneliness, and would have been more-or-less content had she remained a puppet or a slave, but she is more than that now. She is no mere extension of my own personality, and is capable of fully autonomous action. I am all the more proud of her, and myself, for that."

"Who is she, really?" Temple demanded. "And who are you?"

"Your questions are based on false grounds," the vampire told him, "But I shall give you honest answers. You think you want to know who we were when we were alive, assuming that we are, in some sense, still the same individuals now—but even though I retain some of the memories of the man who inhabited this body when it was alive, I am not him. The Countess retains none of the memories of her living predecessor, so she might, I suppose, be reckoned a purer individual than I. In one way of reckoning, she really is Madame Marcian Gregoryi, for Marcian Gregoryi was the name of my living predecessor—a name that I discarded when I decided to become Count Szandor Tzingaryi. In another sense, my companion is Addhema, a female equivalent of Adam, into whom new sentience was breathed by my mesmeric authority when her predecessor's body reverted to common clay."

"So the Bishop is right: you are not humans reborn or resurrected, but demons who have put on borrowed human flesh?"

"*Demon* is such a harsh term, Mr. Temple—and if it is supposed to imply that we are minions of Satan, accursed followers of a self-appointed anti-God, we are certainly nothing of the kind. If the consciousness that emerges to inhabit a new-born babe as it grows to childhood is to be reckoned a creation of God rather than a vile possessor, I cannot see why Addhema and I should not be accorded the same privilege—but I confess that I do not know quite what I am, any more than you can be sure that you know what manner of being you are. I am, however, as enthusiastic to find out as any former victim of superstition and dread who has glimpsed a glimmer of enlightenment and is avid to follow that star."

"Mortdieu claims that he is no longer Napoléon Bonaparte," Temple said, reflectively, "for all that he has the same vaulting ambition—but if Ned's judgment is reliable, Sawney Ross is definitely still Sawney Ross, however sour his complexion may be."

"I would be surprised if Ross makes that claim himself," Szandor retorted, "but he would be entitled to the delusion, if he so desired."

"You have met other representatives of nature's Grey Men," Temple said, his tone making it a statement rather than a question. "Have they told you that they are not the same men now as they were when they were alive?"

"Some have," the other reported, "but the oldest of them have forgotten everything save for their own self-deceptive legends. The Jew insists that he was cursed by Christ on the road to Golgotha, Saint-Germain that he was the greatest of all the alchemical followers of

Hermes Trismegistus—but the Jew is no older than 600 years, and Saint-Germain no older than 200. You have no idea how I have yearned to meet Cain, Pythagoras or Apollonius of Tyana—or any of the old Greek demi-gods—but the sad truth is that Grey Men are mortal too, whether they develop from the living or from the dead, by what might or might not be variations of the same basic metamorphic process."

"You think that Saint-Germain and others like him are merely Grey Men whose predecessors did not die?" Temple asked, curiously

"I cannot be certain about the two examples in question, but I know that there are—or have been—Grey Men who claim that they never died. How they can be certain of that, I don't know, although I suppose they can be certain that their bodies were never buried. But what, exactly, is death, Mr. Temple? Is it the cessation of the heartbeat, the exhaustion of the breath, or merely the extinction of consciousness within the body? If it is the last, then a man might die without his heart ever ceasing to beat, or without ever ceasing to draw breath—but if it is a matter of the suspension of consciousness, do we not die every time we go to sleep, only to rise again, perhaps less identical to our former selves than we admit? Perhaps our dream-selves reformulate us every night—and perhaps, when duplication becomes impossible, they succeed in creating a substitute, different in character and in potential from its predecessor."

"Possessed, for instance, of greater *mesmeric authority*?" said Temple, echoing the phrase the other had chosen.

"I am not at all sure how exceptional I might be in that regard," Szandor told him. "Lazarus seems to have no such power, and trustworthy reportage credits none to

Mortdieu—but their second incarnations are very young, as yet. Then again, Mesmer's discoveries barely scratched the surface of the phenomenon that he mislabeled animal magnetism, and present-day practitioners of hypnotism are similarly groping in near-darkness. The secret report that Franklin and his associates prepared as a result of their investigation of Mesmer is only a little more honest than the one that was published, but at least it admits that the power of suggestion is greater than anyone had imagined, whether or not there is any tangible fluid on which it might be exercised. I am uncomfortably aware of the possibility that, if there were greater mesmerists abroad, they as could easily hide from me, or persuade me of their non-existence, as I can hide from common men, or persuade them of my non-existence—but I will not allow that awareness to inhibit my ambition to try my powers in a spirit of disciplined experimentation, with collaborators of the highest intelligence."

"Your apparent shapeshifting is due to the power of suggestion, then?" Temple deduced. "You have not actually remolded your flesh in Singer's image?"

"You are attempting to draw a distinction that is far too explicit," the vampire told him. "Sight is a less trustworthy sense than humans, in the grip of their dependency, are ready to assume. Seeing is believing, you say, without knowing how truly you speak. Once a belief is securely planted, sight proceeds in association with that belief. Children must learn to see in order to bring a coherent image of the world out of the confusion that surrounds them, and what they learn to see, or not to see, depends on what they are taught to believe, and what they are taught not to believe. Your eyes are not passive instruments, Mr. Temple, but active seekers of form and meaning; nor is your mind a blank canvas awaiting sensory paint, but a net set to trawl an understanding that is largely pre-existent. When I appear to dissolve into a cloud of dust or a wisp of mist, or fade into a near-fleshless skeleton, I do not really evaporate or shrink—that is merely your mind's way of coping with the seeming paradox of the rude destruction of its own confabulations. I am no mere illusion, Mr. Temple—I really am George Singer, insofar as Singer any longer exists, and am becoming more comfortable in that guise every time Andrew Crosse looks at me with the gladness that comes from having a friend that he once believed dead returned to him alive. In the same way, the lovely Addhema, whom I made in the image of my ideal of beauty, really is Countess Marcian Gregoryi, in all the glory of her precious flesh, and she becomes even more herself every time a man looks at her and finds her beauty wondrous."

Temple was not at all sure that he understood the implications of these claims, but he was glad of the information, which he took to be honest. There were more pragmatic issues at stake, which he needed to address. "What do you intend to do tomorrow, Mr. Singer?" he said. "You are not here simply to observe, I think."

"I am here to assist," the vampire replied, equably. "I am here to do what I can in order to ensure that Frankenstein's demonstration is the spectacular success that he, Faraday and Crosse desire so dearly."

"Mesmerically?"

"Of course—but not by means of trickery. It is no part of my plan to persuade the audience that they have seen something that has not actually happened. That would defeat my object."

"So you intend to exert your mesmeric authority upon the resurrected man?"

184

"I do—except that the first subject Frankenstein has chosen is a female, little more than a girl. He selected her on the basis of her youth and the condition of the corpse, rather than her sex, but I am pleased with his choice. I believe that I shall find it easier to render a young female articulate than an old man."

"And what will you have her say?" Temple wanted to know.

"Ideally, whatever she pleases—but if it should transpire that her mind is virtually blank, devoid of accessible memory or tangible ambition, then I shall do my best to put words in her mouth. You need not fear that any words that I implant will lack politeness and piety; I need the demonstration to succeed in every possible sense."

Again, Temple was ready to believe him—but there were other matters still to be addressed, while the opportunity was there. "Why did your rivals kidnap Jean-Pierre Séverin?" he asked.

"I don't know," the vampire replied, "But if my guess is worth more than yours, I'd wager that they want to engineer his metamorphosis into a Grey Man, and chose him because they believe that nature has already primed him for such a transformation. If they fail...well, you already know that they tried to trap you too, and I'd also wager that you warned Treguern to beware when you visited him in the hospital, having concluded that the bully-boys missed an opportunity in wounding him and leaving him behind."

Temple did no bother to confirm that Szandor would have won his bet. "My superiors would never agree to any alliance with vampires," he said.

"Of course not," Szandor replied. "That is way I have come to you. Your superiors will, I suppose, be less ready to dispense with your services if you can tell them that the most beautiful woman in London is in your personal employ, and if you can make deft use of the information she supplies. No one need know that she has returned from the dead, and she is more than capable of making any such accusation seem absurd if it is leveled in her presence. I am offering you a lifeline with which to shore up your precarious position, Mr. Temple—you might do well to take it, else you might be forced to retire from the game...or enter into Tom Brown's employ."

Never, Temple thought—knowing, of course, that that was exactly what he had been intended to think, in spite of the old proverb counseling a man to prefer the Devil he knows to the Devil he does not. He knew, too, that what his visitor had said about the fake Countess was also true about the fake Singer; any public accusation that he or any other person might make regarding Singer's true identity could easily be made to seem absurd in the presence of the man in question, who would have Crosse's testimony to back his imposture. And yet, had not Jean-Pierre Sévérin demonstrated that a sufficiently rapid hand could defeat even a mesmerically-authoritative eye?

As if he were party to Temple, private thoughts, the vampire resumed his discourse: "You are doubtless thinking that you thwarted my plans once, and might do so again—and so you might, if you were sufficiently dexterous. I invite you to wonder, however, whether Sévérin and Treguern might have done more harm than good by bursting in when they did at Miremont. Treguern would have been unhappy to see an alliance forged between myself and Lord Byron, and the *vehmgerichte* would certainly not have been glad to see one forged between myself and the Grafina von Boehm, but you have little sympathy for either. On the other hand, you and your masters might yet have reason to be direly displeased that Colonel Bozzo-Corona has been alerted to shades of light and darkness whose existence he had not previously suspected. Like Saint-German, he had become convinced by his own legend, and had committed himself to it in a fashion that was not entirely sane. How Séverin's captors would have loved to trap the Colonel in a secure net! Now that he is alert, though, he is more likely to trap them. He has made alliance with Tom Brown before, in the guise of the Gentlemen of the Night; were he to do so again..."

"Colonel Bozzo-Corona is a much respected man," Temple said, furrowing his brow as much in anxiety as puzzlement.

"So he is," the ersatz Singer agreed, "but he is three-quarters grey already, and a more avid vampire than I ever was, at least in monetary terms. There's no miser like a grey miser, Mr. Temple, and none more dangerous—especially if he has the army of the *Habits Noirs* at his beck and call."

Temple knew better than to protest that the *Habits Noirs* were an item of urban folklore, although he had never heard any suggestion that Colonel Bozzo-Corona was involved with them. "Still," he said, slowly, "I would be a fool to believe that you could possibly have the interests of the living, rather than the interests of the dead-alive, at heart."

"You'd be a fool if you were to believe that the two do not coincide, at least in this instance," the vampire retorted. "There are men of ill-will among the ranks of the dead-alive as well as the living, and I mount no defense of the likes of Mortdieu, who dreams of conquest—but there are men of good will too, perhaps in as high a proportion as among the living. I am not asking you to trust me, Mr. Temple, but only to bear with me for a little while, in order to determine whether we might both profit from a better understanding."

Get thee behind me, Satan! Temple thought—but he could not muster the conviction to say it aloud, or to mean it. Perhaps that was the effect of the vampire's steady stare, but whatever the source of the belief might have been, the detective was certain in his own mind that Count Szandor was not Satan, nor any minion of the Lord of Hell. Szandor was a creature who had come into the world like any other, unaware of his own origins, nature and potential. The flesh he inhabited had died once, but it was alive again now, and fully entitled to the consideration due to living, thinking individuals. He was not a demon, nor a monster—perhaps less so, in fact, than John Devil the Quaker, with whom Temple had once reluctantly called a truce. Gregory Temple was a secret policeman now, and everyone knew that secret policemen had to make occasional pacts with their adversaries, for the sake of the greater good.

"I make no promises for the longer term," Temple said, finally, "but for the time being, I won't attempt to denounce you before tomorrow's demonstration, or make any other move against you."

"And if the *vehmgerichte* or *Civitas Solis* should make a move?" the vampire prompted.

"They're foreign agents operating on English soil," Temple said, firmly. "It would be my sworn duty to prevent them, just as it would be my duty to arrest any agent of Tom Brown's."

"There's no need to worry about Tom Brown," the false Singer assured him. "He's set against *Civitas Solis* and the *vehm* alike. He might stir up a little mischief, that being his nature, but he's not about to lend any material support to our adversaries. And that, I think, concludes our business for now, Mr. Temple. If all goes well, we shall certainly talk again—and you'll also have the opportunity to question Addhema at your leisure. For now, I'll bid you goodnight—we shall both need sleep if we're to be fully awake tomorrow."

About that, at least, the vampire was right, for Temple could feel the extent of his exhaustion. He was not displeased when the candle-light went out, snuffed by a subtle breath. Nor was he surprised that he did not hear the door of his little room open or close, that absence leaving behind the suggestion, if not the suspicion, that he had been visited by a ghost.

Chapter Five
The Demonstration

The next time Temple was woken up it was by one of his own men, anxious that he was late in making a scheduled round. Having ascertained that his pistol was safe beneath his pillow, Temple made haste to get dressed, and ate a swift breakfast in the servants' parlor. Then he checked his men, making certain that each of them knew exactly what his duties were to be between nine in the morning and midnight before sending those who had not yet slept to bed.

Once again, he made his own tour of the house's surrounds, shivering in the cold morning air, but there was nothing to be seen outside the house, and he still had no idea which of the people within it might be agents of foreign powers. All he could do was wait, and hope that he could react quickly enough if anything untoward did occur.

The demonstration being scheduled to take place at noon, Frankenstein and his associates were busy in their laboratory, making preparations. The members of the Commission of Inquiry were at a loose end, and occupied themselves as they pleased. The Bishop insisted on taking a walk in the fresh air, but it was a little too fresh for most of his companions, so the scientists busied themselves in learned discussion while the parliamentarians—including those who had brought companions from London—investigated the possibility of obtaining sexual favors from Fyne Court's serving girls. So far as Temple could tell, they had little success; Somerset folk did not, in the main, accord much status to Members of Parliament, and Messrs. Hastings, Southborne and Medstead were not conspicuously equipped with any personal charisma.

One way or another, however, the time dragged by until the moment came for the interested parties to assemble in what was known as "the small drawing-room," where chairs had been neatly set out in four rows. The first row was reserved for the members of the commission, the second for a number of other invited guests from the surrounding area, including representatives of the Taunton Literary and Philosophical Society. The third row was occupied by selected members of the guests' households, including two young wives and a female "housekeeper," who added a little feminine glamour to the proceedings. Temple and his men had been allotted chairs in the fourth row, along with Crosse's wife and children, but Temple preferred to stand at one side of the improvised stage, while posting one of his men opposite and another at the room's main door, situated opposite the stage.

Crosse brought Frankenstein and his other co-conspirators into the room through a door behind the stage. He was carrying the corpse to be reanimated cradled in his arms, and did not seem to find the burden excessive. It was not until the girl had been laid on the table that her shroud was removed, revealing her to have been some 13 or 14 years of age. She was not naked, but had been clad in a loose-fitting chemise in order to offer token protection to her modesty.

She had been plain rather than pretty, with the muscles of a farm-girl rather than the slender arms and delicate hands of a lady of leisure, but death had not marred her unduly. Temple had been told, privately, that she had drowned, but had not been long immersed in the water following her demise, and might even have been revived had those who pulled her out known how to proceed in that regard. Temple felt sorry for her parents and siblings, none of whom were present, but also felt a slight tug of hope at the thought that life might yet be returned to the corpse.

The girl's body was still damp, and rather glutinously so, by virtue of having been immersed in a special solution for some time, but it was rapidly wired up to a complex electrical apparatus including a series of Voltaic piles. Before switching on the electric current, however, Frankenstein carefully introduced two fluids into the corpse, one red and one clear, using a clyster.

The hush of expectation that had descended seemed to stretch as the anticipation as prolonged, but Frankenstein was finally ready for the administration of the crucial shock. The day was bright now that the morning mist had cleared, and the room's windows faced south, so the sunlight streamed into the room in full measure, adding a suggestion of everyday normality to events that might have looked far more sinister if carried out in a gloomy cellar or an eerie attic.

The first shock only caused the corpse to shudder convulsively; when it was over, the body gave no more sign of life than before. The second was more effective, but not in any particularly striking sense. The shudder died away, but only to give way to movements of a less abrupt kind, like the stirring of a sleeping body in the grip of a bad dream. A third administration was necessary, however, and even then the reanimated corpse could not sit up unaided; Crosse had to lift her up, and he continued to support her.

When she had first been laid down, the girl had seemed more off-white than grey, in spite of a certain discoloration of her skin, but she was noticeably darker in complexion now. Her eyes were open, and the whites stood out quite clearly to the sides of the near-black iris and jet black pupil, within the shadowed orbits.

She stared at the assembled crowd, and seemed to be able to see them, although her waxen features registered no flicker of surprise, delight or anxiety. A tremor ran through the assembly regardless; some, at least, had already seen more than they expected.

Frankenstein had stepped back, his work done, and Faraday was also content to stand by, watching and waiting. It was George Singer who stepped forward to examine the girl closely, picking up her limp hands one by one and staring into her face. His eyes met hers, and interrogated them. His voice it was, too, that began to ask her questions.

"Do you know where you are?" he asked her—although that did not seem to Temple to be the logical place to start.

The dead girl hesitated, as if unsure how to move her mouth or activate her vocal cords—but in the end, her lips parted, and she whispered: "No."

"Can you tell us your name?"

There was a further hesitation. Temple realized that Crosse and his associates had made no attempt to introduce the girl to the crowd, and that even he had not been told her name—the name, that is, with which she had been baptized when alive. It hardly mattered; the word that was eventually formed, seemingly with some difficulty, by the grey lips was: "No."

George Singer seemed oddly pleased with that reply, although Temple heard several members of the audience emit sighs of disappointment.

"Do you remember anything at all?" the vampire continued.

This time, the hesitation was extended, but Temple thought that the grey girl was undergoing a manifest change as the crowd watched with bated breath, almost as if she were recovering herself...or entering into herself. Her gaze became keener and more intelligent, her stance surer and more self-composed. She drew back from the arms that had been holding her up, standing of her own accord—and she looked into George Singer's eyes, as if she recognized something within them.

"You too have died," she said, "but you have mastered the art of appearance."

Singer seemed severely discomfited by this remark, and Temple knew that he would never have made her say any such thing by means of dictation. Temple also knew, however, that the statement would sound like perfect nonsense to almost all the members of the audience.

"What do you remember?" Singer persisted.

"I remember darkness," the girl replied. "I remember the water—the cold, cloying water. I remember death's embrace—but I am glad to be back in the world of space and time. Is that what you want me to say? Are those the words you are trying to put into my mouth? Am I your slave, to do your bidding?"

Temple had tensed all his muscles, ready to act. He knew that the vampire's plan was going awry—that the mesmeric authority that he was trying to impose upon the dead girl was meeting a determined rebellion, and not merely rebellion, but a measure of resentment and contempt. Whatever spirit had come to take possession of the corpse was stronger than anyone, including the vampire, could have expected. The detective could see, however, that George Singer was intrigued as well as anxious, eager to know what this unexpected newcomer might have to tell him, even though the script that he had written had been torn up and thrown away.

"No, my dear," Singer said, with the utmost tenderness, "you are not my slave, and are not required to do my bidding. You are a free agent, like any other sentient being, with the power of choice—but you're a stranger here, for all that you have lived before. I beg you to be patient, and docile, until you understand what is happening around you."

Again, there was hesitation—and then the grey girl laughed. It was a sardonic laugh, with as much mockery as amusement in it.

That was too much for the Bishop of Salisbury. He leapt to his feet, brandishing a crucifix in his right hand and a Bible in his left, and began to intone a rapid formula of exorcism, in the Latin of the Roman church rather than the English of his own. Temple reckoned that he might be lacking a bell and a candle, if the rite were to be performed to perfection, but he assumed that it would not be utterly lacking in efficacy, if exorcisms had any efficacy at all.

The latter question was difficult to determine. The grey girl certainly reacted to the Bishop's intervention, but not as any demon, resentful but cravenly intimidated by the power of God, might have been expected to react. "Why should I begone?" she asked him, quietly but firmly. "Can you believe that the world is yours, and that you alone have the privilege of determining what it can and shall contain? Do you not understand that you are nothing more than a mere larva, bearing within you the seed of something strange? Begone yourself, you poor pathetic fool!"

Perhaps, Temple thought, if the grey girl had had a weapon to hand, she might have used it in conjunction with her final dismissal, but she was bare-handed, and possessed of no more strength than the frail body she inhabited. All she could muster was a gesture, half-contemptuous and half-bellicose: a mere symbol of aggression.

To at least one of the members of her terrified audience, however, that symbolic gesture was sufficient to warrant a violent reply.

Temple's own men, disciplined by long training, merely reached for their cudgels without taking them out—but Stephen Southborne had brought a dagger to the séance, in case of need, and he drew it. With a single fluid motion, which spoke of practice, he hurled it, aiming for the grey girl's breast.

The vampire would not tolerate that; with a lightning movement, he snatched her out of the path of the flying blade. It missed the resurrected girl by a foot—but Singer was not the only one who had obeyed a protective impulse. Victor Frankenstein had leapt forward, intending to snatch her out of harm's way himself, but had found her already gone, and he stumbled, leaning forward with his arms outstretched.

The dagger struck him in the neck, and buried itself deeply, while red arterial blood spurted forth to either side of the embedded blade.

Southborne went as pale as a ghost, and Hastings had to prop him up to prevent him falling in a swoon. The ladies present were not the only ones who gasped or screamed. Even the vampire seemed stunned; the hands that had reached out so forcefully to pluck the intended victim out of the way relaxed their grip and fell nervelessly to his sides.

The grey girl's mocking contempt changed to raging wrath upon the instant. She leapt away from Singer, shoved Michael Faraday aside, and hurled herself from the stage as if to attack the audience. Few of the crowd's members were still seated, but chairs tumbled in every direction as some moved to their left and others to their right, desperate to get out of her way.

Temple was by no means calm, but he had sufficient self-control to take note of the absurdity of the situation. The girl was no more than five feet tall, slender and weak, while there were many in the crowd who stood nearly a foot higher, with well-toned muscles and the vigor of sportsmen—and yet, not one of the men in the assembly had the courage to take a stand. What they saw coming at them, with their educated eyes, was no mere creature of flesh and blood but a monster, perhaps released from Hell.

Again, Temple wondered whether the girl might have struck out with lethal force had she had a club or a sword, but, as things were, she merely attempted to strike those within reach with the flat of her hand, as if to slap their faces as a punishment for impertinence. None of the attempted blows landed; her intended victims were too quick in their evasions.

The Bishop of Salisbury fell over bruisingly, and so did Peter Barlow, among others, but all of them were tumbled by the jostling elbows or flailing arms of their fellow living men, victims of mere confusion. The grey girl did not lay a hand on anyone as she moved through the four rows of scattered chairs—and once she was through the crowd, she headed straight for the door.

One of Temple's men was guarding the door, and now he did draw his cudgel, spreading his arms and bracing his knees in a street-fighter's crouch.

"Don't hurt her!" Temple howled.

He only meant to instruct the man to handle her gently when he seized her, but the man construed the order differently, and stood aside. The door was standing ajar; there must have been servants gathered beyond it, eavesdropping on the momentous affair—but they were already fleeing. When the girl snatched at the door-knob and drew the batten wide, there was no one visible in the corridor beyond.

Within a second, the girl had disappeared.

In the meantime, Faraday had picked himself up and had joined Andrew Crosse and George Singer, crouching over Frankenstein's fallen body.

"Follow the girl, but *don't hurt her!*" Temple cried to the guardian of the door, as he ran to Frankenstein's side. He knew as soon as he arrived beside the fallen man that there was no hope for him—or, at least, no hope for his life.

"Pick him up!" Faraday instructed Crosse and Singer. "Take him to the laboratory! We must immerse him as soon as possible, even before we draw the dagger from his neck."

Temple did not hesitate; while Crosse and the vampire did as they were told, he turned to the crowd, and posed himself in such a fashion as to forbid any interference. The Bishop of Salisbury was still down, nursing his bruises, but Robert Hastings made as if to protest. "Hold hard!" Temple told him. "You came for a demonstration, and you shall have more than you bargained for, if you consent to wait. Those of you who still suspect trickery will have your final doubts dispelled."

"You must catch and destroy that demon, Mr. Temple!" was Hastings' only reply.

"She has done no harm," Temple said. "I'd rather arrest Mr. Southborne, and commit him to the assizes on a charge of manslaughter, but I dare say that he will claim privileged immunity, since he is on parliamentary business here—and besides, the crime of manslaughter might need to be redefined by parliament, if the Necromancers of London can bring Frankenstein back from the dead."

The Bishop was on his feet by this time, and seemed to be on the point of preaching an angry sermon to Temple and anyone else who would listen, but the room was already emptying as the crowd dispersed.

Having satisfied himself that there was nothing more to be done in the drawing-room, Temple hurried after Faraday and his companions, and reached the laboratory in time to see Frankenstein's body being immersed in the same bath of fluid from which the girl's body had been removed. There were two other tanks nearby, each containing a male corpse, but neither body had been as fresh as Frankenstein's by the time the treatment had begun, and they seemed very somber by comparison.

"Have you learned his technique well enough to bring him back?" Temple demanded of Faraday.

"I believe so," Faraday replied. "We can but try."

The false George Singer took Temple's arm and drew him aside. "That did not go as well as I had hoped," he said, when they were out of earshot of Faraday and Crosse. "I had not expected to meet with such resistance, and had a very different performance planned. Who would have thought that a corpse could be revived so swiftly, with a seemingly-mature intelligence? We must interrogate her together, when your men bring her back; there's much to be learned here."

"*If* they bring her back," Temple said, grimly. "They'll not be the only ones searching for her, and if she falls into the hands of the Germans or the Churchmen, they'll want to keep her for themselves—unless, of course, you can exert your mesmeric authority over *them*."

"I'll do what I can," the vampire said, "but we'll need to keep an eye on Frankenstein too—if he can be revived, with his mind relatively unimpaired, he might be the most valuable witness of all to the mysteries of his own condition."

"The Commission of Inquiry is spoiled, though," Temple observed. "For one of its members to kill the man under investigation, even by accident, is fatal to its pretentions. The Bishop's antics can be set aside, but not Southborne's. He could not have done more had he been secretly commissioned to wreck the investigation."

"Perhaps that's so, in a purely technical sense—but if the members can be persuaded to extend their stay here long enough to watch three more revivals instead of two, imagine what an impact the testimony of Frankenstein might have, delivered from beyond the grave! Imagine what a tale they'd carry back to Canning and the King!"

"If theatricality is what you want," Temple told him, a trifle bitterly, "you might do worse than reveal yourself, and regale the audience with anecdotes of your checkered past."

Singer shook his head. "More than human I might be," he said, "but I'm greatly outnumbered here, without my lovely counterpart to charm my adversaries. I do hope the girl will come to no harm—there are people here, more lethally armed than the idiot Bishop and the headstrong parliamentarian, who might prefer to kill her rather than question her."

"Whatever you might think of the Bishop," Temple said, "there will be many members of that audience who believe that he proved his case—that the girl really was possessed by a malevolent demon. Southborne was probably not the only one who felt a reflexive urge to destroy her. Are you quite sure yourself that the intelligence which took such rapid control of her, in spite of your own efforts, was *not* a demon?"

"As sure as I am that I'm not a demon myself," Singer replied, wryly. "I dare say, though, that this is not the first time such a mistake has been made. Find the girl, Mr. Temple, if you can—I must play my part here."

Temple did not care for the implication that he was under the vampire's orders now, but he was eager to discover what progress the search was making, so he went out in search of his men.

There was no shortage of witnesses to tell him which way the chase had gone, at least while he was still in the house and its shadow, but once he reached the wooded part of the estate he had to use his talents as a tracker.

Recently dead though she was, the grey girl was evidently agile, for she had crossed the boundary wall of Fyne Court's grounds and disappeared into thicker woods, with at least half a dozen men in her wake.

Five minutes after clambering over the wall himself, Temple met someone coming the other way, apparently having abandoned the chase. It was not one of his own men, but one who had traveled with the expedition as Southborne's valet.

"I apologize for my master's hot-headedness, sir," the man said, as he approached the detective. "It was recklessness, not malice. He is exactly what he seems to be."

"Unlike you, I presume," Temple said, looking the man up and down.

"I wondered whether you had identified me when I gave you the piece of paper," the other replied. "We've met before, alas—but Tom was pressed for time, and had to take what opportunity he could to intrude a spy into the party. The others did no better, I think—you've doubtless spotted the German by now, and you must have known already that Snow Harris is in the pocket of *Civitas Solis*."

All of this was news to Temple, but he did his utmost not to show a flicker of surprise, while he tried to figure out where he might have seen the valet before. Sharper's seemed by far the likeliest venue, and the memory eventually clicked into place.

"I've seen you playing the villain to Sam Hopkey's hero," Temple said, trying to sound as if he had never been in doubt about it, "and you're doubtless another veteran of the Old Bailey. How did you know that Singer is an impostor?" He was careful not to say *vampire* in case he, too, might give away far too much.

"Tom knew witnesses to his death who had not been suborned. When he heard of his alleged return, he knew that Szandor must be involved, and that Crosse must have been hypnotized into forgetfulness. You will not seek to have me arrested, I hope, Mr. Temple—I've done nothing against the law, and have done you a good turn. Tom's orders were to protect you, and to trust you if alliances had to be made. The foreigners are the real enemy."

"I don't doubt that the *vehmgerichte* and Balsamo's followers are Tom Brown's enemies just now," Temple retorted, "but I'm not so sure that they're mine, even though one or other of them may well have taken Séverin by stealth. Why have you given up chasing the grey girl?"

"Given up, sir?" the other queried. "I haven't given up—I'm just looking elsewhere. Whatever that creature is, it doesn't lack cunning. If I were in her place, I'd have doubled back already. Your men aren't exactly subtle in their procedures, if you'll forgive the observation."

"And what will you do with her if you find her?"

The other raised an eyebrow, mugging as if he were onstage in Jenny Paddock's cabaret theatre. "Do you take me for one of the pantomime villains I play, sir? Do you imagine that my mind is bent on rape? I can assure you that I'll be the perfect gentleman, as solicitous as a benevolent uncle."

"You mean that you'll help her escape—all the way to London, if you can."

The valet shrugged. "Won't be easy, sir," he said, "given that I'm more-or-less alone. You wouldn't care to come to some arrangement, I suppose—just between ourselves?"

"No, I wouldn't," Temple said, through gritted teeth—although he was not entirely certain of the wisdom of his reflexive hostility.

"There's gratitude for you," the valet replied, seemingly unoffended. "Watch out for the vampire, sir—he's a tricky one, by all accounts." And with that, he continued on his way back toward Fyne Court, leaving Temple alone with the chatter of birdsong and rustlings in the undergrowth that might have been anything at all.

Chapter Six
A Voice from Beyond

Temple stood where he was for three minutes more, listening. There was no sign of anyone else returning from the hunt, and the girl's pursuers had passed out of earshot, probably on a wild goose chase.

Satisfied that there was no point in continuing, Temple turned to follow Southborne's valet, and nearly jumped out of his skin. The grey girl had obviously been standing behind him for a minute or more, waiting for him to turn round.

"I believe I need your help, sir," she said.

"Yes," he said, a trifle numbly, "I believe you do,"

"I heard you shouting to the men who were chasing me, instructing them not to hurt me," she said, explaining her decision to approach him, "but I don't know who you are."

"Gregory Temple," the ex-detective told her. "I'm in the employ of His Majesty's government. I escorted a seven-man commission here from London, to bear witness to your resurrection."

"My resurrection?"

Temple hesitated, then said: "Yes—that's what has happened to you. Were you not aware of that?"

"Are you saying that I really did die? That it was not a dream?"

"Yes—you were drowned."

"Murdered?"

"An accident, I believe. Do you have any reason to think that you might have been murdered?"

"No." The denial did not seem certain.

"But you remember who you are—were—now? You've recovered your memory?"

The grey girl stared at him, quizzically. "I'm not the person I remember," she said, echoing what Szandor had told him, and what General Mortdieu had apparently told Ned Knob. "Yes, I do remember her—but she was a feeble thing. I feel quite different now. I feel...but I don't have the words to describe it. I do have words that aren't my own, though...words that were somehow *put into my head.*"

"By a mesmerist," Temple told her. "He was intent on controlling you, and expected to find you far more vulnerable than you were. He had a script all prepared for you, but you wouldn't respond to his prompts. Perhaps his attempted insistence brought forth an instinctive resistance of some sort. He did save your life, though, when that fool Southborne threw the dagger."

"Yes," the grey girl said, vaguely. "He talked about supplying me with words before..."

"Before?" Temple queried. "Before you died, you mean? You had met him before?" Suddenly, he wondered very forcefully whether the girl's drowning had been something other than an accident. If so, it would not take much imagination to guess who might have been responsible, whether directly or indirectly.

"It was prophesied that I would die," the girl said, still seemingly lost in something akin to a dream, albeit with elements of cruel reality contained within it. "It was also prophesied that I would emerge from the chrysalis of death as a different kind of being, as unlike my old self as a butterfly is to a caterpillar."

So she had already been primed, Temple thought, *with the sentiments she expressed to Hastings and the*

Bishop—they merely failed to emerge on cue. Szandor was taking no chances; he intended to rig the entire exhibition—but if he was prepared to commit murder to do it, I ought to bring him to justice, if I can.

There were, however, more urgent matters at hand. What was he to do with the girl, now that she was in his custody? How could he keep her safe, and away from all the other parties avid to interrogate her?

"Are you cold?" he asked her.

She nodded to indicate that she was, although she did not seem entirely certain. She knew, at least, that she ought to be feeling the cold.

Temple took off his jacket and wrapped her in it. He could not immediately think of any place of safety to which they might go, let alone any in which he could leave her while he attended to his duties back at Fyne Court. "What's your name?" he asked

"I *was* Helen," she replied.

"Well, she-who-was-Helen, we need to find a hiding-place for you. If your memories are intact, you must know the neighborhood far better than any of the people chasing you just now—perhaps better than the servants at Fyne Court. Is there anywhere close at hand where you might be safe, until I can help you get away?"

"I know these woods," she said. "They won't catch me here. Her father was the finest poacher in the county." She spoke with pride; presumably, that was not an idea that Szandor had planted in her head.

"In that case," Temple said, "We need to arrange a meeting place—somewhere to which I can bring a carriage, or at least a pair of horses. Can you ride?"

"Of course I can," she replied. "They don't own a horse, but her father and her brother have worked in stables. She's ridden a post horse—they're the fastest."

206

"That's good," Temple said. "Horses it shall be. Pick a good spot, where we won't be seen."

"Take the Taunton road," she said, after a moment's pause for thought. "There's a broken signpost by a sunken path, about a mile from the Court. Take the sunken road, as far as the ford in the hollow. Wait there—I'll try to make sure that you haven't been followed before I show myself. Best not wait for dusk, though—it's a treacherous place in the dark."

Once they were mounted, Temple thought, it would be very difficult for anyone to chase them, provided that their horses were fit enough and fast enough. "I'll get away when I can," he promised, "but it probably won't be before noon."

She took off his jacket and handed it back. "Best return as you came," she said. "I'll be fine, I think. I do feel the cold, but...I'm not sure that it can harm me now."

Temple hesitated, wondering whether it might not be better simply to take the girl back to Fyne Court, and protect her there as best he could—but he was even more convinced now that he could not trust the vampire, and was certainly not about to put his trust in Southborne's valet. While Szandor was disguised as Singer, he could not count on Crosse or Faraday either. He cursed his misfortune in being so far from the capital. If only the Necromancers of London had been invited to do their work close to home, instead of being exiled to a supposedly safe distance!

Frankenstein, he knew, would not be ripe for revival for at least 72 hours, and perhaps considerably longer. He might have time to get the girl to London and return, although that would certainly violate his instructions and put his official position in even greater jeopardy. He needed a secure hiding-place much nearer to Fyne Court, from which he could come and go at will.

"Go, then," he said to the girl. "I'll come when I can. I'll do everything possible to keep you safe."

The grey girl disappeared into the undergrowth, sand Temple went back to the house. It was a further hour before his men returned, quite empty-handed. Crosse had volunteered to mobilize his servants to beat the woods, but Temple had declined the offer, saying that it would be better not to frighten the girl, and that the wisest course was simply to send someone to wait for her at her parent's house, to which she would undoubtedly return.

It took the detective until 2 p.m. to make his preparations with what he considered to be necessary discretion—by which time he had reason enough to borrow a pair of horses, ostensibly in order to relieve the man he had sent to the village.

He waited for a full hour at the appointed place, but the girl never showed up. Eventually, he returned to the house cursing his bad judgment, but privately convinced that someone else had captured her. If so, she had not been brought back to the house.

The agents of *Civitas Solis* were unlikely, in Temple's judgment, to have any kind of priory nearby, but that did not mean that they did not have friends in the vicinity, especially if William Snow Harris had already been affiliated to their cause. If that really were the case, Harris would undoubtedly take it upon himself to sound out Faraday and Crosse with a view to their recruitment—but with luck, he would try to sound out Singer too, and get more than he bargained for.

Temple did relieve the man he had left at Helen's old home, but instructed him to send another man out as soon as he got back to Fyne Court, so that Temple need not be too long away. He used the interval to question Helen's parents about her life, and about any strangers she might have met in the days leading up to her death. Of the latter matter they clamed to know nothing at all, but they answered all of his questions as one might expect of a poacher and his wife confronted with the former cream of Scotland Yard: evasively and with a great deal of suspicion.

Once he was back at Fyne Court, Temple set about interviewing the members of the Commission, to determine what their thoughts might be on the matter of continuing and completing the Inquiry. Six were immediately willing, being curious themselves as to what might become of Victor Frankenstein—Southborne, in particular, expressed a strong interest in seeing him revived—and the seventh, the Bishop of Salisbury, was easily convinced that there was God's work to be done in any event, albeit best done in a quieter fashion than he had so far contrived.

Eventually, Temple found an opportunity to talk to George Singer again. "What did you do to that girl?" he demanded.

Singer seemed to consider a flat denial, but then shrugged his shoulders. "Nothing too terrible, as you have seen," he answered. "If I contrived her death, it was in the knowledge—or, at least, the conviction—that it would not be irreversible. It appears that I was more successful than I hoped in planting seeds cf suggestion in her mind prior to death, in the hope that they would enhance her capacity to return. Sometimes, I even surprise myself. Have you caught her, then?"

"I think Balsamo's followers might have spirited her away."

"Really? I thought you capable of outwitting them—but no matter. Tomorrow might go better; I had no opportunity to plant any seeds in the minds of the other two poor fellows. On the other hand, they might not revive at all, and if they do, their mental faculties might be beyond the reach of my talents as a mesmerist, redoubtable though they are."

As things turned out, however, the second day's demonstration did not go well at all. The attempted resurrection failed completely. That would have disconcerted Faraday and Crosse in any case, but it was doubly disconcerting in the circumstances, for they could not be sure that they had not erred in some respect, where Frankenstein would have succeeded.

"We have his instructions," Faraday opined, in Temple's presence, "but not his genius. He would have displayed a surer touch—of that we may be certain."

"But the method works," Singer put in. "Given that, you will surely succeed—if not tomorrow, then some time thereafter."

"But dare we take the risk of trying to restore Frankenstein to life, until we have made certain that we are capable of success?" Crosse asked

"Dare we take the risk of *not* making the attempt?" Singer countered. "We did not expect to reach this situation, but now that we have, the members of the spoiled Commission of Inquiry must still be satisfied—and I cannot see that we can satisfy them now, except by bringing Victor back to life. The gauntlet has been thrown at our feet, and we are honor-bound pick it up. We must meet the challenge."

"What do you think, Mr. Temple?" Crosse asked, although Faraday frowned at the notion of consulting a layman on what he considered to be largely a matter of science.

"My first duty is to protect the Commission," Temple said. "I suspect that my superiors might judge that I have already failed in that—but I have a corollary duty to protect the demonstrators who are presenting their evidence to the Commission. In that respect, I wonder whether there might be any danger to Frankenstein in trying to revive him too soon?"

"Too soon?" Faraday muttered. "Like Singer, I'm more afraid of leaving it too late."

"If the fluid and moderate electrical excitation do not restore his pulse, however, we dare not take him out of the womb," Crosse said. "Not tomorrow, at any rate. Even the poor soul we lost today showed slight signs of life before fading into oblivion."

"Some sort of bodily circulation is definitely necessary to restored life," Singer stated, without specifying the reasons for his certainty, "but I'm confident that Frankenstein will recover that more rapidly than the common run of the dead. We shall be glad to have him in reserve, if the third trial fails—no one will pay much heed to that, in the circumstances; the denouement will depend entirely on the fourth act."

He was correct in his estimation; the third trial also failed, although it came within a whisker of success. The dead man revived sufficiently to sit up, but not to stand upright or to talk, and soon lapsed into inertia again. No one seemed to care; many of the observers invited from outside the Court had not even bothered to turn up. The exhibition that everyone wanted to see was the unscheduled fourth one, when Victor Frankenstein would be brought back from the dead—or not.

Faraday and Crosse seemed to be divided in their opinions as to the wisdom of trying to revive Frankensein a mere three days after his death, but that gave Singer a casting vote of sorts, and his mind was made up.

"Three days is a propitious interval," the vampire said. "It carries symbolic meaning for the Bishop, and for his supposedly-devout companions. Besides, the freshness of the body might well be more important than the length of exposure to the preliminary treatment. If we fail, we shall still have the possibility of trying again, but if we succeed...well, think of that, gentlemen. What if we succeed?"

The Necromancers of London could not prevail against the Vampire of Szeged; his arguments would probably have been sufficient even without his additional means of persuasion—and so it was that the audience assembled for a fourth time on the afternoon following the second failure, abuzz with anticipation.

There had been no sign of the grey girl anywhere in the neighborhood, but Southborne's valet had taken the trouble to tell Temple that Tom Brown had been alerted to the circumstances, and would have the roads west of the capital under careful surveillance. "He'd better pray, then," Temple had observed, sourly, "that they have not taken her to the Bristol Channel to put her aboard a boat or a ship." The spy had not had any reason to dispute that possibility.

The audience for the demonstration was larger than any of its predecessors, several of the household servants having found excuses to be in the room, and many of the Commission's hangers-on, including the two whores, having also worked their way into the company. Victor Frankenstein had become a famous man, albeit as a Gothic villain whose shady reputation was akin to Lord

Byron's notoriety. No one doubted that his return from the world beyond would be a momentous occasion, or that any news he might bring back from the afterlife could be anything other than significant. The Bishop was not the only person carrying a crucifix, though, and there was actually a queue of people wanting his blessing before the ceremony began.

The general procedure was identical to the three previous occasions, but it was conducted with a manifest dignity that increased its ritual air. As on the first day, it required three administrations of electrical current to restore any semblance of life to the corpse, but, as on the first day, three sufficed.

The room was filled with a pregnant silence as Crosse and Singer lent the individual who had been Victor Frankenstein the support he needed to sit upright. Singer was not so quick to ask questions this time, however; he remained at Frankenstein's side, but watched as if mesmerized himself while the new Grey Man surveyed the audience with his bleak but trenchant gaze.

In the end, it was Faraday who stepped forward to ask: "Do you know me, Victor?"

The Grey Man turned his head in order to study Faraday carefully. There was a long pause before he finally said: "Yes."

Temple repressed a perverse urge to giggle.

"Who am I?" Faraday asked, innocently.

"Michael Faraday," said the Grey Man, forming the syllables slowly, almost as if he were uncertain of the use of his vocal apparatus.

"And who are you?" Faraday asked.

After another pause, Frankenstein said: "Victor."

Temple could not help noting that Faraday had already called him by that name, but the scientist seemed to be satisfied that the response was no mere echo.

"Do you remember what happened here three days ago?" Faraday asked—unwisely, in Temple's opinion. The detective looked at Southborne; the latter's face was quite white, as if he fully expected the living corpse to point an accusing finger at him, in the fashion of a ghost in a stage melodrama.

"We brought the girl back to life," was Frankenstein's answer. Perhaps, Temple thought, he had not had time to form a memory of what had happened thereafter.

"We did," Faraday confirmed. "And now, we have performed the same service for you—with even greater success."

The Bishop of Salisbury stood up, much more self-controlled now than before. "Might I ask a question, Mr. Faraday?" he asked, his voice only slightly tremulous.

Faraday had no option but to agree.

"Where have you been for the last three days, Doctor Frankenstein?" the Churchman asked.

Frankenstein fixed the Bishop with a basilisk stare. "Do you want to know what Hell is like, Your Eminence?" he asked, evidently gaining swiftly in facility as he made further use of his tongue. "Can you not be patient for a little while longer?"

That is not Frankenstein speaking! Temple thought. *If it is not a demon, then it is someone or something which seems to be masquerading as a demon—but why?* His gaze went reflexively to the vampire, who had only just moved away from Frankenstein slightly, perceiving that the Grey Man was no longer in need of support. Singer seemed as puzzled as Temple was himself, presumably for the same reason.

The Bishop was trying hard to remain unintimidated. "Yes," he said, bravely. "I would like to have testimony of what Hell is like, from the mouth of one of its denizens, recently emerged."

"Why," said the Grey Men, "this is Hell, nor am I out of it."

Temple knew perfectly well, as more than half the audience members must have done, that the Grey Man was quoting Marlowe's Mephistopheles—a mocking ploy surely calculated to increase the suspicion that this entire scene had been staged, and was all trickery. He wondered, momentarily, whether Frankenstein might possibly have been slain by a stage dagger, and whether the blood he had shed might have been fake.

Something is wrong here, he thought, *but what on Earth is the motivation behind it? This is not Szandor's doing, for he wants the Commission to make a favorable report, in order that he might insinuate himself into the company of the duly-licensed Necromancers of London.*

He could not help remembering the possibility that Szandor had mentioned to him, that there might be vampires even older than he, who could deceive him as easily as he could deceive the living.

The scientists seemed uneasy at this turn of events, and Thomas Young took it upon himself to intervene. "How does you present state of being differ, in terms of your sensory perceptions, from the one you knew before?" he asked, having first solicited permission by raising his hand.

"I am still learning to use my faculties," the Grey Man said, in a pensive tone, as if to imply that this was a question he permitted himself to take seriously. "It will take time, I think, to learn this new way of being and overcome my own bewilderment. I suspect that there is much to be learned, but I cannot tell, as yet, what it might be."

William Snow Harris stood up then, either to continue speaking on behalf of science, or to play a role on behalf of *Civitas Solis*. He did not bother to ask Faraday's permission before asking: "How does it feel, Doctor Frankenstein, to have been resurrected from the dead? Are you glad to have been returned to life?"

"Feel?" the Grey Man repeated. "Am I glad? How do I know? Do you think my feelings are comparable with yours? Can you imagine that I might be able to use the words my predecessor knew to describe an experience that your language has never had occasion to represent? We shall need a new language now, Mr. Harris."

"You know my name," Snow Harris observed, dully.

"You were formally introduced to my predecessor," the Grey Man pointed out, "as were Mr. Hastings, Mr. Southborne, Mr. Medstead, Mr. Young, Mr. Barlow and, of course, His Eminence the Bishop. The memories are a trifle dim, at present, but they are intact, I think." He seemed to be collecting himself, testing his muscles and his mind alike. His eyes had lingered on the Bishop after pronouncing his title, and he suddenly said: "May I ask *you* a question, Your Eminence?"

The Bishop still had a grip on his courage. "Yes," he said.

"Was Lazarus possessed by a demon when he came forth from the tomb?" the Grey Man demanded.

"Lazarus came forth in answer to Christ's call," the Bishop replied.

"And how do you know," Frankenstein countered, "that I did not?"

The Bishop looked around, as if fearful of finding Christ lurking somewhere in the room.

Would it be any greater surprise if he were? Temple wondered.

Whether it was his courage or his ingenuity that failed him, the Bishop made no reply.

"The Age of Miracles is over," Hasting stated, flatly.

"Nonsense," the Grey Man retorted. "It has hardly begun. Unless you mean that the resurrection of the dead has henceforth been a matter of rare and random chance, without perceptible causation. If that is what you signify by *miracle* then yes, the Age of Miracles is over, and a new Age has begun, in which resurrection will be a matter of technique and artistry, and life after death will cease to be a mere flickering phantom, putting on flesh and purpose."

This is more than Szandor could have hoped for, Temple thought, realizing that the tide was turning, having only feigned an intention to ebb. *What weight can the Commission's verdict have, now that the dead-alive have an advocate of their own as compelling, in his own way, as General Mortdieu.*

No daggers were being thrown this time; even if Victor Frankenstein's reputation had not gone before the Grey Man, he would have cut a far more imposing figure than the poor bewildered child.

Put him in a suit and top hat instead of a shroud, Temple thought, *and he might address the House of Commons, or the House of Lords, on his own account, challenging them both to assess him as a demon or a miracle of virtue…or a man of science still.*

217

"And what do you intend to do with your new life, Doctor Frankenstein?" Temple was momentarily surprised to find that he had asked the question aloud.

The Grey Man turned to face him. "Gregory Temple," he said, as if struggling to recall the name. "The guardian of the Commission...and public safety. You have met my...the person who calls himself Lazarus. You have heard his account of his intentions. Mine are, I fear, just as vague. How can I know what intentions I might ultimately have until I know what possibilities might lie before me? For the moment, what can I do but ally myself firmly with Mr. Faraday, Mr. Crosse and Mr. Singer, in order to investigate myself, and the possibility of saving others from oblivion, as I have been saved?"

Temple had no alternative in mind, but others apparently did, for the door through which the grey girl had fled three days before was suddenly thrust open, and three men costumed as monks came in. They were carrying swords. Only one of the three pushed back his cowl, permitting Gregory Temple to recognize him as the man who called himself Giuseppe Balsamo.

"Have no fear, my friends," Balsamo said, addressing the audience. "The house is more secure by far now than it was when it only had Temple's four men and your own servants to guard it against the Prussians. I can give the Necromancers of London safer conduct by far than His Majesty's secret police, and with better motives. I must politely request the rest of you to pack your bags and leave within the hour. You are, I fear, in danger from more than one source, and I cannot guarantee the safety of such a large and ill-assorted company."

Temple's men were looking at him for a lead. He signaled to them to stand and wait, taking no overt action for the time being. He was obliged to step forward himself, however, and confront the upstart monk. "You are on English soil, Signor Balsamo," he said, "and I am the recognized authority here. I must ask you to withdraw, and take your men with you."

"This is no mere national concern, as you know very well, Mr. Temple," Balsamo replied. "I belong to no nation, but to the Brotherhood of Humankind."

"You belong to a company of brigands and child-stealers," Temple retorted. "Whatever delusions you have carried forward from the past, you are no better now than Tom Brown's company of criminals or the Illuminati's *vehm*. There is no legitimate authority here but the Crown's." So saying, he drew his cudgel—and his four men drew theirs. He was not foolish enough to think he had the numerical advantage, though, and was not surprised to see at last a dozen members of the audience, masters and servants alike, lay bare an assortment of blades, Not all, he knew, would be affiliates of *Civitas Solis*—but Balsamo would not have made a move had he not thought the situation controllable in the short term.

The wild cards were, however, the four men standing on the stage. Balsamo must have thought that he had a good chance of commanding their obedience—but he might not have been aware of George Singer's imposture, and he certainly had no idea whatsoever of what the Grey Man might do. That was the heart of his gamble.

What the Grey Man actually did was to turn around, pick up a heavy Leyden Jar, and hurl it, with amazing force, directly at Giuseppe Balsamo's head.

Balsamo ducked, but the damage had been done, in symbolic terms. Southborne's valet was not the only man who immediately leapt forward to tackle the invading monks, and Temple's men did not wait for a signal this time. Within half a second, the riot was in full swing.

Chapter Seven
Order out of Chaos

Temple's duty was explicit in the orders he had received from his political masters: to protect the members of the Parliamentary Commission from any harm. That was the purpose of the first orders he howled to his men, instructing them to gather the seven members of the Commission together and to deploy a phalanx around them, to the extent that it was possible for five men to do that.

In practice, of course, it was by no means so simple. For one thing, the members of the Commission were concerned for their companions and servants, and wanted to keep them close, swelling the ranks of those potentially in need of protection considerably. For another, some of the members, and their servants too, were avid to defend themselves, and had weapons with which to do it. Temple had no hesitation in allowing the three members of parliament to join his protective cordon, although he immediately set out to assert his authority over them, in order to keep them in formation. He had only a second's hesitation about allowing Southborne's valet to do likewise; for the moment, it did not matter in the least that the man was in the play of John Devil. Snow Harris's servant, on the other hand, Temple immediately disarmed, and found the time to whisper in the scientist's ear that if he manifested the slightest gesture of support for the warrior monks, he would be knocked out and carried to safety as luggage, to be charged with treason at a later date.

In fact, Snow Harris seemed to be as astonished by the turn of events as anyone else, and glad enough to cleave to his immediate fellows rather than his rumored associates. Without any sign of internal dissent, therefore, the company was formed up, and Temple then directed his attention to getting it safely to the main door of the room and through it. His intention was to make for the stables, if that were practicable, or to find a redoubt that could be suitably barricaded if escape from the grounds proved impossible.

The first part of the operation proved easy enough, there being no organized resistance to it. There were a number of minor brawls taking place between the tumbled chairs and the door, but it proved easy enough for Temple and his fellow point-man to clear all obstructions from the way, without engaging in any earnest combat. Temple was not in the least surprised by that, for he did not suppose for a moment that *Civitas Solis* cared a fig for the members of the Commission; their target was, and had always been, the Necromancers of London—and, most particularly of all, the resurrected Victor Frankenstein.

In different circumstances, Temple might well have taken a stand with Crosse and Faraday, to make certain of their escape, but he could not do that. Indeed, he was barely able to spare a couple of backward glances, as he shepherded his flock toward the door, to see what had become of Frankenstein and his companions. He was unsurprised to see, even at a glance, that it was George Singer who had taken charge of that party, nor that, once Singer had a blade in his hand, it would be direly difficult for anyone to get past him. Neither Crosse nor Faraday was armed, but the Grey Man had shown that he was capable of fighting, and several of Crosse's household servants had immediately rallied to their master's support, making the whole company a fighting-force to be reckoned with, especially on what was effectively home ground. As Temple ushered his own people out into the corridor, therefore, he was able to observe that Crosse's party was making a similarly disciplined retreat through the door behind the stage.

Balsamo had obviously not been bluffing when he claimed that the house was surrounded; there were more monks' habits to be seen in the corridors and even more outside the house—but none of their wearers attempted to attack Temple's company, being content to retreat from them and melt away, intent on discovering and seizing other prey.

Temple brought his charges to the stable complex without anyone sustaining or dealing out any harm more dangerous than a bruise. He supervised the harnessing of the two largest carriages in the garage, and the saddling of a dozen extra horses, rudely pushing back other guests intent on making their own escape, demanding that they wait their turn. One of two protested that he was stealing their horses, to which he replied that he was requisitioning them in the name of the crown, and that they would be able to recover them from the constabulary in Taunton, that being his immediate objective as a place of refuge. When the carriages were loaded, however, and the majority of the horses mounted, he delegated authority for the convoy's safe conduct to his second-in-command, intent on returning to the house.

"That might be unwise, sir," Tom Brown's man said, leaning down from the horse on to which he had climbed. "I should be able to find help closer at hand than Taunton, and you might do better to return with half a dozen experienced brawlers at your back."

"Too late, in all probability," Temple told him. "Go—and if you return with half a dozen would-be brawlers at your back, don't expect to find me in sympathy with you."

He watched the convoy until it was safely through the gate, and then turned back, heading for Crosse's laboratory. At first, the only people he met in the corridors of the house were other escapees intent on following the Commissioners with all possible haste, but he eventually found his way barred by two sword-bearing monks, who had been delegated to form a kind of rearguard while their fellows attempted to storm the laboratory. He knew that he was close to Crosse's lair, but could not see the laboratory door as yet. The sound of raised voices informed him that the battle was not yet finished, however, and an overheard reference to a battering-ram suggested that Frankenstein's followers had barricaded the door, ready to withstand a siege.

Time was pressing, Temple knew. Help would arrive eventually, from Tom Brown's men if not the constables from Taunton—and the agents of the *vehm* would also oppose their rivals fiercely, if they had not been taken out of the equation in advance. Some kinds of assistance, Temple knew, might create more problems than they solved, in the longer term, but the immediate objective was clear enough: to prevent *Civitas Solis* from kidnapping Victor Frankenstein and the Necromancers of London.

It was with that thought in mind that Temple squared himself for a flight, holding out his truncheon in a threatening manner. "I am an officer of the Crown," he informed the two men blocking his way, dutifully. "To cross swords with me is to advertise your eligibility for the gallows."

"You'd have to catch us first," replied one of the monks, unmistakably an Englishman.

"He's just an old man," the second monk observed, as if to bolster his companion's confidence, before addressing Temple directly, saying: "Back away, old man—there's no disgrace in a retreat from superior forces." He too was speaking English like a native.

"Don't kill him," said a voice that came from behind Temple, which certainly did not belong to an Englishman. "This one we should take alive."

Temple suspected that the sentiment behind the instruction was not respect for English law, and was not entirely glad to hear this order—but he was quick to seize whatever slight advantage it might offer him. Satisfied that the two men ahead of him would at least hesitate before trying to run him through, he attacked them without warning, swinging his cudgel in a manner that was by no means as reckless or random as it must have seemed.

The detective was conscious as he moved of the fact that he *was* an old man, but he remembered the fight that Jean-Pierre Séverin had undertaken on his behalf in the grounds of a Paris hotel, and knew that old reflexes can sometimes make up in skill what they lack in promptness. He cracked one of his adversaries on the side of the knee, sending him sprawling on the floor, and smashed the other on the right elbow, disabling his sword-arm. With his free hand he shoved the second man back against the wall, and was past him in a trice, long before the man behind him could take any constructive action. *There!* he thought. *I'm not ready for my dotage as yet!*

He did not even bother to look back to see what the third man was doing; he simply ran on, determined to attack the besiegers of the laboratory from behind even if he were being pursued. He would have undoubtedly have carried out this rough-hewn plan, had he not had occasion to pass an open door, through which a weighted rope was suddenly thrown to tangle his legs.

On another occasion, he might have evaded the inexpert cast, but he was traveling at full tilt for fear of his presumed pursuer, and the slightest loss of balance was always likely to be fatal. He stumbled to his knees, and although he braced himself with his arms, ready to spring up again, he was not given the chance.

Suddenly, there seemed to be monkish habits all around him, and hard blows descending on his back and shoulders. He sustained at least four impacts to the body before his skull was struck, causing him a great deal of pain. When the head was struck, however, he did not lose consciousness, being merely dazed and agonized. Once again, he was acutely aware of his age, and the diminution of is forces attendant upon it, but he also felt a near-supernatural stubbornness, an iron determination not to give way to the multitudinous pains clawing at his body and mind.

He was aware of being picked up and carried awkwardly into the room from which the rope had be thrown, then dumped on a settee. He was abandoned there, not knowing whether to be grateful or to feel insulted that his adversaries did not even think it necessary to knock him unconscious.

"We'll come back for him later," said one of the Englishmen.

Temple was aching too badly in too many places to be able to pull himself together immediately, and contented himself with gripping his injured head in his bloodstained fingers for at least five minutes. He kept his

eyes open, not without difficulty—there was blood trick-
ling down his forehead too, and the pain was literally
blinding—but all he could see was a confusion of
blurred shapes. To begin with, there was a great deal of
noise, but it abated by degrees, and the shapes gradually
coalesced into items of furniture.

Finally, certain that he was alone and unguarded,
Temple blinked away a few bloody tears and made a
Herculean effort to raise himself into a sitting position.
He succeeded, but at some cost, and had to maintain
immobility for a few minutes more, gathering himself all
over again. When he could finally see clearly, his first
glance told him that the room was still empty—but his
second picked out a human form recently arrived in the
doorway.

The newcomer's eyes met his, and the other—who
might otherwise have passed on—immediately hurried
into the room.

"Mr. Temple!" said a Grey Man that Temple first
mistook for Victor Frankenstein. "Are you badly hurt?"

Temple blinked again, and his gaze traveled over
his interlocutor's dust-stained riding-costume and grey
features with mute incomprehension. "Lazarus?" he said,
finally. "Is that you?"

"Yes it is," replied Frankenstein's Adam. "We've
arrived too late, it seems—but I've brought help, if
there's any assistance that can usefully be given. Do you
know where my maker is?"

"He was in the laboratory, I think, only a few minutes ago—ten or fifteen, perhaps. I had the impression
that he was barricaded in, with Faraday, Crosse and the
vampire."

"Vampire?"

"Count Szandor, now masquerading as George Singer, Crosse's old friend and former colleague. Are they not there? Has the door been forced? Have the mad monks taken them?"

"No," Lazarus replied, "they're no longer in the laboratory—but the door has not been broken down, and what has become of them I cannot tell. I gather that the demonstration was not a success."

"Oh yes," Temple said, forcing a sardonic laugh. "It was a tremendous success. Had it been more modest, events would presumably have transpired in far better order. *Civitas Solis* would never have risked an open assault had the prize not seemed too tempting to resist. You know, I suppose, than your maker is now a Grey Man himself, more immediately articulate than any of his kind, with the possible exception of General Mortdieu?"

"I knew that he had died and was due to be resurrected," Lazarus confirmed, bending over to examine Temple's head-wound more carefully with his eyes and fingers. "I came as rapidly as I could, with what assistance I could gather." As he spoke the final words he turned to look at someone else who had come along the corridor, and was now framed in the doorway. It was Jean-Pierre Séverin. Like Lazarus before him, the great swordsman hurried forward as soon as he recognized Temple.

"I'm sorry, my friend," the Frenchman said. "Had we got here a mere ten minutes earlier...but the Comtesse's men are scouring the house and grounds. If they cannot catch up with Balsamo's brigands there, they will soon be on their trail."

"The Comtesse's men?" Temple echoed, in frank bewilderment.

Séverin blushed slightly behind his white beard and moustache. "It's the strangest alliance imaginable," he said, "but it was the Comtesse's men who freed me from the Germans who sent hirelings to capture me on the Dover Road, and Lazarus persuaded me to accept a truce while there are greater matters at stake."

"Don't worry, old friend," said Temple, with a hollow laugh. "The Comtesse is in my direct employ now, it seems, and I have somehow become fast friends with her master, the vampire. Had I succeeded in reaching the laboratory where I believed he and Frankenstein to be under siege, I would have fought with him shoulder to shoulder, in spite of what happened at Miremont. Do you know whether the Commissioners reached safety? They were on the Taunton road."

"We came from another direction," Lazarus told him, "but have no fear—the Commission is irrelevant now. Open warfare has been declared, and it only remains for the various armies to mobilize and take up their positions. Wellington will take a stand himself, no doubt, with 10,000 redcoats behind him."

"It might come to that, now," Temple admitted. "If we could capture a few of Balsamo's men and bring them to trial…"

"I doubt that Mr. Canning is ready for that, as yet," Lazarus told him, moving back after satisfying himself that Temple's head-wound, though bloody, was superficial. "We'll do far better if we can recover Frankenstein, Crosse and Faraday, and establish the Necromancers of London at the heart of the Royal Institution, with or without the mysterious Mr. Singer."

Temple made as if to get to his feet, but his limbs were not yet ready to support him without excessive complaint. "That fool Southborne," he muttered. "If he hadn't panicked at the sight of the grey girl…have you any news of her, by the way?"

"None," Lazarus admitted. "The events of the first demonstration were reported to us, but we have no idea what happened to the subject after her escape from the house."

"I saw her briefly," Temple told him. "We arranged to meet, so that I could get her to a place of safety, but she didn't make it to the rendezvous. I seem to have failed in every possible respect but one—although my superiors will doubtless be pleased to hear that I did my duty according to my orders."

A third man came in then, but this one barely glanced at Temple before addressing himself to Lazarus. "The Grafina is negotiating a treaty with Tom Brown's men," he announced.

Temple recognized the man as Guido, the vampires' principal mortal hireling, and was slightly surprised to see him rather cheerful. "What are you so pleased about?" hee growled.

"Why should I not be glad?" Guido retorted. "The opposition has been tempted to a reckless move, and thus helped enormously to establish a common cause between the rest of us. We had presumed that Balsamo and Belcamp would make their peace, and might even make a treaty with the Illuminati, at least while their Prussian dupes were forced to operate on alien soil. Now, *Civitas Solis* stands alone, with everyone against them—at least for the time being. It's only a few short months since my master stood alone, without a friend in the world, but he will be the lynch-pin of a mighty alliance now, if…"

"If only you can find him," Temple growled. "Is Malo de Treguern with you, perchance?"

"Alas, no," said Lazarus. "The Church has its own politics, and it does not matter how much the Knights of St. John hate the heretics of *Civitas Solis*—they will never join forces with an army as seemingly diabolical as ours."

"I'm not at all sure that I shall join it myself," Temple said, "if John Devil is a member of its High Command."

"With all due respect, Mr. Temple," said Lazarus, politely, "we do not really need you. You would not be half as useful to us as Séverin."

Temple immediately looked up at the Frenchman, who did not let him down. "I stand with Mr. Temple," he declared, stoutly. "I will follow his counsel."

Guido shook his head, as if to signify that it was quite irrelevant, but Lazarus looked at him disapprovingly and said: "If we cannot find Frankenstein, there is no center around which we might form. I am not the only articulate Grey Man in Europe, by any means, but none of us has Frankenstein's status and importance. While he and Faraday are missing, along with Crosse and Szandor, the greater part of the genius of this affair is lost. We do need Séverin—and Mr. Temple might be useful too, if he is willing to help us even for a little while."

If *Civitas Solis* have the men of science," Guido said, confidently, returning to the door as he spoke, "we'll get them back in no time at all, with or without the two old men. The alchemists might outnumber our own small company, but once Tom Brown's resources are added to ours, we can locate and storm any hidey-hole where they might have taken refuge."

"I wish I could believe him," Lazarus said to Temple, as he moved toward the door in his turn, "but we have no idea what resources *Civitas Solis* might have in the vicinity, and their expertise in hiding dates back centuries."

Once the Grey Man had gone, Jean-Pierre Sévérin sat down on the settee beside Temple. "This is direly confusing," he said. "I came to London to warn you that the vampires were in England, fully expecting that you and I might join forces to hunt them down together and dispose of them forever. Now, it seems, they are doing all they can to help us, in a war against enemies I never knew I had."

"They didn't know they were your enemies either," Temple told him, "until their curiosity was aroused. We've lived too long for our own good, it seems; people have begun to look askance at us, sensing something unnatural. It will do us no good to protest that old age has merely been kind to us, because that is the precise object of their research. As an Englishman and a policeman, I have His Majesty's secret agents behind and beside me, but as a Parisian, you, alas, have no one to turn to but the likes of Vidocq."

"I have René de Kervoz behind and beside me," the Frenchman muttered, "and I have received an offer of assistance from Colonel Bozzo-Corona. While I am on English soil I have you, too, Mr. Temple, do I not? If we cannot hunt vampires together, we can still act as one in some other worthy cause."

"You do have me," Temple conceded, "but, as you can see, I'm likely to be as useless to you as I am to Lazarus and his allies. I don't have your uncanny skill in a fight, so I have little to bring to any partnership."

"But I don't have your renowned intelligence," Sévérin countered. "It's my opinion that if anyone can figure out a path through this maze of confusion, and bring order out of its chaos, it's you—not Michael Faraday, or the boastful Count Szandor, or even my old friend Germain Patou, but you. We might make a powerful team, my friend, even in a contest full to overflowing with younger men, secret societies and the ranks of the dead-alive"

Temple finally contrived to stagger to his feet. "You're very kind," he said, "but my bruises are telling me, in no uncertain terms, how far past my best I am, in spite of my seeming resilience. Since younger men than us—and deader ones—seem to have this matter in hand, for now, I suggest that we go down to the servants' pantry to discover whether Cook and Caddick have survived the battle. Either way, we'll be fed and watered, ready to fight another day, if the chance or necessity arises."

"Agreed," said the one-time fencing-master, helping Temple to hobble to the door. "Just show me the way."

Chapter Eight
The Necromancers in London

When Gregory Tremple finally completed the discomfiting business of making his official report, he hastened to St. Thomas's hospital, where Jean-Pierre Séverin was waiting for him at Malo de Treguern's bedside. The great swordsman had already told his compatriot the full story, and Treguern, his curiosity sated, was now protesting loudly against the injustice of his doctors.

"They say that I am an old man," the knight protested. "They think me half-mad, because I wear the Hospitallers' cross so proudly, and owe such fidelity to the Order's ideals. They will not let me go, although the wound no longer troubles me, for fear that it will open again. I have shown them all my other scars, but they will not believe that I have the same healing power now that I had then."

"They might be right, my friend," Temple told him, touching the fingers of his right hand to his own wounded head. "At any rate, you cannot blame them for their anxiety. They are not convinced, as yet, that wounds they have formerly taken to be mortal no longer mark a necessary end to human life."

Treguern took exception to that. "If you are implying that I might be turned into an abomination if I should happen to die," he said, "I must object in no uncertain terms. I would like you to give me your word, Mr. Temple, that you will oppose as sternly as you can any attempt to resurrect me after my death. I will not suffer this body to become the abode of a demon."

"I'll give you my word, for what it's worth," Temple replied, "but now that I've seen and heard two further example of the dead-alive, I'm more convinced than ever that there is no principle of evil at work here. I do not claim that the dead-alive are intrinsically virtuous, nor do I deny that some might be more dangerous in their new state of being than they were when alive, but they are thinking beings, capable of moral judgment and entitled to moral consideration. If I were to die..."

"You should not say such things, even in jest," Treguern insisted, cutting off the sentence. He would doubtless have said more, but was interrupted himself by the arrival of another visitor: an old man wearing a quilted coat and a woolen scarf, who seemed a trifle unsteady on his feet as he walked, but whose eyes were bright, penetrating in their gaze.

Temple and Séverin both recognized the man, but it was Malo de Treguern who actually addressed him by name, saying: "Colonel Bozzo-Corona! What on Earth are you doing here?"

"I am in London on business, traveling with my beloved grand-daughter. little Fanchette. When I heard that one of my oldest friends, a warrior knight, was lying in a hospital bed far from his native Britanny, in danger of dying alone, how could I not come to see him? But I see that you do have friends, and the finest imaginable: a great swordsman and a brilliant detective. I'm delighted to see you again, Monsieur Séverin, Monsieur Temple."

Temple bowed, following Séverin's example.

"You have had quite an adventure, I hear," the Colonel said to Temple. "I had adventures myself once, but I am too old now—every affair I undertake seems likely to be my last. We cannot simply lie down and let fate take its course, though; it is the nature of a man to strive, and, if necessary, to fight."

Temple did not know what to say, but Treguern was more forthright. "Have you, too, come here searching for the elixir of life—or, at least, the secret of progressing to an unholy artificial afterlife?" he asked.

"Me?" said the Colonel. "No, I'm fully reconciled to my own fate—but I still have business matters requiring my attention. Business is the curse of the modern era, don't you think? An evil, but a very necessary evil. A man must have ambition, and ambition, nowadays, requires business. No matter how much we might regret the fact that mere money has become the measure of everything, and that the sheer beauty of a treasure no longer counts for anything by comparison with its market price, we can but accept it...and without money, one cannot do good works, can one, Frère Treguern?"

"One does not need money to do good works," Treguern replied—as the Colonel must have known that he would. "It simply makes them easier to perform."

The Colonel smiled. "You must let me help you, my friend," he said. "Come and stay with me when the doctors release you—I have rented a very comfortable house in Hampstead village. You would be welcome there too, Monsieur Sévérin—and you must come to dinner soon, Mr. Temple. We old men must stick together, must we not? The mere passage of time has given us common cause and united our interests."

Temple thanked the Colonel kindly, although he did not see how he would be able to find time for mere socializing until Balsamo's brigands and their presumed prisoners had been located—a task that had so far proved beyond the scope of Tom Brown, let alone the secret police and the vampire's agents. He was distracted, however, when a young orderly came up to him and handed him a folded sheet of paper, before returning in haste without waiting to be questioned as to its origin.

With the collective gaze of three pairs of curious eyes upon him, Temple unfolded the note. *SHARPER'S AT SIX*, it read, in its entirety. Temple did not doubt that it was an invitation, if not a summons, nor did he doubt that it came from Tom Brown—or, at least, that it had been sent with John Devil's knowledge and approval.

"What is it?" Séverin asked.

"Official business," Temple muttered.

"A state secret!" said the Colonel, marveling. "Why, how exciting. Are you on the trail of Faraday's abductors? That news caused great consternation in the scientific circles of Paris, I can assure you. If the agents of the Terror had not cut off Lavoisier's head during the Revolution, he would be under 24 hour guard today."

Ignoring this strangely ambiguous item of whimsy, Temple said: "I must go." He raised a hand to interrupt Jean-Pierre Séverin before the other could make a formal declaration of his intention to accompany the man whose bosom companion the now considered himself to be. "I need to go alone," he added. "There is no danger—but there might be, if I were to take anyone with me."

He did not give Séverin time to argue, nor either of the others time to comment further, but hurried off.

He walked across Tower Bridge at a brisk pace, and then hired a cab to take him home. He knew that it would take time to make himself up, and then to get to what was nowadays Jenny Paddock's Cabaret Theatre.

He did not make himself up as Solomon Green, the character he had invented specifically for use in the den of iniquity in question. Too many people now knew that Green had been Gregory Temple in disguise. Instead, he made himself up as a sunburned sailor, with every appearance of 20 years' experience in the slave trade. That was the guise he presented to Jenny Paddock when he approached her counter and demanded a tot of rum.

He was served by a young girl, who could not possibly have seen through his imposture, but he saw from the corner of his eye that the mistress of the establishment was looking at him quizzically, and hurried away into the shadows, selecting the same sheltered vantage-point from which Solomon Green had formerly observed the comings-and-goings in the heart of the criminal Underworld.

He had been in the booth for ten minutes before two other individuals sat down to either side of him. They were wrapped up very warmly, having just come in from the icy cold, with felt hats pulled down low over their features and scarves over their mouths. They did not unwrap themselves to display their faces, and left it to Temple to summon the waitress and order two glasses of gin. Neither of them, to judge by their contrasted height and build, could possibly be Henri de Belcamp. One was too bulky by far, and even the smaller of the two was a little too tall and not sufficiently slender.

"Thank you for coming, Mr. Temple," said the smaller of the two, in a voice not much above a whisper, but nevertheless quite distinct. "Tom has given us all a guarantee of safe conduct, so you need have no fear."

For a moment or two, Temple could not identify the voice, and when he did, he was not quite ready to believe it. "Szandor?" he said, interrogatively.

"In person," the vampire replied. "You must have been worried about me, in spite of the Countess's confident assurances that I would be safe. Please tell her, when you next see her, that her confidence was not misplaced."

Temple had only seen Countess Marcian Gregoryi once since his return to London, but he was, indeed, due to see her again very soon. She had already demonstrated her talent for gathering information interesting to the agents of the Crown, and Temple was no longer so sure that his masters would dispense with his services at the slightest excuse.

"Have you escaped from *Civitas Solis*, then?" Temple asked.

"They never caught us," Szandor replied, blithely. "Fyne Court was built in the 17th century, when Jacobean tragedies were still being performed in London's theaters. It was a time when priests' holes and secret passages were *de rigueur*, along with the ghosts of knightly ancestors. When Balsamo's men were able to get into the laboratory—without the necessity of breaking down the door—they found us gone, as if vanished into thin air. We thought it politic to lie low thereafter, though. Our hopes of conducting our research openly, in the confines of the Royal Institution, had been badly dented, if not actually dashed by the fiasco."

"So you threw in your lot with John Devil," Temple growled.

"We have not thrown in our lot with anyone, Mr. Temple," said the other man, speaking for the first time. "We are conducting our own investigations in our own way."

Again, Temple had difficulty identifying the voice. Again, his conclusion seemed more guesswork than reasoned confusion. "Lazarus?" he ventured.

The other actually laughed. "I suppose we are similar now," he said. "There is a certain justice in that, I must reluctantly admit."

"Frankenstein," said Temple, dully. Once, the thought that he was in a booth in Will Sharper's Grog Shop, sandwiched between a vampire and a man returned from the dead would have terrified him. Now, it seemed almost a relief to know that his drinking companions were no petty criminals.

"Tom Brown differs from his erstwhile friends in *Civitas Solis* and his erstwhile enemies in the *vehm*," the vampire said, "in that he is no monopolist. I do not say that he is not a profiteer, but he really does not want to have the afterlife securely within his own gift. He is a Romantic heart."

"And you believe that he is a better protector than His Majesty's Secret Service or the Duke of Wellington's legions?" Temple asked, bitterly, knowing full well that the answer was yes.

"We would like to have your amity as well, Mr. Temple," Frankenstein said.

"Indeed we would," the vampire said, supportively. "Of, at least, your undertaking not to join forces with Malo de Treguern or Colonel Bozzo-Corona."

"The Colonel told me himself, only a few hours ago, that he was here in London on business, and had no interest in the afterlife," Temple said, although he had not really believed it at the time, and was even less convinced now that Szandor had brought up the Colonel's name.

"Business with the Gentlemen of the Night," the vampire confirmed. "But there's probably not a man in their ranks who does not owe a double allegiance to the All-Father and John Devil. We live in a world of confused loyalties, Mr. Temple—which can sometimes break a man in two, if he's not careful. Please tell the Countess to mobilize all her resources to the task of keeping track of Colonel Bozzo-Corona and his shifty soldiers—and you might do worse to put some of your other men on to him as well. He's deluded as to his origins and nature, of course, as we have all been in the past, but his mind is exceedingly sharp, and he's an extraordinarily clever and patient planner. Unlike Tom, he is most certainly a monopolist, and one who stops at nothing."

"Is that what you brought me here to tell me?" Temple asked, unable to sound grateful, although he felt a trifle curmudgeonly on that account.

"We brought you here to reassure you as to our health," the Grey Man put in, "and to let you know that, whatever other crimes Balsamo might have committed, he is not presently holding any significant hostages."

"How are you, Dr. Frankenstein?" Temple asked, with genuine curiosity. "Have you mastered your new faculties and feelings? Do you know yet what you are, and what you might make of your second lease of life?"

"I'm making progress," the Grey Man told him.

"What about the girl?" Temple asked. "Have you managed to recover her from *her* captors?"

"No, alas," said Szandor. "We cannot even be sure that she was captured, although I know how much it would wound you to think that she missed her rendezvous with you of her own accord. Tom will find her in the end—and he has agreed that when he does, he'll hand her over to us in order that she and Victor might compare notes and assist in one another's re-education."

"You cannot trust him," Temple said, flatly. "Treachery is in his bones; it's all he can do to prevent his *alter egos* from betraying one another."

"That's as may be," the vampire replied, equably, "but who can we trust? We can only go forward as best we can, careful not to betray our own destiny."

"You, a vampire, speak of destiny now?" said Temple. "You speak approvingly of men who are not monopolists, and disapprovingly of men who are. It's difficult to believe that you're the same skeletal figure I talked to in Miremont."

"Change is possible for all of us, Mr. Temple," the other murmured. "Even for you. You know as well as we do that the world has already been turned upside-down; the question that remains is whether we can adapt ourselves to the new order. I am determined to do so, and so are my friends."

"You do know, don't you," Temple said to the Grey Man who had once been Victor Frankenstein, "that this man is not George Singer, but a Grey Man of sorts, camouflaged by mesmeric glamour?"

"Yes, I do," Frankenstein replied. "He is my brother now, or my half-brother, at least; we are alike in the most important matter of all. Who else is there in London who can give me a sound education in the art of life after death?"

Temple looked up as someone materialized at the table bearing a tray, and set out another round of drinks, almost as if in answer to the Grey Man's question.

"Compliments of the house, gentlemen," said the newcomer, who was not the little waitress but Jenny Paddock herself. "Mr. Hopkey apologizes for the fact that he has not time to say hello, but he is making himself up for tonight's performance." The hostess was looking directly at Temple, evidently able now to see through his disguise.

"Mr. Hopkey is neither here nor there," Temple told her, coldly. "What of John Devil's apologies?"

"My husband is dead, sir," Jenny Paddock replied, striking an offended pose, "and I'll thank you not to insult the name of my poor, dear Tom under his own roof."

Temple was not entirely sure whether the "Tom" she had in mind just then was Thomas Paddock or Tom Brown.

"Thank you, Mistress Paddock," the vampire put in. "My friend meant no offense. Once we've drunk these down, we'll be on our way—we all have our ships to catch, literally or figuratively speaking."

"You'll miss the performance," Jenny Paddock said, seeming genuinely wounded by such neglect. "That would be a shame, for *The Vampyre* is a fine melodrama, rumored to be based on a story by Lord Byron himself."

"I saw the first performance of the original production at the Porte-Saint-Martin," Szandor said, smoothly. "I was seated directly behind Monsieur Nodier and Monsieur Dumas. Without meaning any disrespect to Mr. Hopkey's troupe, I doubt that they could better that occasion. I no longer like the play as much as I did then—the Byronic image of the vampire has grown a little stale, has it not?"

"As you please, sir," said Jenny Paddock, stiffly.

"It's a pity that Sawney Ross and Ned Knob aren't here to see their protégés perform the play," Temple observed, obedient to a mischievous whim. "You and he were intimate at one time, I believe, Mistress Paddock— at least until Pretty Molly came between you."

The hostess did not deign to reply to that, but returned to her counter with her dignity seemingly intact.

The three men reached out for their glasses, in no particular hurry. Temple would have downed his without ceremony, but Szandor raised his, with the unmistakable gesture of a man about to propose a toast.

Temple paused and waited. The Grey Man followed his example. Temple wondered, vaguely, whether Grey Men were capable of getting drunk. He supposed not, on the assumption that alcohol probably did not have the same effect on dead-alive as on living flesh.

"To the Necromancers of London!" Szandor declared, still speaking in his curiously distinct whisper. "Long may they thrive!"

"To the Future!" added the Grey Man who had once been Victor Frankenstein. "Long may it last!"

Feeling compelled to complete the ritual, Gregory Temple only hesitated a moment before saying: "To Life! Long may it retain the empery of the flesh!"

No one objected; everyone drank. As the fiery beverage assaulted his throat, Gregory Temple could not help but wonder whether his words were mere wisps of straw, about to be blown away by the irresistible tide of destiny and the marvelous discoveries soon to be made by the Necromancers of London.

SF & FANTASY

Guy d'Armen. *Doc Ardan: The City of Gold and Lepers*
G.-J. Arnaud. *The Ice Company*
Aloysius Bertrand. *Gaspard de la Nuit*
Richard Bessière. *The Gardens of the Apocalypse*
Félix Bodin. *The Novel of the Future*
André Caroff. *The Terror of Madame Atomos*
Didier de Chousy. *Ignis*
C. I. Defontenay. *Star (Psi Cassiopeia)*
Charles Derennes. *The People of the Pole*
Georges Dodds/Paul Wessels (anthologists). *The Missing Link*
Harry Dickson. *The Heir of Dracula*
Jules Dornay. *Lord Ruthven Begins*
Sâr Dubnotal *vs. Jack the Ripper*
Alexandre Dumas. *The Return of Lord Ruthven*
J.-C. Dunyach. *The Night Orchid; The Thieves of Silence*
Henri Duvernois. *The Man Who Found Himself*
Henri Falk. *The Age of Lead*
Paul Féval. *Anne of the Isles; Knightshade; Revenants; Vampire City;
The Vampire Countess; The Wandering Jew's Daughter*
Paul Féval, *fils. Felifax, the Tiger-Man*
Arnould Galopin. *Doctor Omega*
Nathalie Henneberg. *The Green Gods*
V. Hugo, P. Foucher & P. Meurice. *The Hunchback of Notre-Dame*
Michel Jeury. *Chronolysis*
Octave Joncquel & Theo Varlet. *The Martian Epic*
Gérard Klein. *The Mote in Time's Eye*
Jean de La Hire. *Enter the Nyctalope; The Nyctalope on Mars; The
Nyctalope vs. Lucifer*
André Laurie. *Spiridon*
Georges Le Faure & Henri de Graffigny. *The Extraordinary Adven-
tures of a Russian Scientist Across the Solar System* (2 vols.)
Gustave Le Rouge. *The Vampires of Mars*
Jules Lermina. *Mysteryville; Panic in Paris; To-Ho and the Gold De-
stroyers*
Jean-Marc & Randy Lofficier. *Edgar Allan Poe on Mars; The Katri-
na Protocol; Pacifica; Robonocchio; Tales of the Shadowmen* (an-
thologists; 7 vols.)
Xavier Mauméjean. *The League of Heroes*
John-Antoine Nau. *Enemy Force*

Marie Nizet. *Captain Vampire*
C. Nodier, A. Beraud & Toussaint-Merle. *Frankenstein*
Henri de Parville. *An Inhabitant of the Planet Mars*
J. Polidori, C. Nodier, E. Scribe. *Lord Ruthven the Vampire*
P.-A. Ponson du Terrail. *The Vampire and the Devil's Son*
Maurice Renard. *The Blue Peril; Doctor Lerne; The Doctored Man;.*
A Man Among the Microbes; The Master of Light
Albert Robida. *The Adventures of Saturnin Farandoul; The Clock of*
the Centuries.
J.-H. Rosny Aîné. *Helgvor of the Blue River; The Givreuse Enigma;*
The Mysterious Force; The Navigators of Space; Vamireh; The
World of the Variants; The Young Vampire
Brian Stableford. *The New Faust at the Tragicomique;The Empire of*
the Necromancers (The Shadow of Frankenstein; Frankenstein and
the Vampire Countess; Frankenstein in London); Sherlock Holmes &
The Vampires of Eternity; The Stones of Camelot; The Wayward
Muse. (anthologist) *The Germans on Venus; News from the Moon*
Han Ryner. *The Superhumans*
Jacques Spitz. *The Eye of Purgatory*
Kurt Steiner. *Ortog*
Villiers de l'Isle-Adam. *The Scaffold; The Vampire Soul*
Philippe Ward. *Artahe*
Philippe Ward & Sylvie Miller. *The Song of Montségur*

MYSTERIES & THRILLERS

M. Allain & P. Souvestre. *The Daughter of Fantômas*
A. Anicet-Bourgeois, Lucien Dabril. *Rocambole*
A. Bisson & G. Livet. *Nick Carter vs. Fantômas*
V. Darlay & H. de Gorsse. *Lupin vs. Holmes: The Stage Play*
Paul Féval. *Gentlemen of the Night; John Devil; The Black Coats*
('Salem Street; The Invisible Weapon; The Parisian Jungle; The
Companions of the Treasure; Heart of Steel; The Cadet Gang)
Emile Gaboriau. *Monsieur Lecoq*
Steve Leadley. *Sherlock Holmes: The Circle of Blood*
Maurice Leblanc. *Arsène Lupin vs. Countess Cagliostro; Lupin vs.*
Holmes (The Blonde Phantom; The Hollow Needle)
Gaston Leroux. *Chéri-Bibi; The Phantom of the Opera; Rouletabille*
& the Mystery of the Yellow Room
William Patrick Maynard. *The Terror of Fu Manchu*
Frank J. Morlock. *Sherlock Holmes: The Grand Horizontals*

P. de Wattyne & Y. Walter. *Sherlock Holmes vs. Fantômas*
David White. *Fantômas in America*

SCREENPLAYS

Mike Baron. *The Iron Triangle*
Emma Bull & Will Shetterly. *Nightspeeder; War for the Oaks*
Gerry Conway & Roy Thomas. *Doc Dynamo*
Steve Englehart. *Majorca*
James Hudnall. *The Devastator*
Jean-Marc & Randy Lofficier. *Royal Flush*
J.-M. & R. Lofficier & Marc Agapit. *Despair*
Andrew Paquette. *Peripheral Vision*
R. Thomas, J. Hendler & L. Sprague de Camp. *Rivers of Time*

NON-FICTION

Stephen R. Bissette. *Blur 1-5. Green Mountain Cinema 1*
Win Scott Eckert. *Crossovers* (2 vols.)
Jean-Marc & Randy Lofficier. *Shadowmen* (2 vols.)
Randy Lofficier. *Over Here*

HEXAGON COMICS

Franco Frescura & Luciano Bernasconi. *Wampus*
Franco Frescura & Giorgio Trevisan. *CLASH*
L. Bernasconi, J.-M. Lofficier & Juan Roncagliolo Berger. *Phenix*
Claude Legrand, J.-M. Lofficier & L. Bernasconi. *Kabur*
Franco Oneta. *Zembla*
L. Buffolente, Lofficier & J.-J. Dzialowski. *Strangers: Homicron*
Danilo Grossi. *Strangers: Jaydee*
Claude Legrand & Luciano Bernasconi. *Strangers: Starlock*

ART BOOKS

Jean-Pierre Normand. *Science Fiction Illustrations*
Raven Okeefe. *Raven's L'il Critters*
Randy Lofficier & Raven OKeefe. *If Your Possum Go Daylight...*
Daniele Serra. *Illusions*

www.ingramcontent.com/pod-product-compliance
Lightning Source LLC
Chambersburg PA
CBHW060351030726
47497CB00003B/677